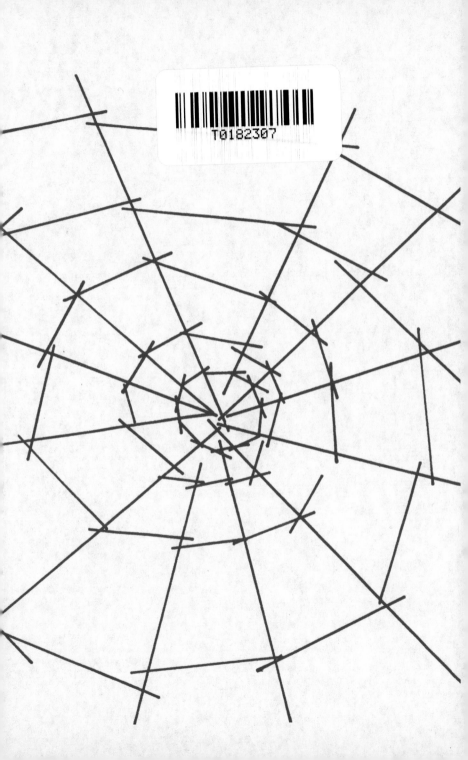

BOOKS BY PAUL BOWLES

NOVELS

The Sheltering Sky

Let It Come Down

The Spider's House

Up Above the World

NOVELLA

Too Far from Home

SHORT STORIES

The Delicate Prey

*A Hundred Camels in the
  Courtyard*

The Time of Friendship

*Pages from Cold Point and
  Other Stories*

A Distant Episode

*Things Gone and Things
  Still Here*

Midnight Mass and Other Stories

Call at Corazón and Other Stories

Collected Stories, 1939–1976

Unwelcome Words

A Thousand Days for Mokhtar

AUTOBIOGRAPHY

Without Stopping

Days: A Tangier Diary

LETTERS

In Touch: The Letters of Paul Bowles
  (edited by Jeffrey Miller)

POETRY

Two Poems

Scenes

The Thicket of Spring

*Next to Nothing: Collected Poems,
  1926–1977*

NONFICTION, TRAVEL, ESSAYS,
MISCELLANEOUS

Yallah! (written by Paul Bowles,
  photographs by Peter W.
  Haeberlinb)

*Their Heads Are Green and
  Their Hands Are Blue*

Points in Time

Paul Bowles: Photographs
  (edited by Simon Bischoff)

the delicate prey and other

stories paul bowles

AN **ecco** BOOK

HARPER **PERENNIAL**

NEW YORK • LONDON • TORONTO • SYDNEY

HARPER ● PERENNIAL

Grateful acknowledgment is made to the editors of the following maga-
zines in which some of these stories originally appeared: *Harper's Bazaar,
Horizon, Life and Letters, Mademoiselle, Partisan Review, Penguin New
Writing, View, Wake, World Review,* and *Zero.*

A hardcover edition of this book was reissued in 1972 by Ecco Press.

HarperCollins books may be purchased for educational, business, or sales
promotional use. For information please write: Special Markets
Department, HarperCollins Publishers, 10 East 53rd Street, New York, NY
10022.

First Harper Perennial edition published 2006.

Library of Congress Cataloging-in-Publication Data has been applied for.

ISBN-10: 0-06-113734-0 (pbk.)
ISBN-13: 978-0-06-113734-1 (pbk.)

06 07 08 09 10 RRD 10 9 8 7 6 5 4 3 2 1

for my mother, who first read me the stories of Poe

contents

the delicate prey *and* other stories

at paso rojo

When old Señora Sanchez died, her two daughters Lucha and Chalía decided to visit their brother at his ranch. Out of devotion they had agreed never to marry while their mother lived, and now that she was gone and they were both slightly over forty there seemed just as little likelihood of a wedding in the family as there ever had. They would probably not admit this even to themselves, however. It was with complete understanding of his two sisters that Don Federico suggested they leave the city and go down to Paso Rojo for a few weeks.

Lucha arrived in black crêpe. To her, death was one of the things that happen in life with a certain regularity, and it therefore demanded outward observance. Otherwise her life was in no way changed, save that at the ranch she would have to get used to a whole new staff of servants.

3

"Indians, poor things, animals with speech," she said to Don Federico the first night as they sat having coffee. A bare-footed girl had just carried the dessert dishes out.

Don Federico smiled. "They are good people," he said deliberately. Living at the ranch so long had lowered his standards, it was said, for even though he had always spent a month or so of each year in the capital, he had grown increasingly indifferent to the social life there.

"The ranch is eating his soul little by little," Lucha used to say to Señora Sanchez.

Only once the old lady had replied. "If his soul is to be eaten, then let the ranch do it."

She looked around the primitive dining room with its dry decorations of palm leaves and branches. "He loves it here because everything is his," she thought, "and some of the things could never have been his if he had not purposely changed to fit them." That was not a completely acceptable thought. She knew the ranch had made him happy and tolerant and wise; to her it seemed sad that he could not have been those things without losing his civilized luster. And that he certainly had lost. He had the skin of a peasant—brown and lined everywhere. He had the slowness of speech of men who have lived for long periods of time in the open. And the inflections of his voice suggested the patience that can come from talking to animals rather than to human beings. Lucha was a sensible woman; still, she could not help feeling a certain amount of regret that her little brother, who at an earlier point in his life had been the best dancer among the members

4

of the country club, should have become the thin, sad-faced, quiet man who sat opposite her.

"You've changed a great deal," she suddenly said, shaking her head from side to side slowly.

"Yes. You change here. But it's a good place."

"Good, yes. But so sad," she said.

He laughed. "Not sad at all. You get used to the quiet. And then you find it's not quiet at all. But you never change much, do you? Chalía's the one who's different. Have you noticed?"

"Oh, Chalía's always been crazy. She doesn't change either."

"Yes. She is very much changed." He looked past the smoking oil lamp, out into the dark. "Where is she? Why doesn't she take coffee?"

"She has insomnia. She never takes it."

"Maybe our nights will put her to sleep," said Don Federico.

Chalía sat on the upper veranda in the soft night breeze. The ranch stood in a great clearing that held the jungle at bay all about, but the monkeys were calling from one side to the other, as if neither clearing nor ranch house existed. She had decided to put off going to bed—that way there was less darkness to be borne in case she stayed awake. The lines of a poem she had read on the train two days before were still in her mind: "*Aveces la noche*. . . . Sometimes the night takes you with it, wraps you up and rolls you along, leaving you washed in sleep at the morning's edge." Those lines were comforting. But there was the terrible line yet to come: "And

5

sometimes the night goes on without you." She tried to jump from the image of the fresh sunlit morning to a completely alien idea: the waiter at the beach club in Puntarenas, but she knew the other thought was waiting there for her in the dark.

She had worn riding breeches and a khaki shirt open at the neck, on the trip from the capital, and she had announced to Lucha her intention of going about in those clothes the whole time she was at Paso Rojo. She and Lucha had quarreled at the station.

"Everyone knows Mamá has died," said Lucha, "and the ones who aren't scandalized are making fun of you."

With intense scorn in her voice Chalía had replied, "You have asked them, I suppose."

On the train as it wound through the mountains toward *tierra caliente* she had suddenly said, apropos of nothing: "Black doesn't become me." Really upsetting to Lucha was the fact that in Puntarenas she had gone off and bought some crimson nail polish which she had painstakingly applied herself in the hotel room.

"You can't, Chalía!" cried her sister, wide-eyed. "You've never done it before. Why do you do it now?"

Chalía had laughed immoderately. "Just a whim!" she had said, spreading her decorated hands in front of her.

Loud footsteps came up the stairs and along the veranda, shaking it slightly. Her sister called: "Chalía!"

She hesitated an instant, then said, "Yes."

6

"You're sitting in the dark! Wait. I'll bring out a lamp from your room. What an idea!"

"We'll be covered with insects," objected Chalía, who, although her mood was not a pleasant one, did not want it disturbed.

"Federico says no!" shouted Lucha from inside. "He says there are no insects! None that bite, anyway!"

Presently she appeared with a small lamp which she set on a table against the wall. She sat down in a nearby hammock and swung herself softly back and forth, humming. Chalía frowned at her, but she seemed not to notice.

"What heat!" exclaimed Lucha finally.

"Don't exert yourself so much," suggested Chalía.

They were quiet. Soon the breeze became a strong wind, coming from the direction of the distant mountains; but it too was hot, like the breath of a great animal. The lamp flickered, threatened to go out. Lucha got up and turned it down. As Chalía moved her head to watch her, her attention was caught by something else, and she quickly shifted her gaze to the wall. Something enormous, black and swift had been there an instant ago; now there was nothing. She watched the spot intently. The wall was faced with small stones which had been plastered over and whitewashed indifferently, so that the surface was very rough and full of large holes. She rose suddenly and approaching the wall, peered at it closely. All the holes, large and small, were lined with whitish funnels. She could see the long, agile legs of the spiders that lived inside, sticking out beyond some of the funnels.

7

"Lucha, this wall is full of monsters!" she cried. A beetle flew near to the lamp, changed its mind and lighted on the wall. The nearest spider darted forth, seized it and disappeared into the wall with it.

"Don't look at them," advised Lucha, but she glanced about the floor near her feet apprehensively.

Chalía pulled her bed into the middle of the room and moved a small table over to it. She blew out the lamp and lay back on the hard mattress. The sound of the nocturnal insects was unbearably loud—an endless, savage scream above the noise of the wind. All the vegetation out there was dry. It made a million scraping sounds in the air as the wind swept through it. From time to time the monkeys called to each other from different sides. A night bird scolded occasionally, but its voice was swallowed up in the insistent insect song and the rush of wind across the hot countryside. And it was absolutely dark.

Perhaps an hour later she lit the lamp by her bed, rose, and in her nightgown went to sit on the veranda. She put the lamp where it had been before, by the wall, and turned her chair to face it. She sat watching the wall until very late.

At dawn the air was cool, full of the sound of continuous lowing of cattle, nearby and far. Breakfast was served as soon as the sky was completely light. In the kitchen there was a hubbub of women's voices. The dining room smelled of kerosene and oranges. A great platter heaped with thick slices of pale pineapple was in the center of the table. Don Federico sat at the end, his back to the wall. Behind him was a small niche, bright with candles, and the Virgin stood there in a blue and silver gown.

"Did you sleep well?" said Don Federico to Lucha.

"Ah, wonderfully well!"

"And you?" to Chalía.

"I never sleep well," she said.

A hen ran distractedly into the room from the veranda and was chased out by the serving girl. Outside the door a group of Indian children stood guard around a square of clothesline along which was draped a red assortment of meat: strips of flesh and loops of internal organs. When a vulture swooped low, the children jumped up and down, screaming in chorus, and drove it into the air again. Chalía frowned at their noise. Don Federico smiled.

"This is all in your honor," he said. "We killed a cow yesterday. Tomorrow all that will be gone."

"Not the vultures!" exclaimed Lucha.

"Certainly not. All the cowboys and servants take some home to their families. And they manage to get rid of quite a bit of it themselves."

"You're too generous," said Chalía. "It's bad for them. It makes them dissatisfied and unhappy. But I suppose if you didn't give it to them, they'd steal it anyway."

Don Federico pushed back his chair.

"No one here has ever stolen anything from me." He rose and went out.

After breakfast while it was still early, before the sun got

9

too high in the sky, he regularly made a two-hour tour of the ranch. Since he preferred to pay unexpected visits to the vaqueros in charge of the various districts, he did not always cover the same regions. He was explaining this to Lucha as he untethered his horse outside the high barbed-wire fence that enclosed the house. "Not because I hope to find something wrong. But this is the best way always to find everything right."

Like Chalía, Lucha was skeptical of the Indian's ability to do anything properly. "A very good idea," she said. "I'm sure you are much too lenient with those boys. They need a strong hand and no pity."

Above the high trees that grew behind the house the red and blue macaws screamed, endlessly repeating their elliptical path in the sky. Lucha looked up in their direction and saw Chalía on the upper porch, tucking a khaki shirt into her breeches.

"Rico, wait! I want to go with you," she called, and rushed into her room.

Lucha turned back to her brother. "You won't take her? She couldn't! With Mamá . . ."

Don Federico cut her short, so as not to hear what would have been painful to him. "You both need fresh air and exercise. Come, both of you."

Lucha was silent a moment, looking aghast into his face. Finally she said, "I couldn't," and moved away to open the gate. Several cowboys were riding their horses slowly up from the paddock toward the front of the house. Chalía appeared on the lower porch and hurried to the gate, where Lucha stood looking at her.

"So you're going horseback riding," said Lucha. Her voice had no expression.

"Yes. Are you coming? I suppose not. We should be back soon; no, Rico?"

Don Federico disregarded her, saying to Lucha: "It would be good if you came."

When she did not reply, but went through the gate and shut it, he had one of the cowboys dismount and help Chalía onto his horse. She sat astride the animal beaming down at the youth.

"Now, you can't come. You have no horse!" she cried, pulling the reins taut violently so that the horse stood absolutely still.

"Yes, Señora. I shall go with the señores." His speech was archaic and respectful, the speech of the rustic Indian. Their soft, polite words always annoyed her, because she believed, quite erroneously, that she could detect mockery underneath. "Like parrots who've been taught two lines of Gongora!" she would laugh, when the subject was being discussed. Now she was further nettled by hearing herself addressed as Señora. "The idiot!" she thought. "He should know that I'm not married." But when she looked down at the cowboy again she noticed his white teeth and his very young face. She smiled, saying, "How hot it is already," and undid the top button of her shirt.

The boy ran to the paddock and returned immediately, riding a larger and more nervous horse. This was a joke to the other cowboys, who started ahead, laughing. Don Federico and Chalía rode side by side, and the boy went along behind them, by turns whistling a tune and uttering soothing words to his skittish horse.

The party went across the mile or so of open space that lay between the house and the jungle. Then the high grass swept the riders' legs as the horses went downward to the river, which was dry save for a narrow stream of water in the middle. They followed the bed downstream, the vegetation increasing the height along the banks as they progressed. Chalía had enameled her fingernails afresh before starting out and was in a good humor. She was discussing the administration of the ranch with Don Federico. The expenses and earning capacity interested her particularly, although she had no clear idea of the price of anything. She had worn an enormous soft straw sombrero whose brim dropped to her shoulders as she rode. Every few minutes she turned around and waved to the cowboy who still remained behind, shouting to him: "Muchacho! You're not lost yet?"

Presently the river was divided into two separate beds by a large island which loomed ahead of them, its upper reaches a solid wall of branches and vines. At the foot of the giant trees among some gray boulders was a score or so of cows, looking very small indeed as they lay hunched up in the mud or ambled about seeking the thickest shade. Don Federico galloped ahead suddenly and conferred loudly with the other vaqueros.

Almost simultaneously Chalía drew in her reins and brought her horse to a halt. The boy was quickly abreast of her. As he came up she called to him: "It's hot, isn't it?"

The men rode on ahead. He circled around her. "Yes, señora. But that is because we are in the sun. There"—he indicated the island—"it is shady. Now they are almost there."

She said nothing, but took off her hat and fanned herself with the brim. As she moved her hand back and forth she watched her red nails. "What an ugly color," she murmured.

"What, señora?"

"Nothing." She paused. "Ah, what heat!"

"Come, señora. Shall we go on?"

Angrily she crumpled the crown of the sombrero in her fist. "I am not señora," she said distinctly, looking at the men ahead as they rode up to the cows and roused them from their lethargy. The boy smiled. She went on. "I am señorita. That is not the same thing. Or perhaps you think it is?"

The boy was puzzled; he was conscious of her sudden emotion, but he had no idea of its cause. "Yes, señorita," he said politely, without conviction. And he added, with more assurance, "I am Roberto Paz, at your orders."

The sun shone down upon them from above and was reflected by the mica in the stones at their feet. Chalía undid another button of her shirt.

"It's hot. Will they came back soon?"

"No, señorita. They return by the road. Shall we go?" He turned his horse toward the island ahead.

"I don't want to be where the cows are," said Chalía with

13

petulance. "They have *garrapatas*. The *garrapatas* get under your skin."

Roberto laughed indulgently. "The *garrapatas* will not molest you if you stay on your horse, señorita."

"But I want to get down and rest. I'm so tired!" The discomfort of the heat became pure fatigue as she said the words; this made it possible for the annoyance she felt with him to transform itself into a general state of self-pity and depression that came upon her like a sudden pain. Hanging her head she sobbed: "Ay, *madre mía!* My poor mamá!" She stayed that way a moment, and her horse began to walk slowly toward the trees at the side of the river bed.

Roberto glanced perplexedly in the direction the others had taken. They had all passed out of sight beyond the head of the island; the cows were lying down again. "The señorita should not cry."

She did not reply. Since the reins continued slack, her horse proceeded at a faster pace toward the forest. When it had reached the shade at the edge of the stream, the boy rode quickly to her side. "Señorita!" he cried.

She sighed and looked up at him, her hat still in her hand. "I'm very tired," she repeated. "I want to get down and rest."

There was a path leading into the forest. Roberto went ahead to lead the way, hacking at stray vines and bushes with his machete. Chalía followed, sitting listlessly in the saddle, calmed by the sudden entrance into the green world of silence and comparative coolness.

They rode slowly upward through the forest for a quarter of an hour or so without saying anything to each other. When they came to a gate Roberto opened it without dismounting and waited for Chalía to pass through. As she went by him she smiled and said: "How nice it is here."

He replied, rather curtly, she thought: "Yes, Señorita."

Ahead, the vegetation thinned, and beyond lay a vast, open, slightly undulating expanse of land, decorated here and there, as if by intent, with giant white-trunked ceiba trees. The hot wind blew across this upland terrain, and the cry of cicadas was in the air. Chalía halted her horse and jumped down. The tiny thistlelike plants that covered the ground crackled under her boots. She seated herself carefully in the shade at the very edge of the open land.

Roberto tied the two horses to a tree and stood looking at her with the alert, hostile eyes of the Indian who faces what he does not understand.

"Sit down. Here," she said.

Stonily he obeyed, sitting with his legs straight on the earth in front of him, his back very erect. She rested her hand on his shoulder. "*Qué calor*," she murmured.

She did not expect him to answer, but he did, and his voice sounded remote. "It is not my fault, señorita."

She slipped her arm around his neck and felt the muscles grow tense. She rubbed her face over his chest; he did not move or say anything. With her eyes shut and her head pressing hard against him, she felt as if she were hanging to consciousness only by the ceaseless shrill scream of the cicadas. She remained thus, leaning over more heavily upon him as he braced himself with his hands against the earth behind him. His face had become an impenetrable mask; he seemed not to be thinking of anything, not even to be present.

Breathing heavily, she raised her head to look at him, but found she did not have the courage to reach his eyes with her gaze. Instead she watched his throat and finally whispered, "It doesn't matter what you think of me. It's enough for me to hold you like this."

He turned his head stiffly away from her face, looking across the landscape to the mountains. Gruffly he said, "My brother could come by this place. We must go back to the river."

She tried to bury her face in his chest, to lose herself once more in the delicious sensation. Without warning, he moved quickly and stood up, so that she tumbled forward with her face against the ground.

The surprise of her little fall changed her mood instantly. She sprang up, dashed blindly for the nearer of the two horses, was astride it in an instant, and before he could cry, "It's the bad horse!" had pounded the animal's flanks with her heels. It raised its head wildly; with a violent bound it began to gallop over the countryside. At the first movement she realized dimly that there had been a change, that it was not the same horse, but in her excitement she let her observation stop there. She was delighted to be moving swiftly across the plain against the hot wind. Roberto was left behind.

"*Idiota!*" she screamed into the air. "*Idiota! Idiota!*" with

16

all her might. Ahead of her a tremendous vulture, panic-stricken at the approaching hoof sounds, flapped clumsily away into the sky.

The saddle, having been strapped on for less vigorous action, began to slip. She gripped the pommel with one hand, and seizing her shirt with the other gave it a convulsive tug that ripped it completely open. A powerful feeling of exultation came to her as she glanced down and saw her own skin white in the sunlight.

In the distance to one side, she dimly saw some palm trees reaching above a small patch of lower vegetation. She shut her eyes: the palms looked like shiny green spiders. She was out of breath from the jolting. The sun was too hot. The saddle kept slipping further; she could not right it. The horse showed no sign of being aware of her existence. She pulled on the reins as hard as she could without falling over backward, but it had no effect on the horse, which continued to run at top speed, following no path and missing some of the trees by what seemed no more than inches.

"Where shall I be in an hour?" she asked herself. "Dead, perhaps?" The idea of death did not frighten her the way it did some people. She was afraid of the night because she could not sleep; she was not afraid of life and death because she did not feel implicated to any extent in either one. Only other people lived and died, had their lives and deaths. She, being inside herself, existed merely as herself and not as a part of anything else. People, animals, flowers and stones were objects, and they all belonged to the world outside. It was their juxtapositions that made hostile or friendly patterns. Sometimes she looked at her own hands and feet for several minutes, trying to fight off an indefinite sensation they gave her of belonging also to the world outside. But this never troubled her deeply. The impressions were received and accepted without question; at most she could combat them when they were too strong for her comfort.

Here in the hot morning sun, being pulled forward through the air, she began to feel that almost all of her had slipped out of the inside world, that only a tiny part of her was still she. The part that was left was full of astonishment and disbelief; the only discomfort now lay in having to accept the fact of the great white tree trunks that continued to rush by her.

She tried several times to make herself be elsewhere: in her rose garden at home, in the hotel dining room at Puntarenas, even as a last resort which might prove feasible since it too had been unpleasant, in her bed back at the ranch, with the dark around her.

With a great bound, the horse cleared a ditch. The saddle slipped completely around and hung underneath. Having no pommel to cling to, she kept on as best she could, clutching the horse's flanks with her legs and always pulling on the reins. Suddenly the animal slowed down and stepped briskly into a thicket. There was a path of sorts; she suspected it was the same one they had used coming from the river. She sat listlessly, waiting to see where the horse would go.

Finally it came out into the river bed as she had expected, and trotted back to the ranch. The sun was directly overhead when they reached the paddock. The horse stood outside, waiting to be let in, but it seemed that no one was around.

Making a great effort, she slid down to the ground and found she had difficulty in standing because her legs were trembling so. She was furious and ashamed. As she hobbled toward the house she was strongly hoping Lucha would not see her. A few Indian girls appeared to be the only people about. She dragged herself upstairs and shut herself in her room. The bed had been pushed back against the wall, but she did not have the force to pull it out into the center where she wanted it.

When Don Federico and the others returned, Lucha, who had been reading downstairs, went to the gate. "Where's Chalía?" she cried.

"She was tired. One of the boys brought her back a while ago," he said. "It's just as well. We went halfway to Cañas."

Chalía had her lunch in bed and slept soundly until late in the afternoon. When she emerged from her room onto the veranda, a woman was dusting the rocking chairs and arranging them in a row against the wall.

"Where's my sister?" demanded Chalía.

"Gone to the village in the truck with the señor," the woman replied, going to the head of the stairs and beginning to dust them one by one, as she went down backward.

Chalía seated herself in a chair and put her feet up on the porch railing, reflecting as she did so that if Lucha had been there she would have disapproved of the posture. There was a bend in the river—the only part of it that came within sight of the house—just below her, and a portion of the bank was visible to her through the foliage from where she sat. A large breadfruit tree spread its branches out almost to the opposite side of the stream. There was a pool at the turn, just where the tree's trunk grew out of the muddy bank. An Indian sauntered out of the undergrowth and calmly removed his trousers, then his shirt. He stood there a moment, stark naked, looking at the water, before he walked into it and began to splash and swim. When he had finished bathing he stood again on the bank, smoothing his blue-black hair. Chalía was puzzled, knowing that few Indians would be so immodest as to bathe naked in full view of the upstairs veranda. With a sudden strange sensation as she watched him, she realized it was Roberto and that he was wholly conscious of her presence at that moment.

"He knows Rico is gone and that no one can see him from downstairs," she thought, resolving to tell her brother when he came home. The idea of vengeance upon the boy filled her with a delicious excitement. She watched his deliberate movements as he dressed. He sat down on a rock with only his shirt on and combed his hair. The late afternoon sun shone through the leaves and gave his brown skin an orange cast. When finally he had gone away without once glancing up at the house, she rose and went into her room. Maneuvering the bed into the middle of the floor once more, she began to walk around it; her mood was growing more and more turbulent as she circled about the room.

She heard the truck door slam, and a moment later, voices downstairs. With her finger to her temple, where she always put it when her heart was beating very fast, she slipped out onto the veranda and downstairs. Don Federico was in the commissary, which he opened for a half hour each morning and evening. Chalía stepped inside the door, her mouth already open, feeling the words about to burst from her lungs. Two children were pushing their copper coins along the counter, pointing at the candy they wanted. By the lamp a woman was looking at a bolt of goods. Don Federico was on a ladder, getting down another bolt. Chalía's mouth closed slowly. She looked down at her brother's desk by the door beside her, where he kept his ledgers and bills. In an open cigar box almost touching her hand was a pile of dirty bank notes. She was back in the room before she knew it. She shut the door and saw that she had four ten-colon notes in her hand. She stuffed them into her breeches pocket.

At dinner they made fun of her for having slept all the afternoon, telling her that now she would lie awake again all night.

She was busy eating. "If I do, so much the worse," she said, without looking up.

"I've arranged a little concert after dinner," said Don Federico. Lucha was ecstatic. He went on: "The cowboys have some friends here, over from Bagaces, and Raul has finished building his marimba."

The men and boys began to assemble soon after dinner. There was laughter, and guitars were strummed in the dark on the terrace. The two sisters went to sit at the end near the dining room, Don Federico was in the middle with the vaqueros, and the servants were ranged at the kitchen end. After several solo songs by various men with guitars, Raul and a friend began to play the marimba. Roberto was seated on the floor among the cowboys who were not performing.

"Suppose we all dance," said Don Federico, jumping up and seizing Lucha. They moved about together at one end of the terrace for a moment, but no one else stirred.

"A *bailar!*" Don Federico shouted, laughing.

Several of the girls started to dance timidly in couples, with loud giggling. None of the men would budge. The marimba players went on pounding out the same piece over and over again. Don Federico danced with Chalía, who was stiff from her morning ride; soon she excused herself and left. Instead of going upstairs to bed she crossed onto the front veranda and sat looking across the vast moonlit clearing. The night was thick with eternity. She could feel it there, just beyond the gate. Only the monotonous, tinkling music kept the house within the confines of time, saved it from being engulfed. As she listened to the merrymaking progress, she had the impression that the men were taking more part in it. "Rico has probably opened them a bottle of rum," she thought with fury.

At last it sounded as though everyone were dancing. Her curiosity having risen to a high pitch, she was about to rise and return to the terrace, when a figure appeared at the other end of the veranda. She needed no one to tell her it was Roberto. He was walking soundlessly toward her; he seemed to hesitate

22

as he came up to her, then he squatted down by her chair and looked up at her. She had been right: he smelled of rum.

"Good evening, señorita."

She felt impelled to remain silent. Nevertheless, she said, "Good evening." She put her hand into her pocket, saying to herself that she must do this correctly and quickly.

As he crouched there with his face shining in the moonlight, she bent forward and passed her hand over his smooth hair. Keeping her fingers on the back of his neck, she leaned still further forward and kissed his lips. The rum was very strong. He did not move. She began to whisper in his ear, very low: "Roberto, I love you. I have a present for you. Forty *colones*. Here."

He turned his head swiftly and said out loud, "Where?"

She put the bills into his hand, still holding his head, and whispered again: "Sh! Not a word to anyone. I must go now. I'll give you more tomorrow night." She let go of him.

He rose and went out the gate. She went straight upstairs to bed, and as she went to sleep the music was still going on.

Much later she awoke and lit her lamp. It was half past four. Day would soon break. Feeling full of an unaccustomed energy, Chalía dressed, extinguished the lamp and went outdoors, shutting the gate quietly behind her. In the paddock the horses stirred. She walked by it and started along the road to the village. It was a very silent hour: the night insects had ceased their noises and the birds had not yet begun their early-morning twitter. The moon was low in the sky, so that it

23

remained behind the trees most of the time. Ahead of her Venus flared like a minor moon. She walked quickly, with only a twinge of pain now and then in her hip.

Something dark lying in the road ahead of her made her stop walking. It did not move. She watched it closely, stepping cautiously toward it, ready to run the other way. As her eyes grew accustomed to its form, she saw that it was a man lying absolutely still. And as she drew near, she knew it was Roberto. She touched his arm with her foot. He did not respond. She leaned over and put her hand on his chest. He was breathing deeply, and the smell of liquor was almost overpowering. She straightened and kicked him lightly in the head. There was a tiny groan from far within. This also, she said to herself, would have to be done quickly. She felt wonderfully light and powerful as she slowly maneuvered his body with her feet to the right-hand side of the road. There was a small cliff there, about twenty feet high. When she got him to the edge, she waited a while, looking at his features in the moonlight. His mouth was open a little, and the white teeth peeked out from behind the lips. She smoothed his forehead a few times and with a gentle push rolled him over the edge. He fell very heavily, making a strange animal sound as he hit.

She walked back to the ranch at top speed. It was getting light when she arrived. She went into the kitchen and ordered her breakfast, saying: "I'm up early." The entire day she spent around the house, reading and talking to Lucha. She thought Don Federico looked preoccupied when he set out on his morning tour of inspection, after closing the commissary.

24

She thought he still did when he returned; she told him so at lunch.

"It's nothing," he said. "I can't seem to balance my books."

"And you've always been such a good mathematician," said Chalía.

During the afternoon some cowboys brought Roberto in. She heard the commotion in the kitchen and the servants' cries of "*Ay, Dios!*" She went out to watch. He was conscious, lying on the floor with all the other Indians staring at him.

"What's the matter?" she said.

One of the cowboys laughed. "Nothing of importance. He had too much—" the cowboy made a gesture of drinking from a bottle, "and fell off the road. Nothing but bruises, I think."

After dinner Don Federico asked Chalía and Lucha into his little private office. He looked drawn, and he spoke more slowly than usual. As Chalía entered she saw that Roberto was standing inside the door. He did not look at her. Lucha and Chalía sat down; Don Federico and Roberto remained standing.

"This is the first time anyone has done this to me," said Don Federico, looking down at the rug, his hands locked behind him. "Roberto has stolen from me. The money is missing. Some of it is in his pocket still, more than his monthly wages. I know he has stolen it because he had no money yesterday and because," he turned to Chalía, "because he can account for having it only by lying. He says you gave it to him. Did you give Roberto any money yesterday?"

25

Chalía looked puzzled. "No," she said. "I thought of giving him a *colon* when he brought me back from the ride yesterday morning. But then I thought it would be better to wait until we were leaving to go back to the city. Was it much? He's just a boy."

Don Federico said: "It was forty *colones*. But that's the same as forty *centavos*. Stealing . . ."

Chalía interrupted him. "Rico!" she exclaimed. "Forty *colones!* That's a great deal! Has he spent much of it? You could take it out of his wages little by little." She knew her brother would say what he did say, a moment later.

"Never! He'll leave tonight. And his brother with him."

In the dim light Chalía could see the large purple bruise on Roberto's forehead. He kept his head lowered and did not look up, even when she and Lucha rose and left the room at a sign from their brother. They went upstairs together and sat down on the veranda.

"What barbarous people they are!" said Lucha indignantly. "Poor Rico may learn some day how to treat them. But I'm afraid one of them will kill him first."

Chalía rocked back and forth, fanning herself lazily. "With a few more lessons like this he may change," she said. "What heat!"

They heard Don Federico's voice below by the gate. Firmly it said, "*Adiós*." There were muffled replies and the gate was closed. Don Federico joined his sisters on the veranda. He sat down sadly.

"I didn't like to send them away on foot at night," he said, shaking his head. "But that Roberto is a bad one. It was better to have him go once and for all, quickly. Juan is good, but I had to get rid of him too, of course."

"*Claro, claro,*" said Lucha absently. Suddenly she turned to her brother full of concern. "I hope you remembered to take away the money you said he still had in his pocket."

"Yes, yes," he assured her, but from the tone of his voice she knew he had let the boy keep it.

Don Federico and Lucha said good night and went to bed. Chalía sat up a while, looking vaguely at the wall with the spiders in it. Then she yawned and took the lamp into her room. Again the bed had been pushed back against the wall by the maid. Chalía shrugged her shoulders, got into the bed where it was, blew out the lamp, listened for a few minutes to the night sounds, and went peacefully to sleep, thinking of how surprisingly little time it had taken her to get used to life at Paso Rojo, and even, she had to admit now, to begin to enjoy it.

pastor dowe at tacaté

Pastor Dowe delivered his first sermon in Tacaté on a bright Sunday morning shortly after the beginning of the rainy season. Almost a hundred Indians attended, and some of them had come all the way from Balaché in the valley. They sat quietly on the ground while he spoke to them for an hour or so in their own tongue. Not even the children became restive; there was the most complete silence as long as he kept speaking. But he could see that their attention was born of respect rather than of interest. Being a conscientious man he was troubled to discover this.

When he had finished the sermon, the notes for which were headed "Meaning of Jesus," they slowly got to their feet and began wandering away, quite obviously thinking of other things. Pastor Dowe was puzzled. He had been assured by Dr.

Ramos of the University that his mastery of the dialect was sufficient to enable his prospective parishioners to follow his sermons, and he had had no difficulty conversing with the Indians who had accompanied him up from San Gerónimo. He stood sadly on the small thatch-covered platform in the clearing before his house and watched the men and women walking slowly away in different directions. He had the sensation of having communicated absolutely nothing to them.

All at once he felt he must keep the people here a little longer, and he called out to them to stop. Politely they turned their faces toward the pavilion where he stood, and remained looking at him, without moving. Several of the smaller children were already playing a game, and were darting about silently in the background. The pastor glanced at his wrist watch and spoke to Nicolás, who had been pointed out to him as one of the most intelligent and influential men in the village, asking him to come up and stand beside him.

Once Nicolás was next to him, he decided to test him with a few questions. "Nicolás," he said in his dry, small voice, "what did I tell you today?"

Nicolás coughed and looked over the heads of the assembly to where an enormous sow was rooting in the mud under a mango tree. Then he said: "Don Jesucristo."

"Yes," agreed Pastor Dowe encouragingly. "*Bai*, and Don Jesucristo what?"

"A good man," answered Nicolás with indifference.

"Yes, yes, but what more?" Pastor Dowe was impatient; his voice rose in pitch.

29

Nicolás was silent. Finally he said, "Now I go," and stepped carefully down from the platform. The others again began to gather up their belongings and move off. For a moment Pastor Dowe was furious. Then he took his notebook and his Bible and went into the house.

At lunch Mateo, who waited on table, and whom he had brought with him from Ocosingo, stood leaning against the wall smiling.

"Señor," he said, "Nicolás says they will not come again to hear you without music."

"Music!" cried Pastor Dowe, setting his fork on the table. "Ridiculous! What music? We have no music."

"He says the father at Yalactín used to sing."

"Ridiculous!" said the pastor again. "In the first place I can't sing, and in any case it's unheard of! *Inaudito!*"

"Sí, *verdad?*" agreed Mateo.

The pastor's tiny bedroom was breathlessly hot, even at night. However, it was the only room in the little house with a window on the outside; he could shut the door onto the noisy patio where by day the servants invariably gathered for their work and their conversations. He lay under the closed canopy of his mosquito net, listening to the barking of the dogs in the village below. He was thinking about Nicolás. Apparently Nicolás had chosen for himself the role of envoy from the village to the mission. The pastor's thin lips moved. "A troublemaker," he whispered to himself. "I'll speak with him tomorrow."

Early the next morning he stood outside Nicolás's hut.

Each house in Tacaté had its own small temple: a few tree trunks holding up some thatch to shelter the offerings of fruit and cooked food. The pastor took care not to go near the one that stood near by; he already felt enough like a pariah, and Dr. Ramos had warned him against meddling of that sort. He called out.

A little girl about seven years old appeared in the doorway of the house. She looked at him wildly a moment with huge round eyes before she squealed and disappeared back into the darkness. The pastor waited and called again. Presently a man came around the hut from the back and told him that Nicolás would return. The pastor sat down on a stump. Soon the little girl stood again in the doorway; this time she smiled coyly. The pastor looked at her severely. It seemed to him she was too old to run about naked. He turned his head away and examined the thick red petals of a banana blossom hanging near-by. When he looked back she had come out and was standing near him, still smiling. He got up and walked toward the road, his head down, as if deep in thought. Nicolás entered through the gate at that moment, and the pastor, colliding with him, apologized.

"Good," grunted Nicolás. "What?"

His visitor was not sure how he ought to begin. He decided to be pleasant.

"I am a good man," he smiled.

"Yes," said Nicolás. "Don Jesucristo is a good man."

"No, no, no!" cried Pastor Dowe.

Nicolás looked politely confused, but said nothing.

31

Feeling that his command of the dialect was not equal to this sort of situation, the pastor wisely decided to begin again. "Hachakyum made the world. Is that true?"

Nicolás nodded in agreement, and squatted down at the pastor's feet, looking up at him, his eyes narrowed against the sun.

"Hachakyum made the sky," the pastor began to point, "the mountains, the trees, those people there. Is that true?"

Again Nicolás assented.

"Hachakyum is good. Hachakyum made you. True?" Pastor Dowe sat down again on the stump.

Nicolás spoke finally, "All that you say is true."

The pastor permitted himself a pleased smile and went on. "Hachakyum made everything and everyone because He is mighty and good."

Nicolás frowned. "No!" he cried. "That is not true! Hachakyum did not make everyone. He did not make you. He did not make guns or Don Jesucristo. Many things He did not make!"

The pastor shut his eyes a moment, seeking strength. "Good," he said at last in a patient voice. "Who made the other things? Who made me? Please tell me."

Nicolás did not hesitate. "Metzabok."

"But who is Metzabok?" cried the pastor, letting an outraged note show in his voice. The word for God he had always known only as Hachakyum.

"Metzabok makes all the things that do not belong here," said Nicolás.

The pastor rose, took out his handkerchief and wiped his

32

forehead. "You hate me," he said, looking down at the Indian. The word was too strong, but he did not know how to say it any other way.

Nicolás stood up quickly and touched the pastor's arm with his hand.

"No. That is not true. You are a good man. Everyone likes you."

Pastor Dowe backed away in spite of himself. The touch of the brown hand was vaguely distasteful to him. He looked beseechingly into the Indian's face and said, "But Hachakyum did not make me?"

"No."

There was a long pause.

"Will you come next time to my house and hear me speak?"

Nicolás looked uncomfortable.

"Everyone has work to do," he said.

"Mateo says you want music," began the pastor.

Nicolás shrugged. "To me it is not important. But the others will come if you have music. Yes, that is true. They like music."

"But *what* music?" cried the pastor in desperation.

"They say you have a *bitrola*."

The pastor looked away, thinking: "There is no way to keep anything from these people." Along with all his other household goods and the things left behind by his wife when she died, he had brought a little portable phonograph. It was somewhere in the storeroom piled with the empty valises and cold-weather garments.

33

"Tell them I will play the *bitrola,*" he said, going out the gate.

The little girl ran after him and stood watching him as he walked up the road.

On his way through the village the pastor was troubled by the reflection that he was wholly alone in this distant place, alone in his struggle to bring the truth to its people. He consoled himself by recalling that it is only in each man's own consciousness that the isolation exists; objectively man is always a part of something.

When he arrived home he sent Mateo to the storeroom to look for the portable phonograph. After a time the boy brought it out, dusted it and stood by while the pastor opened the case. The crank was inside. He took it out and wound the spring. There were a few records in the compartment at the top. The first he examined were "Let's Do It," "Crazy Rhythm," and "Strike up the Band," none of which Pastor Dowe considered proper accompaniments to his sermons. He looked further. There was a recording of Al Jolson singing "Sonny Boy" and a cracked copy of "She's Funny That Way." As he looked at the labels he remembered how the music on each disc had sounded. Unfortunately Mrs. Dowe had disliked hymn music; she had called it "mournful."

"So here we are," he sighed, "without music."

Mateo was astonished. "It does not play?"

"I can't play them this music for dancing, Mateo."

Cómo nó, señor! They will like it very much!

"No, Mateo!" said the pastor forcefully, and he put on

34

"Crazy Rhythm" to illustrate his point. As the thin metallic tones issued from the instrument, Mateo's expression changed to one of admiration bordering on beatitude. "*Qué bonito!*" he said reverently. Pastor Dowe lifted the tone arm and the hopping rhythmical pattern ceased.

"It cannot be done," he said with finality, closing the lid.

Nevertheless on Saturday he remembered that he had promised Nicolás there would be music at the service, and he decided to tell Mateo to carry the phonograph out to the pavilion in order to have it there in case the demand for it should prove to be pressing. This was a wise precaution, because the next morning when the villagers arrived they were talking of nothing but the music they were to hear.

His topic was "The Strength of Faith," and he had got about ten minutes into the sermon when Nicolás, who was squatting directly in front of him, quietly stood up and raised his hand. Pastor Dowe frowned and stopped talking.

Nicolás spoke: "Now music, then talk. Then music, then talk. Then music." He turned around and faced the others. "That is a good way." There were murmurs of assent, and everyone leaned a bit farther forward on his haunches to catch whatever musical sounds might issue from the pavilion.

The pastor sighed and lifted the machine onto the table, knocking off the Bible that lay at the edge. "Of course," he said to himself with a faint bitterness. The first record he came to was "Crazy Rhythm." As it started to play, an infant nearby, who had been singsonging a series of meaningless sounds, ceased making its parrotlike noises, remaining silent and transfixed as it stared at the platform. Everyone sat absolutely quiet until the piece was over. Then there was a hubbub of approbation. "Now more talk," said Nicolás, looking very pleased.

The pastor continued. He spoke a little haltingly now, because the music had broken his train of thought, and even by looking at his notes he could not be sure just how far he had got before the interruption. As he continued, he looked down at the people sitting nearest him. Beside Nicolás he noticed the little girl who had watched him from the doorway, and he was gratified to see that she was wearing a small garment which managed to cover her. She was staring at him with an expression he interpreted as one of fascinated admiration.

Presently, when he felt that his audience was about to grow restive (even though he had to admit that they never would have shown it outwardly) he put on "Sonny Boy." From the reaction it was not difficult to guess that this selection was finding less favor with its listeners. The general expression of tense anticipation at the beginning of the record soon relaxed into one of routine enjoyment of a less intense degree. When the piece was finished, Nicolás got to his feet again and raised his hand solemnly, saying: "Good. But the other music is more beautiful."

The pastor made a short summation, and, after playing "Crazy Rhythm" again, he announced that the service was over.

In this way "Crazy Rhythm" became an integral part of Pastor Dowe's weekly service. After a few months the old record was so badly worn that he determined to play it only once at each gathering. His flock submitted to this show of economy with bad grace. They complained, using Nicolás as emissary.

"But the music is old. There will be no more if I use it all," the pastor explained.

Nicolás smiled unbelievingly. "You say that. But you do not want us to have it."

The following day, as the pastor sat reading in the patio's shade, Mateo again announced Nicolás, who had entered through the kitchen and, it appeared, had been conversing with the servants there. By now the pastor had learned fairly well how to read the expressions on Nicolás's face; the one he saw there now told him that new exactions were at hand.

Nicolás looked respectful. "Señor," he said, "we like you because you have given us music when we asked you for it. Now we are all good friends. We want you to give us salt."

"Salt?" exclaimed Pastor Dowe, incredulous. "What for?"

Nicolás laughed good-naturedly, making it clear that he thought the pastor was joking with him. Then he made a gesture of licking. "To eat," he said.

"Ah, yes," murmured the pastor, recalling that among the Indians rock salt is a scarce luxury.

"But we have no salt," he said quickly.

"Oh, yes, señor. There." Nicolás indicated the kitchen.

The pastor stood up. He was determined to put an end to this haggling, which he considered a demoralizing element in his

37

official relationship with the village. Signaling for Nicolás to follow, he walked into the kitchen, calling as he entered, "Quintina, show me our salt."

Several of the servants, including Mateo, were standing in the room. It was Mateo who opened a low cupboard and disclosed a great stack of grayish cakes piled on the floor. The pastor was astonished. "So many kilos of salt!" he exclaimed. "*Cómo se hace?*"

Mateo calmly told him it had been brought with them all the way from Ocosingo. "For us," he added, looking about at the others.

Pastor Dowe seized upon this, hoping it was meant as a hint and could be recognized as one. "Of course," he said to Nicolás. "This is for my house."

Nicolás looked unimpressed. "You have enough for everyone in the village," he remarked. "In two Sundays you can get more from Ocosingo. Everyone will be very happy all the time that way. Everyone will come each time you speak. You give them salt and make music."

Pastor Dowe felt himself beginning to tremble a little. He knew he was excited and so he was careful to make his voice sound natural.

"I will decide, Nicolás," he said. "Good-bye."

It was clear that Nicolás in no way regarded these words as a dismissal. He answered, "Good-bye," and leaned back against the wall calling, "Marta!" The little girl, of whose presence in the room the pastor now became conscious, moved out from the shadows of a corner. She held what appeared to him to be a

38

large doll, and was being very solicitous of it. As the pastor stepped out into the bright patio, the picture struck him as false, and he turned around and looked back into the kitchen, frowning. He remained in the doorway in an attitude of suspended action for a moment, staring at little Marta. The doll, held lovingly in the child's arms, and swaddled in a much-used rag, was making spasmodic movements.

The pastor's ill-humor was with him; probably he would have shown it no matter what the circumstances. "What is it?" he demanded indignantly. As if in answer the bundle squirmed again, throwing off part of the rag that covered it, and the pastor saw what looked to him like a comic-strip caricature of Red Riding Hood's wolf peering out from under the grandmother's nightcap. Again Pastor Dowe cried, "What is it?"

Nicolás turned from his conversation, amused, and told Marta to hold it up and uncover it so the señor could see it. This she did, pulling away the wrapping and exposing to view a lively young alligator which, since it was being held more or less on its back, was objecting in a routine fashion to the treatment by rhythmically paddling the air with its little black feet. Its rather long face seemed, however, to be smiling.

"Good heavens!" cried the pastor in English. The spectacle struck him as strangely scandalous. There was a hidden obscenity in the sight of the mildly agitated little reptile with its head wrapped in a rag, but Marta was still holding it out toward him for his inspection. He touched the smooth scales of its belly with his fingers, and withdrew his hand, saying, "Its jaws should be bound. It will bite her."

39

Mateo laughed. "She is too quick," and then said it in dialect to Nicolás, who agreed, and also laughed. The pastor patted Marta on the head as she returned the animal to her bosom and resumed cradling it tenderly.

Nicolás' eyes were on him. "You like Marta?" he asked seriously.

The pastor was thinking about the salt. "Yes, yes," he said with the false enthusiasm of the preoccupied man. He went to his bedroom and shut the door. Lying on the narrow bed in the afternoon was the same as lying on it at night: there was the same sound of dogs barking in the village. Today there was also the sound of wind going past the window. Even the canopy of mosquito netting swayed a little from time to time as the air came into the room. The pastor was trying to decide whether or not to give in to Nicolás. When he got very sleepy, he thought: "After all, what principle am I upholding in keeping it from them? They want music. They want salt. They will learn to want God." This thought proved relaxing to him, and he fell asleep to the sound of the dogs barking and the wind shrilling past the window.

During the night the clouds rolled down off the mountains into the valley, and when dawn came they remained there, impaled on the high trees. The few birds that made themselves heard sounded as though they were singing beneath the ceiling of a great room. The wet air was thick with wood smoke, but there was no noise from the village; a wall of cloud lay between it and the mission house.

From his bed, instead of the wind passing the window, the

pastor heard the slow drops of water falling upon the bushes from the eaves. He lay still awhile, lulled by the subdued chatter of the servants' voices in the kitchen. Then he went to the window and looked out into the grayness. Even the nearest trees were invisible; there was a heavy odor of earth. He dressed, shivering as the damp garments touched his skin. On the table lay a newspaper:

BARCELONA BOMBARDEADO POR DOSCIENTOS AVIONES

As he shaved, trying to work up a lather with the tepid water Quintina had brought him, full of charcoal ashes, it occurred to him that he would like to escape from the people of Tacaté and the smothering feeling they gave him of being lost in antiquity. It would be good to be free from that infinite sadness even for a few hours.

He ate a larger breakfast than usual and went outside to the sheltered platform, where he sat down in the dampness and began to read the seventy-eighth Psalm, which he had thought of using as the basis of a sermon. As he read he looked out at the emptiness in front of him. Where he knew the mango tree stood he could see only the white void, as if the land dropped away at the platform's edge for a thousand feet or more.

"He clave the rocks in the wilderness, and gave them drink as out of the great depths." From the house came the sound of Quintina's giggling. "Mateo is probably chasing her around the patio," thought the pastor; wisely he had long since given up expecting any Indian to behave as he considered an adult should. Every few seconds on the other side of the pavilion a turkey made its hysterical gobbling sound. The pastor spread his Bible out on the table, put his hands to his ears, and continued to read: "He caused an east wind to blow in the heaven: and by His power He brought in the south wind."

"Passages like that would sound utterly pagan in the dialect," he caught himself thinking. He unstopped his ears and reflected: "But to their ears *everything* must have a pagan sound. Everything I say is transformed on the way to them into something else." This was a manner of thinking that Pastor Dowe had always taken pains to avoid. He fixed his eyes on the text with determination, and read on. The giggling in the house was louder; he could hear Mateo too now. "He sent divers sorts of flies among them; . . . and frogs, which destroyed them." The door into the patio was opened and the pastor heard Mateo coughing as he stood looking out. "He certainly has tuberculosis," said the pastor to himself, as the Indian spat repeatedly. He shut his Bible and took off his glasses, feeling about on the table for their case. Not encountering it, he rose, and taking a step forward, crushed it under his heel. Compassionately, he stooped down and picked it up. The hinges were snapped and the metal sides under their artificial leather covering were bent out of shape. Mateo could have hammered it back into a semblance of its form, but Pastor Dowe preferred to think: "All things have their death." He had had the case eleven years. Briefly he summed up its life: the sunny afternoon when he had bought it on the little side street in downtown Havana;

42

the busy years in the hills of southern Brazil; the time in Chile when he had dropped the case, with a pair of dark glasses in it, out the bus window, and everyone in the bus had got out and helped him look for it; the depressing year in Chicago when for some reason he had left it in a bureau drawer most of the time and had carried his glasses loose in his coat pocket. He remembered some of the newspaper clippings he had kept in the case, and many of the little slips of paper with ideas jotted down on them. He looked tenderly down at it, thinking: "And so this is the place and time, and these are the circumstances of its death." For some reason he was happy to have witnessed this death; it was comforting to know exactly how the case had finished its existence. He still looked at it with sadness for a moment. Then he flung it out into the white air as if the precipice were really there. With his Bible under his arm he strode to the door and brushed past Mateo without saying a word. But as he walked into his room it seemed to him that Mateo had looked at him in a strange fashion, as if he knew something and were waiting to see when the pastor would find out, too.

Back in his suffocating little room the pastor felt an even more imperious need to be alone for a time. He changed his shoes, took his cane and went out into the fog. In this weather there was only one path practicable, and that led downward through the village. He stepped ahead over the stones with great caution, for although he could discern the ground at his feet and the spot where he put the tip of his cane each time, beyond that on all sides was mere whiteness. Walking along thus, he reflected, was like trying to read a text with only one

43

letter visible at a time. The wood smoke was sharp in the still air.

For perhaps half an hour Pastor Dowe continued this way, carefully putting one foot before the other. The emptiness around him, the lack of all visual detail, rather than activating his thought, served to dull his perceptions. His progress over the stones was laborious but strangely relaxing. One of the few ideas that came into his head as he moved along was that it would be pleasant to pass through the village without anyone's noticing him, and it seemed to him that it might be managed; even at ten feet he would be invisible. He could walk between the huts and hear the babies crying, and when he came out at the other end no one would know he had been there. He was not sure where he would go then.

The way became suddenly rougher as the path went into a zigzagging descent along the steep side of a ravine. He had reached the bottom before he raised his head once. "Ah," he said, standing still. The fog was now above him, a great gray quilt of cloud. He saw the giant trees that stood around him and heard them dripping slowly in a solemn, uneven chorus onto the wild coca leaves beneath.

"There is no such place as this on the way to the village," thought the pastor. He was mildly annoyed, but more astonished, to find himself standing by these trees that looked like elephants and were larger than any other trees he had seen in the region. Automatically he turned around in the path and started back up the slope. Beside the overpowering sadness of the landscape, now that it was visible to him, the fog up there was a comfort and a protection. He paused for a moment to stare back at the fat, spiny tree trunks and the welter of vegetation beyond. A small sound behind him made him turn his head.

Two Indians were trotting down the path toward him. As they came up they stopped and looked at him with such expectancy on their dark little faces that Pastor Dowe thought they were going to speak. Instead the one ahead made a grunting sound and motioned to the other to follow. There was no way of effecting a detour around the pastor, so they brushed violently against him as they went by. Without once looking back they hurried on downward and disappeared among the green coca leaves.

This unlikely behavior on the part of the two natives vaguely intrigued him; on an impulse he determined to find an explanation for it. He started after them.

Soon he had gone beyond the spot where he had turned back a moment ago. He was in the forest; the plant odor was almost unbearable—a smell of living and dead vegetation in a world where slow growth and slow death are simultaneous and inseparable. He stopped once and listened for footsteps. Apparently the Indians had run on ahead of him; nevertheless he continued on his way. Since the path was fairly wide and well broken in, it was only now and then that he came into contact with a hanging tendril or a projecting branch.

The posturing trees and vines gave the impression of having been arrested in furious motion, and presented a monotonous succession of tortured tableaux vivants. It was as if, for the moment while he watched, the desperate battle for air had

45

been suspended and would be resumed only when he turned away his head. As he looked, he decided that it was precisely this unconfirmable quality of surreptitiousness which made the place so disquieting. Now and then, high above his head, a blood-colored butterfly would float silently through the gloom from one tree trunk to another. They were all alike; it seemed to him that it must be always the same insect. Several times he passed the white grillwork of great spider webs flung across between the plants like gates painted on the dark wall behind. But all the webs looked uninhabited. The large, leisurely drops of water still continued to fall from above; even if it had been raining hard, the earth could not have been wetter.

The pastor was astigmatic, and since he was beginning to be dizzy from watching so many details, he kept his eyes looking straight ahead as he walked, deviating his gaze only when he had to avoid the plant life that had grown across the path. The floor of the forest continued flat. Suddenly he became aware that the air around him was reverberating with faint sounds. He stood still, and recognized the casual gurgle a deep stream makes from time to time as it moves past its banks. Almost immediately ahead of him was the water, black and wide, and considering its proximity, incredibly quiet in its swift flowing. A few paces before him a great dead tree, covered with orange fungus, lay across the path. The pastor's glance followed the trunk to the left; at the small end, facing him, sat the two Indians. They were looking at him with interest, and he knew they had been waiting for him. He walked over to them, greeted them. They replied solemnly, never taking their shining eyes from his face.

As if they had rehearsed it, they both rose at the same instant and walked to the water's edge, where they stood looking down. Then one of them glanced back at the pastor and said simply, "Come." As he made his way around the log he saw that they were standing by a long bamboo raft which was beached on the muddy bank. They lifted it and dropped one end into the stream.

"Where are you going?" asked the pastor. For reply they lifted their short brown arms in unison and waved them slowly in the direction of downstream. Again the one who had spoken before said, "Come." The pastor, his curiosity aroused, looked suspiciously at the delicate raft, and back at the two men. At the same time he felt that it would be pleasanter to be riding with them than to go back through the forest. Impatiently he again demanded, "Where are you going? Tacaté?"

"Tacaté," echoed the one who up to this point had not spoken.

"Is it strong?" queried the pastor, stooping to push lightly on a piece of bamboo. This was merely a formality; he had perfect faith in the Indians' ability to master the materials of the jungle.

"Strong," said the first. "Come."

The pastor glanced back into the wet forest, climbed onto the raft, and sat doubled up on its bottom in the stern. The two quickly jumped aboard and pushed the frail craft from the bank with a pole.

47

Then began a journey which almost at once Pastor Dowe regretted having undertaken. Even as the three of them shot swiftly ahead, around the first bend in the stream, he wished he had stayed behind and could be at this moment on his way up the side of the ravine. And as they sped on down the silent waterway he continued to reproach himself for having come along without knowing why. At each successive bend in the tunnellike course, he felt farther from the world. He found himself straining in a ridiculous effort to hold the raft back: it glided far too easily along the top of the black water. Further from the world, or did he mean further from God? A region like this seemed outside God's jurisdiction. When he had reached that idea he shut his eyes. It was an absurdity, manifestly impossible—in any case, inadmissible—yet it had occurred to him and was remaining with him in his mind. "God is always with me," he said to himself silently, but the formula had no effect. He opened his eyes quickly and looked at the two men. They were facing him, but he had the impression of being invisible to them; they could see only the quickly dissipated ripples left behind on the surface of the water, and the irregular arched ceiling of vegetation under which they had passed.

The pastor took his cane from where it was lying hidden, and gesticulated with it as he asked, "Where are we going?" Once again they both pointed vaguely into the air, over their shoulders, as if the question were of no interest, and the expression on their faces never changed. Loath to let even another tree go past, the pastor mechanically immersed his cane in the water as though he would stop the constant forward thrusting of the raft; he withdrew it immediately and laid it dripping across the bottom. Even that much contact with the dark stream was unpleasant to him. He tried to tell himself that there was no reason for his sudden spiritual collapse, but at the same time it seemed to him that he could feel the innermost fibers of his consciousness in the process of relaxing. The journey downstream was a monstrous letting go, and he fought against it with all his power. "Forgive me, O God, I am leaving You behind. Forgive me for leaving You behind." His nails pressed into his palms as he prayed.

And so he sat in agonized silence while they slid ahead through the forest and out into a wide lagoon where the gray sky was once more visible. Here the raft went much more slowly, and the Indians propelled it gently with their hands toward the shore where the water was shallow. Then one of them poled it along with the bamboo stick. The pastor did not notice the great beds of water hyacinths they passed through, nor the silken sound made as they rubbed against the raft. Out here under the low-hanging clouds there was occasionally a bird cry or a sudden rustle in the high grass by the water's edge. Still the pastor remained sunk within himself, feeling, rather than thinking: "Now it is done. I have passed over into the other land." And he remained so deeply preoccupied with this emotional certainty that he was not aware of it when they approached a high escarpment rising sheer from the lagoon, nor when they drew up onto the sand of a small cove at one side of the cliff. When he looked up the two Indians were standing on the sand, and one of them was saying, "Come." They did not help him get

49

ashore; he did this with some difficulty, although he was conscious of none.

As soon as he was on land they led him along the foot of the cliff that curved away from the water. Following a tortuous track beaten through the undergrowth they came out all at once at the very foot of the wall of rock.

There were two caves—a small one opening to the left, and a wider, higher one to the right. They halted outside the smaller. "Go in," they said to the pastor. It was not very light inside, and he could see very little. The two remained at the entrance. "Your god lives here," said one. "Speak with him."

The pastor was on his knees. "O Father, hear my voice. Let my voice come through to you. I ask it in Jesus' name. . . ." The Indian was calling to him, "Speak in our tongue." The pastor made an effort, and began a halting supplication in the dialect. There were grunts of satisfaction outside. The concentration demanded in order to translate his thoughts into the still unfamiliar language served to clear his mind somewhat. And the comforting parallel between this prayer and those he offered for his congregation helped to restore his calm. As he continued to speak, always with fewer hesitations, he felt a great rush of strength going through him. Confidently he raised his head and went on praying, his eyes on the wall in front of him. At the same moment he heard the cry: "Metzabok hears you now. Say more to him."

The pastor's lips stopped moving, and his eyes saw for the first time the red hand painted on the rock before him, and the charcoal, the ashes, the flower petals and the wooden spoons strewn about. But he had no sensation of horror; that was over. The important thing now was that he felt strong and happy. His spiritual condition was a physical fact. Having prayed to Metzabok was also a fact, of course, but his deploring of it was in purely mental terms. Without formulating the thought, he decided that forgiveness would be forthcoming when he asked God for it.

To satisfy the watchers outside the cave he added a few formal phrases to his prayer, rose, and stepped out into the daylight. For the first time he noticed a certain animation in the features of the two little men. One said, "Metzabok is very happy." The other said, "Wait." Whereupon they both hurried over to the larger of the two apertures and disappeared inside. The pastor sat on a rock, resting his chin on the hand that held the head of his cane. He was still suffused with the strange triumphant sensation of having returned to himself.

He heard them muttering for a quarter of an hour or so inside the cave. Presently they came out, still looking very serious. Moved by curiosity, the pastor risked a question. He indicated the larger cave with a finger and said, "Hachakyum lives there?" Together they assented. He wanted to go further and ask if Hachakyum approved of his having spoken with Metzabok, but he felt the question would be imprudent; besides, he was certain the answer would be in the affirmative.

They arrived back in the village at nightfall, after having walked all the way. The Indians' gait had been far too swift for Pastor Dowe, and they had stopped only once to eat some sapotes they had found under the trees. He asked to be taken to the house of Nicolás. It was raining lightly when they reached the hut. The pastor sat down in the doorway beneath the overhanging eaves of cane. He felt utterly exhausted; it had been one of the most tiring days of his life, and he was not home yet.

His two companions ran off when Nicolás appeared. Evidently he already knew of the visit to the cave. It seemed to the pastor that he had never seen his face so full of expression or so pleasant. "*Utz, utz,*" said Nicolás. "Good, good. You must eat and sleep."

After a meal of fruit and maize cakes, the pastor felt better. The hut was filled with wood smoke from the fire in the corner. He lay back in a low hammock which little Marta, casually pulling on a string from time to time, kept in gentle motion. He was overcome with a desire to sleep, but his host seemed to be in a communicative mood, and he wanted to profit by it. As he was about to speak, Nicolás approached, carrying a rusty tin biscuit box. Squatting beside the hammock he said in a low voice: "I will show you my things." The pastor was delighted; this bespoke a high degree of friendliness. Nicolás opened the box and took out some sample-size squares of printed cloth, an old vial of quinine tablets, a torn strip of newspaper, and four copper coins. He gave the pastor time to examine each carefully. At the bottom of the box were a good many orange and blue feathers which Nicolás did not bother to take out. The pastor realized that he was seeing the treasures of the household, that these items were rare objects of art. He looked at each thing with great seriousness handing it back with a verbal expression of admiration. Finally he said: "Thank you," and fell back into the hammock. Nicolás returned the box to the women sitting in the corner. When he came back over to the pastor he said: "Now we sleep."

"Nicolás," asked the pastor, "is Metzabok bad?"

"*Bai*, señor. Sometimes very bad. Like a small child. When he does not get what he wants right away, he makes fires, fever, wars. He can be very good, too, when he is happy. You should speak with him every day. Then you will know him."

"But you never speak with him."

"*Bai*, we do. Many do, when they are sick or unhappy. They ask him to take away the trouble. I never speak with him," Nicolás looked pleased, "Because Hachakyum is my good friend and I do not need Metzabok. Besides, Metzabok's home is far—three hours' walk. I can speak with Hachakyum here." The pastor knew he meant the little altar outside. He nodded and fell asleep.

The village in the early morning was a chaos of shrill sounds: dogs, parrots and cockatoos, babies, turkeys. The pastor lay still in his hammock awhile listening, before he was officially wakened by Nicolás. "We must go now, señor," he said. "Everyone is waiting for you."

The pastor sat up, a little bit alarmed. "Where?" he cried.

"You speak and make music today."

"Yes, yes." He had quite forgotten it was Sunday.

The pastor was silent, walking beside Nicolás up the road to the mission. The weather had changed, and the early sun was very bright. "I have been fortified by my experience," he

53

was thinking. His head was clear; he felt amazingly healthy. The unaccustomed sensation of vigor gave him a strange nostalgia for the days of his youth. "I must always have felt like this then. I remember it," he thought.

At the mission there was a great crowd—many more people than he had ever seen attend a sermon at Tacaté. They were chatting quietly, but when he and Nicolás appeared there was an immediate hush. Mateo was standing in the pavilion waiting for him, with the phonograph open. With a pang the pastor realized he had not prepared a sermon for his flock. He went into the house for a moment, and returned to seat himself at the table in the pavilion, where he picked up his Bible. He had left his few notes in the book, so that it opened to the seventy-eighth Psalm. "I shall read them that," he decided. He turned to Mateo. "Play the *disco*," he said. Mateo put on "Crazy Rhythm." The pastor quickly made a few pencil alterations in the text of the psalm, substituting the names of minor local deities, like Usukun and Sibanaa for such names as Jacob and Ephraim, and local place names for Israel and Egypt. And he wrote the word Hachakyum each time the word God or the Lord appeared. He had not finished when the record stopped. "Play it again," he commanded. The audience was delighted, even though the sound was abominably scratchy. When the music was over for the second time, he stood and began to paraphrase the psalm in a clear voice. "The children of Sibanaa, carrying bows to shoot, ran into the forest to hide when the enemy came. They did not keep their promises to Hachakyum, and they would not live as He told them to live." The audience was electrified. As he spoke, he looked down and saw the child Marta staring up at him. She had let go of her baby alligator, and it was crawling with a surprising speed toward the table where he sat. Quintina, Mateo, and the two maids were piling up the bars of salt on the ground to one side. They kept returning to the kitchen for more. He realized that what he was saying doubtless made no sense in terms of his listeners' religion, but it was a story of the unleashing of divine displeasure upon an unholy people, and they were enjoying it vastly. The alligator, trailing its rags, had crawled to within a few inches of the pastor's feet, where it remained quiet, content to be out of Marta's arms.

Presently, while he was still speaking, Mateo began to hand out the salt, and soon they all were running their tongues rhythmically over the large rough cakes, but continuing to pay strict attention to his words. When he was about to finish, he motioned to Mateo to be ready to start the record again the minute he finished; on the last word he lowered his arm as a signal, and "Crazy Rhythm" sounded once more. The alligator began to crawl hastily toward the far end of the pavilion. Pastor Dowe bent down and picked it up. As he stepped forward to hand it to Mateo, Nicolás rose from the ground, and taking Marta by the hand, walked over into the pavilion with her.

"Señor," he said, "Marta will live with you. I give her to you."

"What do you mean?" cried the pastor in a voice which cracked a little. The alligator squirmed in his hand.

"She is your wife. She will live here."

Pastor Dowe's eyes grew very wide. He was unable to say

55

anything for a moment. He shook his hands in the air and finally he said: "No" several times.

Nicolás' face grew unpleasant. "You do not like Marta?"

"Very much. She is beautiful." The pastor sat down slowly on his chair. "But she is a little child."

Nicolás frowned with impatience. "She is already large."

"No, Nicolás. No. No."

Nicolás pushed his daughter forward and stepped back several paces, leaving her there by the table. "It is done," he said sternly. "She is your wife. I have given her to you."

Pastor Dowe looked out over the assembly and saw the unspoken approval in all the faces. "Crazy Rhythm" ceased to play. There was silence. Under the mango tree he saw a woman toying with a small, shiny object. Suddenly he recognized his glasses case; the woman was stripping the leatheroid fabric from it. The bare aluminum with its dents flashed in the sun. For some reason even in the middle of this situation he found himself thinking: "So I was wrong. It is not dead. She will keep it, the way Nicolás has kept the quinine tablets."

He looked down at Marta. The child was staring at him quite without expression. Like a cat, he reflected.

Again he began to protest. "Nicolás," he cried, his voice very high, "this is impossible!" He felt a hand grip his arm, and turned to receive a warning glance from Mateo.

Nicolás had already advanced toward the pavilion, his face like a thundercloud. As he seemed about to speak, the pastor interrupted him quickly. He had decided to temporize. "She may stay at the mission today," he said weakly.

"She is your wife," said Nicolás with great feeling. "You cannot send her away. You must keep her."

"*Diga que sí*," Mateo was whispering. "Say yes, señor."

"Yes," the pastor heard himself saying. "Yes. Good." He got up and walked slowly into the house, holding the alligator with one hand and pushing Marta in front of him with the other. Mateo followed and closed the door after them.

"Take her into the kitchen, Mateo," said the pastor dully, handing the little reptile to Marta. As Mateo went across the patio leading the child by the hand, he called after him. "Leave her with Quintina and come to my room."

He sat down on the edge of his bed, staring ahead of him with unseeing eyes. At each moment his predicament seemed to him more terrible. With relief he heard Mateo knock. The people outdoors were slowly leaving. It cost him an effort to call out, "*Adelante*." When Mateo had come in, the pastor said, "Close the door."

"Mateo, did you know they were going to do this? That they were going to bring that child here?"

"*Sí, señor.*"

"You knew it! But why didn't you say anything? Why didn't you tell me?"

Mateo shrugged his shoulders, looking at the floor. "I didn't know it would matter to you," he said. "Anyway, it would have been useless."

"Useless? Why? You could have stopped Nicolás," said the pastor, although he did not believe it himself.

Mateo laughed shortly. "You think so?"

57

"Mateo, you must help me. We must oblige Nicolás to take her back."

Mateo shook his head. "It can't be done. These people are very severe. They never change their laws."

"Perhaps a letter to the administrator at Ocosingo . . ."

"No, señor. That would make still more trouble. You are not a Catholic." Mateo shifted on his feet and suddenly smiled thinly. "Why not let her stay? She doesn't eat much. She can work in the kitchen. In two years she will be very pretty."

The pastor jumped, and made such a wide and vehement gesture with his hands that the mosquito netting, looped above his head, fell down about his face. Mateo helped him disentangle himself. The air smelled of dust from the netting.

"You don't understand anything!" shouted Pastor Dowe, beside himself. "I can't talk to you! I don't want to talk to you! Go out and leave me alone." Mateo obediently left the room.

Pounding his left palm with his right fist, over and over again, the pastor stood in his window before the landscape that shone in the strong sun. A few women were still eating under the mango tree; the rest had gone back down the hill.

He lay on his bed throughout the long afternoon. When twilight came he had made his decision. Locking his door, he proceeded to pack what personal effects he could into his smallest suitcase. His Bible and notebooks went on top with his toothbrush and atabrine tablets. When Quintina came to announce supper he asked to have it brought to his bed, taking care to slip the packed valise into the closet before he unlocked the door for her to enter. He waited until the talking had ceased all over the house, until he knew everyone was asleep. With the small bag not too heavy in one hand he tiptoed into the patio, out through the door into the fragrant night, across the open space in front of the pavilion, under the mango tree and down the path leading to Tacaté. Then he began to walk fast, because he wanted to get through the village before the moon rose.

There was a chorus of dogs barking as he entered the village street. He began to run, straight through to the other end. And he kept running even then, until he had reached the point where the path, wider here, dipped beneath the hill and curved into the forest. His heart was beating rapidly from the exertion. To rest, and to try to be fairly certain he was not being followed, he sat down on his little valise in the center of the path. There he remained a long time, thinking of nothing, while the night went on and the moon came up. He heard only the light wind among the leaves and vines. Overhead a few bats reeled soundlessly back and forth. At last he took a deep breath, got up, and went on.

call at corazón

"But why would you want a little horror like that to go along with us? It doesn't make sense. You know what they're like."

"I know what they're like," said her husband. "It's comforting to watch them. Whatever happens, if I had that to look at, I'd be reminded of how stupid I was ever to get upset."

He leaned further over the railing and looked intently down at the dock. There were baskets for sale, crude painted toys of hard natural rubber, reptile-hide wallets and belts, and a few whole snakeskins unrolled. And placed apart from these wares, out of the hot sunlight, in the shadow of a crate, sat a tiny, furry monkey. The hands were folded, and the forehead was wrinkled in sad apprehensiveness.

"Isn't he wonderful?"

"I think you're impossible—and a little insulting," she replied.

He turned to look at her. "Are you serious?" He saw that she was.

She went on, studying her sandaled feet and the narrow deck-boards beneath them: "You know I don't really mind all this nonsense, or your craziness. Just let me finish." He nodded his head in agreement, looking back at the hot dock and the wretched tin-roofed village beyond. "It goes without saying I don't mind all that, or we wouldn't be here together. You might be here alone . . ."

"You don't take a honeymoon alone," he interrupted.

"*You* might." She laughed shortly.

He reached along the rail for her hand, but she pulled it away, saying, "I'm still talking to you. I expect you to be crazy, and I expect to give in to you all along. I'm crazy too, I know. But I wish there were some way I could just once feel that my giving in meant anything to you. I wish you knew how to be gracious about it."

"You think you humor me so much? I haven't noticed it." His voice was sullen.

"I don't *humor* you at all. I'm just trying to live with you on an extended trip in a lot of cramped little cabins on an endless series of stinking boats."

"What do you mean?" he cried excitedly. "You've always said you loved the boats. Have you changed your mind, or just lost it completely?"

She turned and walked toward the prow. "Don't talk to me," she said. "Go and buy your monkey."

An expression of solicitousness on his face, he was following her. "You know I won't buy it if it's going to make you miserable."

"I'll be more miserable if you don't, so please go and buy it." She stopped and turned. "I'd love to have it. I really would. I think it's sweet."

"I don't get you at all."

She smiled. "I know. Does it bother you very much?"

After he had bought the monkey and tied it to the metal post of the bunk in the cabin, he took a walk to explore the port. It was a town made of corrugated tin and barbed wire. The sun's heat was painful, even with the sky's low-lying cover of fog. It was the middle of the day and few people were in the streets. He came to the edge of the town almost immediately. Here between him and the forest lay a narrow, slow-moving stream, its water the color of black coffee. A few women were washing clothes; small children splashed. Gigantic gray crabs scuttled between the holes they had made in the mud along the bank. He sat down on some elaborately twisted roots at the foot of a tree and took out the notebook he always carried with him. The day before, in a bar at Pedernales, he had written: "Recipe for dissolving the impression of hideousness made by a thing: Fix the attention upon the given object or situation so that the various elements, all familiar, will regroup themselves. Frightfulness is never more than an unfamiliar pattern."

He lit a cigarette and watched the women's hopeless attempts to launder the ragged garments. Then he threw the burning stub at the nearest crab, and carefully wrote: "More than

62

anything else, woman requires strict ritualistic observance of the traditions of sexual behavior. That is her definition of love." He thought of the derision that would be called forth should he make such a statement to the girl back on the ship. After looking at his watch, he wrote hurriedly: "Modern, that is, intellectual education, having been devised by males for males, inhibits and confuses her. She avenges . . ."

Two naked children, coming up from their play in the river, ran screaming past him, scattering drops of water over the paper. He called out to them, but they continued their chase without noticing him. He put his pencil and notebook into his pocket, smiling, and watched them patter after one another through the dust.

When he arrived back at the ship, the thunder was rolling down from the mountains around the harbor. The storm reached the height of its hysteria just as they got under way.

She was sitting on her bunk, looking through the open porthole. The shrill crashes of thunder echoed from one side of the bay to the other as they steamed toward the open sea. He lay doubled up on his bunk opposite, reading.

"Don't lean your head against that metal wall," he advised. "It's a perfect conductor."

She jumped down to the floor and went to the washstand.

"Where are those two quarts of White Horse we got yesterday?"

He gestured. "In the rack on your side. Are you going to drink?"

"I'm going to *have* a drink, yes."

"In this heat? Why don't you wait until it clears, and have it on deck?"

"I want it now. When it clears I won't need it."

She poured the whisky and added water from the carafe in the wall bracket over the washbowl.

"You realize what you're doing, of course."

She glared at him. "What am I doing?"

He shrugged his shoulders. "Nothing, except just giving in to a passing emotional state. You could read, or lie down and doze."

Holding her glass in one hand, she pulled open the door into the passageway with the other, and went out. The noise of the slamming door startled the monkey, perched on a suitcase. It hesitated a second, and hurried under its master's bunk. He made a few kissing sounds to entice it out, and returned to his book. Soon he began to imagine her alone and unhappy on the deck, and the thought cut into the pleasure of his reading. He forced himself to lie still a few minutes, the open book face down across his chest. The boat was moving at full speed now, and the sound of the motors was louder than the storm in the sky.

Soon he rose and went on deck. The land behind was already hidden by the falling rain, and the air smelled of deep water. She was standing alone by the rail, looking down at the waves, with the empty glass in her hand. Pity seized him as he watched, but he could not walk across to her and put into consoling words the emotion he felt.

Back in the cabin he found the monkey on his bunk, slowly tearing the pages from the book he had been reading.

The next day was spent in leisurely preparation for disembarking and changing of boats: in Villalta they were to take a smaller vessel to the opposite side of the delta.

When she came in to pack after dinner, she stood a moment studying the cabin. "He's messed it up, all right," said her husband, "but I found your necklace behind my big valise, and we'd read all the magazines anyway."

"I suppose this represents Man's innate urge to destroy," she said, kicking a ball of crumpled paper across the floor. "And the next time he tries to bite you, it'll be Man's basic insecurity."

"You don't know what a bore you are when you try to be caustic. If you want me to get rid of him, I will. It's easy enough."

She bent to touch the animal, but it backed uneasily under the bunk. She stood up. "I don't mind him. What I mind is you. He can't help being a little horror, but he keeps reminding me that you could if you wanted."

Her husband's face assumed the impassivity that was characteristic of him when he was determined not to lose his temper. She knew he would wait to be angry until she was unprepared for his attack. He said nothing, tapping an insistent rhythm on the lid of a suitcase with his fingernails.

"Naturally I don't really mean you're a horror," she continued.

"Why not mean it?" he said, smiling pleasantly. "What's wrong with criticism? Probably I am, to you. I like monkeys because I see them as little model men. You think men are something else, something spiritual or God knows what. Whatever it is, I notice you're the one who's always being disillu-

65

sioned and going around wondering how mankind can be so bestial. I think mankind is fine."

"Please don't go on," she said. "I know your theories. You'll never convince yourself of them."

When they had finished packing, they went to bed. As he snapped off the light behind his pillow, he said, "Tell me honestly. Do you want me to give him to the steward?"

She kicked off her sheet in the dark. Through the porthole, near the horizon, she could see stars, and the calm sea slipped by just below her. Without thinking she said, "Why don't you drop him overboard?"

In the silence that followed she realized she had spoken carelessly, but the tepid breeze moving with languor over her body was making it increasingly difficult for her to think or speak. As she fell asleep it seemed to her she heard her husband saying slowly, "I believe you would. I believe you would."

The next morning she slept late, and when she went up for breakfast her husband had already finished his and was leaning back, smoking.

"How are you?" he asked brightly. "The cabin steward's delighted with the monkey."

She felt a flush of pleasure. "Oh," she said, sitting down, "did you give it to him? You didn't have to do that." She glanced at the menu; it was the same as every other day. "But I suppose really it's better. A monkey doesn't go with a honeymoon."

"I think you're right," he agreed.

66

Villalta was stifling and dusty. On the other boat they had grown accustomed to having very few passengers around, and it was an unpleasant surprise to find the new one swarming with people. Their new boat was a two-decked ferry painted white, with an enormous paddle wheel at the stern. On the lower deck, which rested not more than two feet above the surface of the river, passengers and freight stood ready to travel, packed together indiscriminately. The upper deck had a salon and a dozen or so narrow staterooms. In the salon the first-class passengers undid their bundles of pillows and opened their paper bags of food. The orange light of the setting sun flooded the room.

They looked into several of the staterooms.

"They all seem to be empty," she said.

"I can see why. Still, the privacy would be a help."

"This one's double. And it has a screen in the window. This is the best one."

"I'll look for a steward or somebody. Go on in and take over." He pushed the bags out of the passageway where the *cargador* had left them, and went off in search of an employee. In every corner of the boat the people seemed to be multiplying. There were twice as many as there had been a few moments before. The salon was completely full, its floor space occupied by groups of travelers with small children and elderly women, who were already stretched out on blankets and newspapers.

"It looks like Salvation Army headquarters the night after a major disaster," he said as he came back into the stateroom.

"I can't find anybody. Anyway, we'd better stay in here. The other cubicles are beginning to fill up."

"I'm not so sure I wouldn't rather be on deck," she announced. "There are hundreds of cockroaches."

"And probably worse," he added, looking at the bunks.

"The thing to do is take those filthy sheets off and just lie on the mattresses." She peered out into the corridor. Sweat was trickling down her neck. "Do you think it's safe?"

"What do you mean?"

"All those people. This old tub."

He shrugged his shoulders.

"It's just one night. Tomorrow we'll be at Cienaga. And it's almost night now."

She shut the door and leaned against it, smiling faintly. "I think it's going to be fun," she said.

"The boat's moving!" he cried. "Let's go on deck. If we can get out there."

Slowly the old boat pushed across the bay toward the dark east shore. People were singing and playing guitars. On the bottom deck a cow lowed continuously. And louder than all the sounds was the rush of water made by the huge paddles.

They sat on the deck in the middle of a vociferous crowd, leaning against the bars of the railing, and watched the moon rise above the mangrove swamps ahead. As they approached the opposite side of the bay, it looked as if the boat might plow straight into the shore, but a narrow waterway presently appeared, and the boat slipped cautiously in. The people

68

immediately moved back from the railing, crowding against the opposite wall. Branches from the trees on the bank began to rub against the boat, scraping along the side walls of the cabins, and then whipping violently across the deck.

They pushed their way through the throng and walked across the salon to the deck on the other side of the boat; the same thing was happening there.

"It's crazy," she declared. "It's like a nightmare. Whoever heard of going through a channel no wider than the boat! It makes me nervous. I'm going in and read."

Her husband let go of her arm. "You can never enter into the spirit of a thing, can you?"

"You tell me what the spirit is, and I'll see about entering into it," she said, turning away.

He followed her. "Don't you want to go down onto the lower deck? They seem to be going strong down there. Listen." He held up his hand. Repeated screams of laughter came up from below.

"I certainly don't!" she called, without looking around.

He went below. Groups of men were seated on bulging burlap sacks and wooden crates, matching coins. The women stood behind them, puffing on black cigarettes and shrieking with excitement. He watched them closely, reflecting that with fewer teeth missing they would be a handsome people. "Mineral deficiency in the soil," he commented to himself.

Standing on the other side of a circle of gamblers, facing him, was a muscular young native whose visored cap and faint air of

69

aloofness suggested official position of some sort aboard the boat. With difficulty the traveler made his way over to him, and spoke to him in Spanish.

"Are you an employee here?"

"Yes, sir."

"I am in cabin number eight. Can I pay the supplementary fare to you?"

"Yes, sir."

"Good."

He reached into his pocket for his wallet, at the same time remembering with annoyance that he had left it upstairs locked in a suitcase. The man looked expectant. His hand was out.

"My money is in my stateroom." Then he added, "My wife has it. But if you come up in half an hour I can pay you the fare."

"Yes, sir." The man lowered his hand and merely looked at him. Even though he gave an impression of purely animal force, his broad, somewhat simian face was handsome, the husband reflected. It was surprising when, a moment later, that face betrayed a boyish shyness as the man said, "I am going to spray the cabin for your señora."

"Thank you. Are there many mosquitoes?"

The man grunted and shook the fingers of one hand as if he had just burned them.

"Soon you will see how many." He moved away.

At that moment the boat jolted violently, and there was great merriment among the passengers. He pushed his way to the prow and saw that the pilot had run into the bank. The tangle of branches and roots was a few feet from his face, its complex forms vaguely lighted by the boat's lanterns. The boat backed laboriously and the channel's agitated water rose to deck level and lapped the outer edge. Slowly they nosed along the bank until the prow once more pointed to midstream, and they continued. Then almost immediately the passage curved so sharply that the same thing happened again, throwing him sideways against a sack of something unpleasantly soft and wet. A bell clanged below deck in the interior of the boat; the passengers' laughter was louder.

Eventually they pushed ahead, but now the movement became painfully slow as the sharpness of the curves in the passage increased. Under the water the stumps groaned as the boat forced its sides against them. Branches cracked and broke, falling onto the forward and upper decks. The lantern at the prow was swept into the water.

"This isn't the regular channel," muttered a gambler, glancing up.

Several travelers exclaimed, "What?" almost in unison.

"There's a pile of passages through here. We're picking up cargo at Corazón."

The players retreated to a square inner arena which others were forming by shifting some of the crates. The husband followed them. Here they were comparatively safe from the intruding boughs. The deck was better lighted here, and this gave him the idea of making an entry in his notebook. Bending over a carton marked *Vermifugo Santa Rosalia*, he wrote: "November 18. We are moving through the blood stream of a giant.

A very dark night." Here a fresh collision with the land knocked him over, knocked over everyone who was not propped between solid objects.

A few babies were crying, but most of them still slept. He slid down to the deck. Finding his position fairly comfortable, he fell into a dozing state which was broken irregularly by the shouting of the people and the jolting of the boat.

When he awoke later, the boat was quite stationary, the games had ceased, and the people were asleep, a few of the men continuing their conversation in small groups. He lay still, listening. The talk was all about places; they were comparing the unpleasant things to be found in various parts of the republic: insects, weather, reptiles, diseases, lack of food, high prices.

He looked at his watch. It was half past one. With difficulty he got to his feet, and found his way to the stairs. Above, in the salon, the kerosene lamps illumined a vast disorder of prostrate figures. He went into the corridor and knocked on the door marked with an eight. Without waiting for her to answer, he opened the door. It was dark inside. He heard a muffled cough nearby, and decided that she was awake.

"How are the mosquitoes? Did my monkey man come and fix you up?" he asked.

She did not answer, so he lit a match. She was not in the bunk on the left. The match burned his thumb. With the second one, he looked at the right-hand bunk. A tin insecticide sprayer lay there on the mattress; its leak had made a large circle of oil on the bare ticking. The cough was repeated. It was someone in the next cabin.

"Now what?" he said aloud, uncomfortable at finding himself upset to this degree. A suspicion seized him. Without lighting the hanging lamp, he rushed to open her valises, and in the dark felt hurriedly through the flimsy pieces of clothing and the toilet articles. The whisky bottles were not there.

This was not the first time she had gone on a solitary drinking bout, and it would be easy to find her among the passengers. However, being angry, he decided not to look for her. He took off his shirt and trousers and lay down on the left-hand bunk. His hand touched a bottle standing on the floor by the head of the bunk. He raised himself enough to smell it; it was beer and the bottle was half full. It was hot in the cabin, and he drank the remaining warm, bitter liquid with relish and rolled the bottle across the room.

The boat was not moving, but voices shouted out here and there. An occasional bump could be felt as a sack of something heavy was heaved aboard. He looked through the little square window with the screen in it. In the foreground, dimly illumined by the boat's lanterns, a few dark men, naked save for their ragged underdrawers, stood on a landing made in the mud and stared toward the boat. Through the endless intricacies of roots and trunks behind them he saw a bonfire blazing, but it was far back in the swamp. The air smelled of stagnant water and smoke.

Deciding to take advantage of the relative silence, he lay down and tried to sleep; he was not surprised, however, by the difficulty he found in relaxing. It was always hard to sleep when she was not there in the room. The comfort of her presence was lacking, and there was also the fear of being awakened by her return. When he allowed himself to, he would quickly begin to formulate ideas and translate them into sentences whose recording seemed the more urgent because he was lying comfortably in the dark. Sometimes he thought about her, but only as an unclear figure whose character lent flavor to a succession of backdrops. More often he reviewed the day just completed, seeking to convince himself that it had carried him a bit further away from his childhood. Often for months at a time the strangeness of his dreams persuaded him that at last he had turned the corner, that the dark place had finally been left behind, that he was out of hearing. Then, one evening as he fell asleep, before he had time to refuse, he would be staring closely at a long-forgotten object—a plate, a chair, a pincushion—and the accustomed feeling of infinite futility and sadness would recur.

The motor started up, and the great noise of the water in the paddle wheel recommenced. They pushed off from Corazón. He was pleased. "Now I shan't hear her when she comes in and bangs around," he thought, and fell into a light sleep.

He was scratching his arms and legs. The long-continued, vague malaise eventually became full consciousness, and he sat up angrily. Above the sounds made by the boat he could hear another sound, one which came through the window: an incredibly high and tiny tone, tiny but constant in pitch and intensity. He jumped down from the berth and went to the window. The channel was wider here, and the overhanging vegetation no longer touched the sides of the boat. In the air, nearby, far away, everywhere, was the thin wail of mosquito wings. He was aghast, and completely delighted by the novelty of the phenomenon. For a moment he watched the tangled black wilderness slip past. Then with the itching he remembered the mosquitoes inside the cabin. The screen did not reach quite to the top of the window; there was ample space for them to crawl in. Even there in the dark as he moved his fingers along the frame to find the handle he could feel them; there were that many.

Now that he was fully awake, he lighted a match and went to her bunk. Of course she was not there. He lifted the Flit gun and shook it. It was empty, and as the match went out, he saw that the spot on the mattress had spread even further.

"Son of a bitch!" he whispered, and going back to the window he tugged the screen vigorously upward to close the crack. As he let go of it, it fell out into the water, and almost immediately he was conscious of the soft caress of tiny wings all about his head. In his undershirt and trousers he rushed out into the corridor. Nothing had changed in the salon. Almost everyone was asleep. There were screen doors giving onto the deck. He inspected them: they appeared to be more firmly installed. A few mosquitoes brushed against his face, but it was not the horde. He edged in between two women who were sleeping sitting with their backs against the wall, and stayed there in acute discomfort until again he dozed. It was not long before he opened his eyes to find the dim light of dawn in the air. His neck ached. He arose and went out onto the deck, to which most of the people from the salon had already crowded.

The boat was moving through a wide estuary dotted with clumps of plants and trees that rose out of the shallow water. Along the edges of the small islands stood herons, so white in the early gray light that their brightness seemed to come from inside them.

It was half past five. At this moment the boat was due in Cienaga, where it was met on its weekly trip by the train that went into the interior. Already a thin spit of land ahead was being identified by eager watchers. Day was coming up swiftly; sky and water were the same color. The deck reeked of the greasy smell of mangoes as people began to breakfast.

And now at last he began to feel pangs of anxiety as to where she might be. He determined to make an immediate and thorough search of the boat. She would be instantly recognizable in any group. First, he looked methodically through the salon, then he exhausted the possibilities on the upper decks. Then he went downstairs, where the gambling had already begun again. Toward the stern, roped to two flimsy iron posts, stood the cow, no longer bellowing. Nearby was an improvised lean-to, probably the crew's quarters. As he passed the small door, he peered through the low transom above it, and saw her lying beside a man on the floor. Automatically he walked on; then he turned and went back. The two were asleep, and half-clothed. In the warm air that came through the screened transom there was the smell of whisky that had been drunk and whisky that had been spilled.

He went upstairs, his heart beating violently. In the cabin, he closed her two valises, packed his own, set them all together by the door and laid the raincoats on top of them. He put on his shirt, combed his hair carefully, and went on deck. Cienaga was there ahead, in the mountains' morning shadow: the dock, a line of huts against the jungle behind, and the railway station to the right beyond the village.

As they docked, he signaled the two urchins who were waving for his attention, screaming, *"Equipajes!"* They fought a bit with one another until he made them see his two fingers held aloft. Then to make them certain, he pointed at each of them in turn, and they grinned. Still grinning, they stood beside him with the bags and coats, and he was among the first of the upper-deck passengers to get on land. They went down the street to the station with the parrots screaming at them from each thatched gable along the way.

On the crowded, waiting train, with the luggage finally in the rack, his heart beat harder than ever, and he kept his eyes painfully on the long dusty street that led back to the dock. At the far end, as the whistle blew, he thought he saw a figure in white running among the dogs and children toward the station, but the train started up as he watched, and the street was lost to view. He took out his notebook, and sat with it on his lap, smiling at the shining green landscape that moved with increasing speed past the window.

under the sky

Inland from the sea on the dry coastal plain lay the town, open, spread out under the huge high sky. People who lived outside in the country, and even some of the more educated town-dwellers, called the town "the Inferno" because nowhere in the region was the heat so intense. No other place around was quite so shadowless and so dusty; it seemed that the clouds above shrank upwards to their farthest possible positions. Many miles above, and to all sides, they hung there in their massive patterns, remote and motionless. In the spring, during the nights, the lightning constantly jumped from one cloud to another, revealing unexpected distances between them. Then, if anyone ever looked at the sky, he was surprised to see how each flash revealed a seemingly more distant portion of the heavens to which still more clouds had receded. But people in the town seldom turned their heads upward. They knew at what time of the year the rains would come, and it was unnecessary to scan those vast regions in order to say what day that would be. When the wind had blown hard for two weeks so that the dust filled the wide empty streets, and the lightning grew brighter each night until finally there was a little thunder, they could be sure the water would soon fall.

Once a year when the lightning was in the sky Jacinto left his village in the mountains and walked down to the town, carrying with him all the things his family had made since his last trip. There were two days of walking in the sierra where it was cool; the third day the road was through the hot lands, and this was the day he preferred, because the road was flat and he could walk faster and leave the others behind. He was taller and prouder than they, and he refused to bend over in order to be able to trot uphill and downhill as they did. In the mountains he labored to keep up with them, but on the plain he strode powerfully ahead and sometimes arrived at the market before sunset.

Now he stood in the public square with a small paper parcel in his hand. He had arrived the day before. Instead of sitting in the sidestreet near the fountain and discussing the sales with the others from his village, he walked into the municipal garden and sat down on a concrete bench marked "1936." He looked up and down the walk. No one paid him any attention. He was barefoot, so the shoeshine boys passed him by.

Tearing open the paper packet he emptied the dried leaves into his left hand. With his right he picked out all the little round, black berries and tossed them away. Then he crushed the

79

leaves and slowly rolled them into five thin cigarettes. This took all his attention for a half hour.

A voice beside him said: "That's pretty."

He looked up. It was a town-dweller; he had never seen him before, so he did not answer.

"All for you?" said the other in the silken town voice that Jacinto had learned to distrust.

"I bought it. I made them," said Jacinto.

"But I like *grifas* too," smiled the stranger. He was poorly dressed and had black teeth.

Jacinto covered the cigarettes completely with one big hand which he placed on the seat of the bench. The stranger pointed to a soldier sleeping on another bench near the iron bandstand.

"He wants one and I want one. You should be more careful. It's three months now for possessing marijuana. Don't you know?"

"No," said Jacinto. "I don't know." Then he slowly handed over two of the cigarettes. The man took them.

"So long," he said.

Jacinto stood up full of fury, and with the other three cigarettes still in his hand, he walked out into the plaza and down the long street that led to the station. It was nearly time for the daily train from the north. Sometimes crazy people got off, who would give a man enough money for two good meals, just for carrying a bundle into the town for them. There was a cemetery behind the roundhouse where some of the railroad employees went to smoke the weed. He remembered it from the preceding year; he had met an inspector there who had taken him to see a girl. She had proved to be ugly—one side of her face was mottled with blue and purple.

At the station the train had already arrived. The people trying to get on were fighting with those who were trying to get off. He wondered why with all those open windows everyone insisted on going through the two little doors at the ends of the cars. It would have been very simple the other way, but these people were too stupid to think of it. His defeat at the hands of the townsman still bothered him; he wanted to have a gun so he could pull it out and shout: "I am the father of all of you!" But it was not likely that he ever would have a gun.

Without approaching the platform where so many people were moving about, he stood and impassively watched the confusion. From the crowd three strange-looking people suddenly emerged. They all had very white skin and yellow hair. He knew, of course, that they were from a faraway place because everyone knows that when people look as strange as that they are from the capital or even farther. There were two women and one man, and as they approached him, he noticed that they were speaking a language which only they could understand. Each one carried a leather bag covered with small squares of colored paper stuck on at different angles. He stepped back, keeping his eyes on the face of the younger woman. He could not be sure whether he found her beautiful or revolting. Still he continued to look at her as she passed, holding on to the man's arm. The other woman noticed him, and smiled faintly as she went by.

He turned angrily and walked toward the tracks. He was angry at her stupidity—for thinking he could have enough money to pay her as much as she would surely want. He walked on until he came to the cemetery. It was empty save for the gray lizards that scurried from the path at his feet. In the farthest corner there was a small square building with a white stone woman on top. He sat in the shade of the little building and took out his cigarettes.

The train whistled; it was starting on its trip to the sea where the people eat nothing but fish and travel on top of the water. He drew in the first few breaths very slowly and deliberately, holding the smoke in his lungs until he felt it burning the edges of his soul. After a few minutes the feeling began to take shape. From the back of his head it moved down to his shoulders. It was as if he were wearing a tight metal garment. At that instant he looked at the sky and saw far above him the tiny black dots that were vultures, moving ever so slowly in circles as they surveyed the plain in the afternoon sunlight. Beyond them stood the clouds, deep and monumental. "Ay!" he sighed, shutting his eyes, and it occurred to him that this was what the dead people, who were lying on all sides of him, looked at day after day. This was all they could see—the clouds, and the vultures, which they did not need to fear, hidden safely as they were, deep in holy ground.

He continued to smoke, going deeper and deeper into delight. Finally he lay back and murmured: "Now I am dead too." When he opened his eyes it was still the same day, and the sun was very low in the sky. Some men were talking nearby. He listened; they were trainmen come to smoke, discussing wages and prices of meals. He did not believe any of the figures they so casually mentioned. They were lying to impress one another, and they did not even believe each other. He smoked half of the second cigarette, rose, stretched, and jumped over the cemetery wall, going back to the station by a roundabout path in order not to have to speak to the trainmen. Those people, when they smoked, always wanted more and more company; they would never let a fellow smoker go quietly on his way.

He went to the cantina by the station, and standing in the street, watched the railway employees playing billiards inside. As night approached, the lightning became increasingly visible. He walked up the long street toward the center of town. Men were playing marimbas in the doorways and in front of the houses—three or four together, and sometimes only one, indolently. The marimbas and the marijuana were the only good things in the town, reflected Jacinto. The women were ugly and dirty, and the men were all thieves and drunkards. He remembered the three people at the station. They would be in the hotel opposite the plaza. He walked a little faster, and his eyes, bloodshot from lack of sleep and too much of the drug, opened a bit wider.

After he had eaten heartily in the market sitting by the edge of the fountain, he felt very well. By the side wall of the cathedral were all the families from the mountains, some already asleep, the others preparing for the night. Almost all the stalls in the market were dark; a few figures still stood in front of the cold fruit-juice stand. Jacinto felt in his pocket for the stub and the whole cigarette, and keeping his fingers around them, walked across to the park. The celestial fireworks were very bright, but there was no thunder. Throughout the town sounded the clink and purr of the marimbas, some near and some far away. A soft breeze stirred the branches of the few lemon trees in the park. He walked along thoughtfully until he came to a bench directly opposite the entrance of the hotel, and there he sat down and brazenly began to smoke his stub. After a few minutes it was easier for him to believe that one of the two yellow-haired women would come out. He flicked away the butt, leaned back and stared straight at the hotel. The manager had put a square loudspeaker over the entrance door, and out of it came a great crackling and hissing that covered the sound of the marimbas. Occasionally a few loud notes of band music rose above the chaos, and from time to time there seemed to be a man's voice speaking behind the noise. Jacinto was annoyed: the women would want to stay inside where they could hear the sound better.

A long time went by. The radio was silenced. The few voices in the park disappeared down the streets. By the cathedral everyone was asleep. Even the marimbas seemed to have stopped, but when the breeze occasionally grew more active, it brought with it, swelling and dying, long marimba trills from a distant part of the town.

It grew very late. There was no sound but the lemon leaves rubbing together and the jet of water splashing into the basin in the center of the market. Jacinto was used to waiting. And halfway through the night a woman stepped out of the hotel, stood for a moment looking at the sky, and walked across the street to the park. From his bench in the dark he watched her as she approached. In the lightning he saw that it was not the younger one. He was disappointed. She looked upward again before moving into the shade of the lemon trees, and in a moment she sat down on the next bench and lighted a cigarette. He waited a few minutes. Then he said: "Señorita."

The yellow-haired woman cried: "Oh!" She had not seen him. She jumped up and stood still, peering toward his bench.

He moved to the end of the seat and calmly repeated the word. "Señorita."

She walked uncertainly toward him, still peering. He knew this was a ruse. She could see him quite clearly each second or so, whenever the sky lighted up. When she was near enough to the bench, he motioned for her to sit down beside him. As he had suspected, she spoke his tongue.

"What is it?" she asked. The talk in the strange language at the station had only been for show, after all.

"Sit down, señorita."

"Why?"

"Because I tell you to."

She laughed and threw away her cigarette.

"That's not a reason," she said, sitting down at the other end of the bench. "What are you doing here so late?" She spoke carefully and correctly, like a priest. He answered this by saying: "And you, what are you looking for?"

"Nothing."

"Yes. You are looking for something," he said solemnly.

"I was not sleeping. It is very hot."

"No. It is not hot," said Jacinto. He was feeling increasingly sure of himself, and he drew out the last cigarette and began to smoke it. "What are you doing here in this town?" he asked her after a moment.

"Passing on my way south to the border," she said, and she told him how she was traveling with two friends, a husband and wife, and how she often took a walk when they had gone to bed.

Jacinto listened as he drew in the smoke and breathed it out. Suddenly he jumped up. Touching her arm, he said: "Come to the market."

She arose, asking: "Why?" and walked with him across the park. When they were in the street, he took her wrist fiercely and pressing it, said between his teeth: "Look at the sky."

She looked up wonderingly, a little fearfully. He went on in a low, intense voice: "As God is my witness, I am going into the hotel and kill the man who came here with you."

Her eyes grew large. She tried to wrest her arm away, but he would not let it go, and he thrust his face into hers. "I have a pistol in my pocket and I am going to kill that man."

"But why?" she whispered weakly, looking up and down the empty street.

"I want his wife."

The woman said: "It is not possible. She would scream."

"I know the proprietor," said Jacinto, rolling his eyes and grinning. The woman seemed to believe him. Now he felt that a great thing was about to happen.

"And you," he said, twisting her arm brutally, "you do not scream."

86

"No."

Again he pointed to the sky.

"God is my witness. You can save the life of your friend. Come with me."

She was trembling violently, but as they stumbled through the street and he let go of her an instant, she began to run. With one bound he had overtaken her, and he made her stop and look at the sky again as he went through his threats once more. She saw his wide, red-veined eyes in a bright flash of lightning, and his utterly empty face. Mechanically she allowed him to push her along through the streets. He did not let go of her again.

"You are saving your friend's life," he said. "God will reward you."

She was sobbing as she went along. No one passed them as they moved unsteadily on toward the station. When they were nearly there they made a great detour past the edge of town, and finally came to the cemetery.

"This is a holy place," he murmured, swiftly crossing himself. "Here you are going to save your friend's life."

He took off his shirt, laid it on the stony ground, and pushed her down. There was nothing but the insistent, silent flashing in the sky. She kept her eyes shut, but she shuddered at each flash, even with her lids closed. The wind blew harder, and the smell of the dust was in her nostrils.

He took her back as far as the park and there he let go of her. Then he said: "Good night, señorita," and walked away very quickly. He was happy because she had not asked for any money.

The next year when he came down to the town he waited at the station four afternoons to see the train come in. The last afternoon he went to the cemetery and sat near the small square building that had the stone woman on top of it. On the ground the dust blew past. The enormous clouds hung in the sky and the vultures were there high above him. As he smoked he recalled the yellow-haired woman. After a time he began to weep, and rolled over onto the earth, clutching the pebbles as he sobbed. An old woman of the town, who came every day to her son's grave, passed near to him. Seeing him, she shook her head and murmured to herself: "He has lost his mother."

señor ong and señor ha

At the end of the town's long street a raw green mountain cut across the sky at a forty-five degree angle, its straight slope moving violently from the cloudy heights down into the valley where the river ran. In the valley, although the land was fertile, there were no farms or orchards, because the people of the town were lazy and did not want to bother clearing away the rocks that strewed the ground. And then, it was always too hot for that sort of work, and everybody had malaria there, so that long ago the town had fallen into its little pattern of living off the Indians who came down from the mountains with food and went back with cheap cloth, machetes and things like mirrors or empty bottles. Life always had been easy; although no one in the town was rich, still, no one ever went hungry. Almost every house had some papayas and a mango tree beside it, and there were plenty of avocadoes and pineapples to be had in the market for next to nothing.

Some of this had changed when the government had begun the building of the great dam up above. No one seemed to know exactly where the dam was; they were building it somewhere up in the mountains; already the water had covered several villages, and now after six years the construction was still going on. This last was the important part, because it meant that when the Indians came down from above they now brought with them not only food but money. Thus it had come about that certain people in the town had suddenly found themselves rich. They could scarcely believe it themselves, but there was the money, and still the Indians went on coming down and leaving more and more of it on the counters of their shops. They did not know what to do with all these unexpected pesos. Most of them bought huge radios which they kept going from early morning until night, all tuned in full strength to Tapachula, so that when they walked the length of the main street they were never out of earshot of the program and could follow it without a break. But still they had money. Pepe Jimenez had bought a bright new automobile in the capital, but by the time he had arrived back in town with it, after driving it over the sixty miles of trail from Mapastenango, it was no longer an object to excite admiration, and he felt that he had made an unwise purchase. Even the main street was too bumpy and muddy for him to drive it up and down, and so it stood rusting in front of Mi Esperanza, the bar by the bridge. When they came out of school Nicho and his companions would play in it, pretending it was a fort. But then a group of larger boys from the upper end of the town had come one day and appropriated the car for their own games, so that the boys who lived by the river no longer dared to approach it.

Nicho lived with his aunt in a small house whose garden ended in a wilderness of plants and vines; just below them rushed the river, dashing sideways from boulder to boulder in its shallow mist-filled canyon. The house was clean and simple, and they lived quietly. Nicho's aunt was a woman of too easygoing a nature. Being conscious of this, she felt that one way of giving her dead sister's child the proper care was to attempt to instil discipline in him; the discipline consisted in calling him by his true name, which was Dionisio.

Nor did she have any conception of discipline as far as her own living was concerned, so that the boy was not astonished when the day came that she said to him: "Dionisio, you will have to stop going to school. We have no more money. Don Anastasio will hire you at ten pesos a month to work in his store, and you can get the noonday meal there too. *Lástima*, but there is no money!"

For a week Nicho sat in the shop learning the prices of the articles that Don Anastasio sold, and then one evening when he went home he found a strange-looking man in the house, sitting in the other rocking chair opposite his aunt. The man looked a little like some of the Indians that came down from the furthest and highest mountains, but his skin was lighter, he was plumper and softer-seeming, and his eyes were almost shut. He smiled at the boy, but not in a way that Nicho thought very friendly, and shook hands without getting up from his chair. That night his aunt looked really quite happy, and as they were getting ready for bed she said to him: "Señor Ong is coming to live with us. You will not have to work any more. God has been good to us."

But it occurred to Nicho that if Señor Ong was to live with them, he would prefer to go on working at Don Anastasio's, in order not to be around the house and so have to see Señor Ong so much. Tactfully he said: "I like Don Anastasio." His aunt looked at him sharply. "Señor Ong does not want you to work. He is a proud man, and rich enough to feed us both. It is nothing for him. He showed me his money."

Nicho was not at all pleased, and he went to sleep slowly, his mind full of misgivings. He was afraid that one day he would fight with Señor Ong. And besides, what would his friends say? Señor Ong was such a strange-looking man. But the very next morning he arrived from the Hotel Paraiso with three boys whom Nicho knew, and each boy carried a large bag on his head. From the garden he watched them accept the generous tips Señor Ong gave them and then run off to school without waiting to see whether Nicho wanted to speak to them or not. "Very bad," he said to himself as he kicked a stone around and around the bare earth floor of the garden. A little while later he went down to the river and sat on top of the highest boulder watching the milky water that churned beneath him. One of his five cockatoos was screaming from the tangle of leaves on the banks. "*Callate!*" he yelled at it; his own ill-humor annoyed him as much as Señor Ong's arrival.

And everything turned out much as he had feared—only worse. Two days later, one of the boys from the upper end of the street said to him in passing: *"Hola, Chale!"* He replied to the greeting automatically and walked on, but a second later he said to himself: *"Chale?* But that means Chinaman! Chink!" Of course. Señor Ong must be a Chinaman. He turned to look at the boy, and thought of hitting him in the back with a stone. Then he hung his head and walked on slowly. Nothing would do any good.

Little by little the joke spread, and soon even his own friends called him *Chale* when they met him, and although it was really he who had become less friendly, he imagined that they all were avoiding him, that no one wanted to see him any more, and he spent most of his time playing by the river. The water's sound was deafening, but at the same time it made him feel a little bit better.

Neither Señor Ong nor his aunt paid much attention to him, save for their constant mealtime demands that he eat. "Now that we have more food than we need, you don't want to eat it," said his aunt angrily. "Eat, Dionisio," smiled Señor Ong. *"Bien,"* said Nicho, full of resentment, but in a tone of mock-resignation, and pulled off a small piece of tortilla which he chewed very slowly.

There seemed to be no question of his returning to school; at least, the subject was never mentioned, for which he was most grateful, since he had no desire to be back in the midst of his friends just to hear them call him *Chale*. The name by itself would have been bearable if only it had not implied the ridicule

93

of his home life; his powerlessness to change that condition seemed much more shameful than any state of affairs for which he himself might have been at fault. And so he spent his days down by the river, jumping like a goat across the rocks, throwing stones to frighten the vultures away from the carcasses the water left for them, finding deep pools to swim in, and following the river downstream to lie idly naked on the rocks in the hot sun. No matter how pleasant to him Señor Ong might be—and already he had given him candy on several occasions, as well as a metal pencil with red lead in it—he could not bring himself to accept his being a part of the household. And then there were the singular visits of strange, rich townspeople, persons whom his aunt never had known, but who now appeared to find it quite natural to come to the house, stay for five or ten minutes talking to Señor Ong, and then go away again without so much as asking after his aunt, who always made a point of being in the back of the house or in the garden when they came. He could not understand that at all. It was still her house. Or perhaps not! Maybe she had given it to Señor Ong. Women often were crazy. He did not dare ask her. Once he was able to bring himself to inquire about the people, who kept coming in increasing numbers. She had answered: "They are friends of Señor Ong," and had looked at him with an expression which seemed to say: "Is that enough for you, busybody?" He was more than ever convinced that there was something more to know about the visitors. Then he met Luz, and being no longer alone, he ceased for a time to think about them.

When, one windy day, he had first seen her standing on the

bridge, her bright head shining against the black mountains behind, he had stopped walking and stood perfectly still in order
to look more carefully: he thought there was a mistake in his
seeing. Never would he have believed it possible for anyone to
look that way. Her hair was a silky white helmet on the top of
her head, her whole face was white, almost as if she had covered
it with paint, her brows and lashes, and even her eyes, were light
to the point of not existing. Only her pale pink lips seemed
real. She clutched the railing of the bridge tightly, an expression of intense preoccupation—or perhaps faint pain—on her
face as she peered out from beneath her inadequate white brows.
And her head moved slowly up and down as if it were trying to
find an angle of vision which would be bearable for those feeble
eyes that suffered behind their white lashes.

A few weeks back he merely would have stood looking at this
apparition; now he watched intently until the girl, who was
about his own age, seemed on the point of pitching forward into
the road, and then he hurried toward her and firmly took her
arm. An instant she drew back, squinting into his face.

"Who?" she said, confused.

"Me. What's the matter?"

She relaxed, let herself be led along. "Nothing," she answered
after a moment. Nicho walked with her down the path to the
river. When they got to the shade, the heavy lines in her forehead disappeared. "The sun hurts your eyes?" he asked her, and
she said that it did. Under a giant breadfruit tree there were
clean gray rocks; they sat down and he began a series of questions.
She answered placidly; her name was Luz; she had come with her

sister only two days ago from San Lucas; she would stay on with her grandfather here because her parents were having quarrels at home. All her replies were given while she gazed out across the landscape, yet Nicho was sure she could not see the feathery trees across the river or the mountains beyond. He asked her: "Why don't you look at me when you talk to me?"

She put her hand in front of her face. "My eyes are ugly."

"It's not true!" he declared with indignation. Then, "They're beautiful," he added, after looking at them carefully for a moment.

She saw that he was not making fun of her, and straightway decided that she liked him more than any boy she had ever known.

That night he told his aunt about Luz, and as he described the colors in her face and hair he saw her look pleased. "*Una hija del sol!*" she exclaimed. "They bring good luck. You must invite her here tomorrow. I shall prepare her a good *refresco de tamarindo*." Nicho said he would, but he had no intention of subjecting his friend to his aunt's interested scrutiny. And while he was not at all astonished to hear that albinos had special powers, he thought it selfish of his aunt to want to profit immediately by those which Luz might possess.

The next day when he went to the bridge and found Luz standing there, he was careful to lead her through a hidden lane down to the water, so that she might remain unseen as they passed near the house. The bed of the river lay largely in the shadows cast by the great trees that grew along its sides. Slowly the two children wandered downstream, jumping from rock to rock. Now and then they startled a vulture, which rose at their approach like a huge cinder, swaying clumsily in the air while they walked by, to realight in the same spot a moment later. There was a particular place that he wanted to show her, where the river widened and had sandy shores, but it lay a good way downstream, so that it took them a long time to get there. When they arrived, the sun's light was golden and the insects had begun to call. On the hill, invisible behind the thick wall of trees, the soldiers were having machine-gun practice: the blunt little berries of sound came in clusters at irregular intervals. Nicho rolled his trouser legs up high above his knees and waded well out into the shallow stream. "Wait!" he called to her. Bending, he scooped up a handful of sand from the river bed. His attitude as he brought it back for her to see was so triumphant that she caught her breath, craned her neck to see it before he had arrived. "What is it?" she asked.

"Look! Silver!" he said, dropping the wet sand reverently into her outstretched palm. The tiny grains of mica glistened in the late sunlight.

"*Qué precioso!*" she cried in delight. They sat on some roots by the water. When the sand was drier, she poured it carefully into the pocket of her dress.

"What are you going to do with it?" he asked her.

"Give it to my grandfather."

"No, no!" he exclaimed. "You don't give away silver. You hide it. Don't you have a place where you hide things?"

Luz was silent; she never had thought of hiding anything. "No," she said presently, and she looked at him with admiration.

He took her hand. "I'll give you a special place in my garden

97

where you can hide everything you want. But you must never tell anyone."

"Of course not." She was annoyed that he should think her so stupid. For a while she had been content just to sit there with Nicho beside her; now she was impatient to get back and deposit the treasure. He tried to persuade her to stay a little longer, saying that there would be time enough if they returned later, but she had stood up and would not sit down again. They climbed upstream across the boulders, coming suddenly upon a pool where two young women stood thigh-deep washing clothes, naked save for the skirts wrapped round their waists, long full skirts that floated gently in the current. The women laughed and called out a greeting. Luz was scandalized.

"They should be ashamed!" she cried. "In San Lucas if a woman did that, everyone would throw stones at her until she was buried under them!"

"Why?" said Nicho, thinking that San Lucas must be a very wicked town.

"Because they would," she answered, still savoring the shock and shame she had felt at the sight of the golden breasts in the sunlight.

When they got back to town they turned into the path that led to Nicho's house, and while they were still in the jungle end of the garden, Nicho stopped and indicated a dead tree whose trunk had partially decayed. With the gesture of a conspirator he pulled aside the fringed curtain of vines that hung down across most of it, revealing several dark holes. Reaching into one of them, he pulled out a bright tin can, flicked off the belligerent ants that raced wildly around it, and held it forth to her.

"Put it in here," he whispered.

It took a while to transfer all the sand from her pocket to the can; when it was done he replaced it inside the dark trunk and let the vines fall straight again to cover the place. Then he conducted Luz quickly up through the garden, around the house, into the street. His aunt, having caught sight of them, called: "Dionisio!" But he pretended not to have heard her and pushed Luz ahead of him nervously. He was suddenly in terror lest Luz see Señor Ong; that was something which must be avoided at any cost.

"Dionisio!" She was still calling; she had come out and was standing in front of the door, looking down the street after them, but he did not turn around. They reached the bridge. It was out of sight of the house.

"*Adiós*," he said.

"*Hasta mañana*," she answered, peering up at him with her strange air of making a great effort. He watched her walk up the street, moving her head from side to side as if there were a thousand things to see, when in reality there were only a few pigs and some chickens roaming about.

At the evening meal his aunt eyed him reproachfully. He averted her gaze; she did not mention his promise to bring Luz to the house for *refrescos*. That night he lay on his mat watching the phosphorescent beetles. His room gave on the patio; it had only three walls. The fourth side was wide open. Branches of the lemon tree reached in and rubbed against the wall above his head; up there, too, was a huge unfolding banana leaf which was

99

pushing its way further into the room each day. Now the patio was dizzy with the beetles' sharp lights. Crawling on the plants or flying frantically between them, they flashed their signals on and off with maddening insistence. In the neighboring room his aunt and Señor Ong occupied the bed of the house, enjoying the privacy of quarters that were closed in on all four sides. He listened: the wind was rising. Nightly it appeared and played on the leaves of the trees, dying away again before dawn. Tomorrow he would take Luz down to the river to get more silver. He hoped Señor Ong had not been spying when he had uncovered the holes in the tree trunk. The mere thought of such a possibility set him to worrying, and he twisted on his mat from one side to the other.

Presently he decided to go and see if the silver was still there. Once he had assured himself either that it was safe or that it had been stolen, he would feel better about it. He sat up, slipped into his trousers, and stepped out into the patio. The night was full of life and motion; leaves and branches touched, making tiny sighs. Singing insects droned in the trees overhead; everywhere the bright beetles flashed. As he stood there feeling the small wind wander over him he became aware of other sounds in the direction of the *sala*. The light was on there, and for a moment he thought that perhaps Señor Ong had a late visitor, since that was the room where he received his callers. But he heard no voices. Avoiding the lemon tree's sharp twigs, he made his way soundlessly to the closed doors and peered between them.

There was a square niche in the *sala* wall across which, when he had first arrived, Señor Ong had tacked a large calendar. This bore a colored picture of a smiling Chinese girl. She wore a blue bathing suit and white fur-topped boots, and she sat by a pool of shiny pink tiles. Over her head in a luminous sky a gigantic four-motored plane bore down upon her, and further above, in a still brighter area of the heavens, was the benevolent face of Generalissimo Chiang. Beneath the picture were the words: ABARROTES FINOS. Sun Man Ngai, Huixtla, Chis. The calendar was the one object Señor Ong had brought with him that Nicho could wholeheartedly admire; he knew every detail of the picture by heart. Its presence had transformed the *sala* from a dull room with two old rocking chairs and a table to a place where anything might happen if one waited long enough. And now as he peeked through the crack, he saw with a shock that Señor Ong had removed the calendar from its place on the wall, and laid it on the table. He had a hammer and a chisel and he was pounding and scratching the bottom of the niche. Occasionally he would scoop out the resulting plaster and dust with his fat little hands, and dump it in a neat pile on the table. Nicho waited for a long time without daring to move. Even when the wind blew a little harder and chilled his naked back he did not stir, for fear of seeing Señor Ong turn around and look with his narrow eyes toward the door, the hammer in one hand, the chisel in the other. Besides, it was important to know what he was doing. But Señor Ong seemed to be in no hurry. Almost an hour went by, and still tirelessly he kept up his methodical work, pausing regularly to take out the debris and pile it on the table. At last Nicho began to feel like sneezing; in a frenzy he turned and ran through the patio to his room, scratching his chest against the branches on the way. The emotion engendered by his flight had taken away his desire to sneeze, but he lay down anyway for fear it might return if he went back to the door. In the midst of wondering about Señor Ong he fell asleep.

The next morning when he went into the *sala* the pretty Chinese girl covered the niche as usual. He stood still listening: his aunt and Señor Ong were talking in the next room. Quickly he pulled out the thumbtack in the lower left-hand corner of the calendar and reached in. He could feel nothing there. Disappointed, he fastened it back and went out into the garden. In the tree his treasure was undisturbed, but now that he suspected Señor Ong of having a treasure too, the little can of sand seemed scarcely worth his interest.

He went to the bridge and waited for Luz. When she came they walked to the river below the garden and sat beside the water. Nicho's mind was full of the image of Señor Ong bending over the niche with his tools, and his fancy was occupied with speculation as to what exactly he had been doing. He was uncertain whether or not to share his secret with Luz. He hoped she would not talk about her silver this morning; to forestall inquiries about it he mentioned curtly that he had looked at it only a half hour ago and that it was intact. Luz sat regarding him perplexedly; he seemed scarcely the same person as yesterday. Finally she said, as he continued to fix his gaze on the black pebbles at his feet: "What's the matter with you today?"

"Nothing." He grasped her arm to belie his word; the gesture betrayed him into beginning the confidence. "Listen. In my house there's a lot of gold hidden." He told her everything: Señor Ong's arrival, his own dislike of him, the visits of the town's rich shopkeepers to the house, and finally the suspicious behavior of Señor Ong in the *sala* the night before. She listened, blinking rapidly all the while. And when he had finished she agreed with him that it was probably gold hidden there in the niche, only she was inclined to think that it belonged to his aunt, and that Señor Ong had stolen it from her. This idea had not occurred to Nicho, and he did not really believe it. Nevertheless, it pleased him. "I'll get it and give it back to her," he declared. "Of course," said Luz solemnly, as if there were no alternative. They sat a while without speaking. Up in the garden all the cockatoos were screaming at once. The prospect of stealing back the gold in order to return it to his aunt excited him. But there were dangers. He began to describe the hideousness of Señor Ong's person and character, extemporaneously adding details. Luz shivered and looked apprehensively toward the shadowy path. "*Hay que tener mucho cuidado*," she murmured. Then suddenly she wanted to go home.

Now there was only one thing to wait for: Señor Ong's absence from the house. In Tlaltepec there lived a Chinese man whom he usually visited each week, going on the early bus in the morning and returning in time for the midday meal. Three days went by. People came to the house and went away again, but Señor Ong sat quietly in the *sala* without once going into the street. Each day Nicho and Luz met on the bridge and sat by the river discussing the treasure with an excitement that steadily grew. "Ay, *qué maravilla!*" she would exclaim, holding her hands far apart. "This much gold!" Nicho would nod in agreement; all the same he had a feeling that when he saw the treasure he would be disappointed.

Finally the morning came when Señor Ong kissed Nicho's aunt on the cheek and went out of the house carrying a newspaper under his arm. "Where is he going?" Nicho asked innocently.

"Tlaltepec." His aunt was scrubbing the floor of the *sala*.

He went into the patio and watched a humming-bird buzz from one to another of the *huele-de-noche's* white flowers. When his aunt had finished in the *sala* she shut the door and started on the floor of the bedroom. In agitation he tiptoed into the room and over to the calendar, whose two lower corners he unfastened from the wall. Again the niche was empty. Its floor consisted of four large flower-decorated tiles. Without touching them he could tell which was the loose one. He lifted it up and felt underneath. It was a paper packet, not very large, and, which was worse, soft to the touch. He pulled out a fat manila envelope, replaced the tile and the calendar, and walked softly out through the patio, into the garden to his tree.

In the large envelope were a lot of little envelopes, and in some of the little envelopes there was a small quantity of odorless white powder. The other little envelopes were empty, held together by a rubber band. That was all there was. Nicho had expected a disappointment, but scarcely so complete a one as this. He was furious: Señor Ong had played a joke on him, had replaced the gold with this worthless dust, just out of devil-try. But when he thought about it, he decided that Señor Ong could not have guessed that he knew about the niche, so that after all this powder must be the real treasure. Also he felt it un-likely that it belonged to his aunt, in which case Señor Ong would be even more angry to find it gone. He took out two of the small empty envelopes, and from each of the others he poured a tiny bit of powder, until these two also contained about the same amount. Then he replaced both empty and full envelopes in the larger folder, and seeing that his aunt was in the kitchen, went back to the *sala* with it. Señor Ong would never notice the two missing envelopes or the powder that Nicho had poured into them. Once back in the garden he hid the two tiny packets under the tin can full of sand, and wandered down to the bridge.

It was too early to expect Luz. A thin gray curtain of rain came drifting up the valley. In another few minutes it would have arrived. The green mountainside at the end of the street glared in the half light. Don Anastasio came walking jauntily down the main street, and turned in at the side street where Nicho's house was. Obeying a blind impulse, he called to him: *"Muy buenos, Don Anastasio!"* The old man wheeled about; he seemed none too pleased to see Nicho. "Good day," he replied, and then he hurried on. Nicho ran from the bridge and stood at the entrance of the street watching him. Sure enough, he was about to go into Nicho's house.

"Don Anastasio!" he shouted, beginning to run toward him.

Don Anastasio stopped walking and stood still, his face screwed up in annoyance. Nicho arrived out of breath. "You wanted to see Señor Ong? He's gone out."

Don Anastasio did not look happy now, either. "Where?" he said heavily.

"I think to Mapastenango, perhaps," said Nicho, trying to sound vague, and wondering if that could be counted as a lie.

"*Qué malo!*" grunted Don Anastasio. "He won't be back today, then."

"I don't know."

There was a silence.

"Can I do anything for you?" faltered Nicho.

"No, no," said Don Anastasio hastily; then he stared down at him. During the week when Nicho had been working at his store, he had had occasion to notice that the boy was unusually quick. "That is," he added slowly, "I don't suppose—did Señor Ong. . . ?"

"Just a minute," said Nicho, feeling that he was about to discover the secret and at the same time become master of the situation. "Wait here," he added firmly. At the moment Don Anastasio showed no inclination to do anything else. He stood watching Nicho disappear around the corner of the house.

In a minute the boy returned panting, and smiled at Don Anastasio.

"Shall we go to the bridge?" he said.

Again Don Anastasio acquiesced, looking furtively up and down the long street as they came out into it. They stood on the bridge leaning over the water below, and Nicho brought one of the little envelopes out of his pocket, glancing up at Don Anastasio's face at the same time. Yes! He had been right! He saw the features fixed in an expression of relief, pleasure and greedy anticipation. But only for an instant. By the time he was handing over the packet to Don Anastasio, the old man's face looked the same as always.

"*Muy bien, muy bien*," he grumbled. The first small drops of rain alighted softly on their heads, but neither noticed them. "Do I pay you or Señor Ong?" said Don Anastasio, pocketing the envelope.

Nicho's heart beat harder for a few seconds: Señor Ong must not know of this. But he could not ask Don Anastasio not to tell him. He cleared his throat and said: "Me." But his voice sounded feeble.

"Aha!" said Don Anastasio, smiling a little; and he ruffled Nicho's hair in paternal fashion. Finding it wet, he looked up vacantly at the sky. "It's raining," he commented, a note of surprise in his voice.

"*Sí, señor*," assented Nicho weakly.

"How much?" said Don Anastasio, looking at him very hard. In the valley the thunder groaned faintly.

Nicho felt he must answer immediately, but he had no idea what to say. "Is a peso all right?"

Don Anastasio stared at him even harder; he felt that the old man's eyes would cut through him in another instant. Then Don Anastasio's countenance changed suddenly, and he said: "A peso. Good." And he handed him a silver coin. "Next week you come to my store with another envelope. I'll give you an extra

107

twenty centavos for making the trip. And—sssst!" He put his fingers to his lips, rolling his eyes upward. "Ssst!" He patted Nicho on the shoulder, looking very pleased, and went up the street.

Señor Ong came back earlier than usual, wet through, and in rather a bad humor. Nicho never had paid any attention to the conversations that passed between his aunt and Señor Ong. Now from the kitchen he listened, and heard him say: "I have no confidence in Ha. They tell me he was in town here two days ago. Of course he swears he was in Tlaltepec all the time."

"Three thousand pesos thrown into the street!" declared his aunt savagely. "I told you so then. I told you he would go on selling here as well as in Tlaltepec. *Yo te lo dije, hombre!*"

"I am not sure yet," said Señor Ong, and Nicho could imagine his soft smile as he said the words. Now that he had stolen from him he disliked him more than ever; in a sense he almost wished Señor Ong might discover the theft and accuse him, thereby creating the opportunity for him to say: "Yes, I stole from you, and I hate you." But he knew that he himself would do nothing to hasten such a moment. He went out through the rain to his tree. The earth's dark breath rose all around him, hung in the wet air. He took out the can of sand and dropped the peso into it.

It rained all day and through the night; Nicho did not see Luz until the following day. Then he adopted a mysterious, baffled air and conducted her to the tree.

"Look!" he cried, showing her the tin can. "The silver has made a peso!"

Luz was convinced and delighted, but she did not seem really surprised. *"Qué bueno!"* she murmured.

"Do you want to take it?" He held up the coin. But he was careful to keep his hand over the envelope in the tree's hollow.

"No, no! Leave it! Maybe it will make more. Put it back! Put it back!"

He was a little crestfallen to find that she took his miracle so nearly for granted. They stamped their feet to knock off the ants that were beginning to climb up their legs.

"And the gold?" she whispered. "Did you get it back for your aunt? Was it heavy? What did Señor Ong say?"

"There was nothing there at all," said Nicho, feeling uncomfortable without knowing why.

"Oh." She was disappointed.

They took a long walk down the river, and came upon an enormous iguana sunning himself on a rock above a pool. Nicho threw a stone, and the monster lumbered away into the leaves. Luz clutched his arm tightly as it disappeared from sight; there was the heavy sound of its body dragging through the underbrush. All at once Nicho shook himself free, pulled off his shirt and trousers, and gave a running leap into the pool. He splashed about, beating wildly at the water with his arms and legs, yelling loudly all the while. With an uncertain gait Luz approached the edge, where she sat down and watched him. Presently she said: "Find some more silver." She did not seem at all shocked by his nudity. He sank to the bottom and scrabbled about, touching only rock. Up again, he shouted: "There isn't any!" Her white head followed his movements as he cavorted around the pool. When he came out, he sat on the opposite side, letting the sun dry him. Behind the hill the machine-gun practice was again in progress.

"In San Lucas do you think they'd throw stones at me?" he shouted.

"Why?" she called. "No, no! *Claro que nó!* For boys it's all right."

The next few days were sunny, and they came each afternoon to the pool.

One morning, the other little envelope in his pocket, Nicho went into the center of town to Don Anastasio's shop. The old man seemed very glad to see him. He opened the envelope behind the counter and lookd carefully at its contents. Then he handed Nicho a peso and a half.

"I have no change," said Nicho.

"The *tostón* is for you," said Don Anastasio gruffly. "There's a cinema tonight. Come back next week. Don't forget."

Nicho ran down the street, wondering when he would have the chance to fill another envelope for Don Anastasio. It was about time for Señor Ong to make a trip to Tlaltepec.

A moment before he got to the bridge a tall woman stepped out of a shop and confronted him. She had very large eyes and a rather frightening face.

"*Hola, chico!*"

"*Sí, señora.*" He stood still and stared at her.

"Have you got something for me?"

"Something for you?" he repeated blankly.

"A little envelope?" She held out two pesos. Nicho looked at them and said: "*No, señora.*"

Her face became more frightening. "Yes. Yes. You have," she insisted, moving toward him. He glanced up and down the street: there was no one. The shop seemed to be empty. It was the hot hour of the day. He was suddenly terrified by her face. "Tomorrow," he cried, ducking to one side in order to dart past her. But she caught hold of his neck. "Today," she said roughly; her long fingernails were pushing into his skin. "Sí, señora." He did not dare look up at her. "On the bridge," she grated. "This afternoon."

"Sí, señora."

She let go and he walked on, sobbing a little with anger and shame for having been afraid.

In the *sala* Señor Ong and his aunt were talking excitedly. He did not go in, but climbed into a hammock in the patio and listened. Don Anastasio's name was mentioned. Nicho's heart skipped ahead: something had happened!

"Now I am almost sure," Señor Ong said slowly. "It is two weeks since he has been here, and Saenz tells me he is perfectly happy. That means only one thing: Ha must be supplying him directly."

"Of course," said his aunt bitterly. "You needn't have waited two weeks to know that. Three thousand pesos dropped into the river. What a waste! *Qué idiota, tú!*"

Señor Ong paid no attention to her. "There's also the Fernandez woman," he mused. "She should have been around a few days ago. I know she has no money, but so far she has always managed to scrape together something."

"That old hag!" said his aunt contemptuously. "With her

111

face now, she'll be lucky if she can raise twenty, not to speak of fifty."

"She can raise it," said Señor Ong with confidence in his voice. "The question is, has Ha already found her and is he giving it to her for less?"

"Don't ask *me* all these questions!" cried his aunt with impatience. "Go to Tlaltepec and ask the old man himself!"

"When I go there," said Señor Ong in a quiet, deadly voice, "it will not be to ask him anything."

At that moment a knock came at the front door; his aunt immediately left the room, shutting the door behind her, and went through the patio into the kitchen. For a few minutes Nicho could hear only the confused sound of low voices talking in the *sala*. Presently someone closed the front door. The visitor was gone.

Before the midday meal Nicho went out into the garden and tossed the two silver coins Don Anastasio had given him into the can of sand. It gave him pleasure to think of showing them to Luz; her credulity made him feel clever and superior. He determined never to tell her about the powder. All through lunch he thought about the tall woman he was to meet on the bridge. When the meal was over, Señor Ong did something unusual: he took up his hat and said: "I am going to see Saenz and have a talk with him." And he went out. Nicho watched him disappear into the main street; then he went into the house and saw his aunt shut herself into the bedroom for her siesta. Without hesitating he walked straight to the niche in the *sala* and took out the big yellow envelope. He knew he was doing a dangerous thing, but he was determined to do it anyway. Quickly he slipped two fat little envelopes into his pocket. He left one in his tree, and with the other he went out and stood on the bridge to wait for the woman. She was not long in spotting him from the shop. As she came toward him, her haggard face seemed to darken the afternoon. He held the little white envelope out to her even as she approached, as if to keep her at a certain distance from him. Frowning mightily, she reached for it, snatched it from his fingers like a furious bird, and violently pushed it inside her bodice. With the other hand she put two pesos into his still outstretched palm; and then she strode away without saying a word. He decided to remain on the bridge, hoping that Luz would appear presently.

When she came, he suddenly did not want to take her to the tree, or even to the river. Instead, grasping her hand, he said: "I have an idea." This was not true: as yet he had no idea, but he felt the need of doing something new, important.

"What idea?"

"Let's take a trip!"

"A trip! Where to?"

They started up the street hand in hand.

"We can take a bus," he said.

"But where?"

"*No importa adonde.*"

Luz was not convinced the idea was sound; her mind was encumbered with visions of her older sister's stern face when she returned. Nevertheless he could see that she would go. As they came to where the houses and shops began, he let go of her hand

113

for fear of meeting one of his friends. He had never walked on the street with her. The sun's light was intense, but a gigantic white cloud was rising slowly up from behind the mountains in front of them. He turned to look at her pale shining head. Her eyes were painful, squinting slits in her face. Surely no one else in the world had such beautiful hair. Glancing at the cloud he whispered to her: "The sun will go in soon."

At the central plaza there was a bus half full of people. From time to time the driver, who stood leaning against its red tin body, shouted: "Tlaltepec! Tlaltepec!" No sooner had they got aboard and taken seats near the back alongside the windows than Luz, in an access of apprehensiveness, asked to get out. But he held her arm and said, hurriedly inventing: "*Oye*, I wanted to go to Tlaltepec because we have something very important to do there. We have to save somebody's life." She listened attentively to his story: the monstrous Señor Ong was going to kill old Señor Ha for not having kept his promise to stay in Tlaltepec. As he recounted the tale, and recalled the wording of Señor Ong's threat, he began to believe the story himself. "When I go there it will not be to ask him anything." The old man would be given no opportunity to explain, no chance to defend himself. As the bus moved out of the plaza, he was as convinced as Luz that they were off to Tlaltepec on an heroic mission.

Tlaltepec was below, in a closed valley with mountains on all sides. The great white cloud, its brilliant edges billowing outward, climbed higher into the sky; as into a cave, the bus entered the precinct of its shadow. Here suddenly everything was green. Scraps of bird-song came in through the open windows, sharp above the rattling of the ancient vehicle.

"Ay, *el pobrecito!*" sighed Luz from time to time.

They came into Tlaltepec, stopped in the plaza. The passengers got out and quickly dispersed in different directions. The village was very quiet. Bright green grass grew in the middle of the streets. A few silent Indians sat around the plaza against the walls. Nicho and Luz walked up the main street, awed by the hush which enveloped the village. The cloud had covered the sky; now it was slowly pulled down like a curtain over the other side of the valley. A sad little churchbell began to ring behind them in the plaza. They turned into a small shop marked *Farmacia Moderna*. The man sitting inside knew Señor Ha: he was the only Chinese in the village. "He lives opposite the convent, in the last house." In Tlaltepec everything was nearby. The bell was still tolling from the plaza. In front of the ruined convent was an open square of sward; basketball posts had been put up at each end, but now they were broken. Before the last house stood a large tree laden with thousands of lavender flowers. In the still air they fell without cease, like silent tears, onto the damp earth beneath.

Nicho knocked on the door. A servant girl came and looked at the two children indifferently, went away. In a moment Señor Ha appeared. He was not quite so old as they had expected; his angular face was expressionless, but he looked closely at both of them. Nicho had hoped he would ask them into the house: he wanted to see if Señor Ha had a calendar like the one at home in the *sala,* but no such hospitality was forthcoming. Luz sat down on the stone step below them and picked up some of the blossoms that had fallen from the tree while Nicho told Señor Ha who he was and why he had come. Señor Ha stood quite still. Even when Nicho said: "And he is going to kill you," his hard little eyes remained in exactly the same position. Nothing in his face moved; he looked at Nicho as though he had not heard a word. For a moment Nicho thought that perhaps he understood nothing but Chinese, but then Señor Ha said, very clearly: "What lies!" And he shut the door.

They walked back to the plaza without saying anything, and sat down on an iron bench to wait for the bus. A warm, mistlike rain moved downward through the air, falling so softly that it was inaudible even in the stillness of the deserted plaza. At one point while they waited Nicho got up and went to the main street in search of some candy. As he came out of the shop, a little man carrying a briefcase walked quickly past and crossed the street. It was Señor Ha.

While they sat eating the candy a battered sedan came out of the main street and bumped across the plaza; on the edge of its back seat, leaning forward talking to the driver, was Señor Ha. They stared. The car turned into the road that led up the mountainside toward the town, and disappeared in the twilight.

"He's going to tell Señor Ong!" cried Nicho suddenly. He let his mouth stay open and fixed the ground.

Luz squeezed his arm. "You don't care," she declared. "They're only Chinamen. You're not afraid of them."

He looked blankly at her. Then with scorn he answered: "No!"

116

They talked very little on the ride up in the rain. It was night by the time they arrived in the town. Wet and hungry, they went down the street toward the bridge, still without speaking. As they crossed the river Nicho turned to her and said: "Come and have dinner at my house."

"My sister . . ."

But he pulled her roughly along with him. Even as he opened the front door and saw his aunt and Señor Ong sitting inside, he knew that Señor Ha had not been there.

"Why are you so late?" said his aunt. "You're wet." Then she saw Luz. "Shut the door, *niña*," she said, looking pleased.

While they ate in the covered part of the patio, Señor Ong continued with what he apparently had been saying earlier in the evening . . . "She looked directly at me without saying a word."

"Who?" said his aunt, smiling at Luz.

"The Fernandez woman. This afternoon." Señor Ong's voice was edged with impatience. "For me that is proof enough. She's getting it somewhere else."

His aunt snorted. "Still you're looking for proof! *Niña*, take more meat." She piled extra food on Luz's plate.

"Yes, there's no doubt now," Señor Ong continued.

"What beautiful hair! *Ay, Dios!*" She smoothed the top of the girl's head. Nicho was ashamed: he knew that he had invited her to dinner because he had been afraid to come home alone, and he knew that his aunt was touching her hair only in order to bring herself good luck. He sighed miserably and glanced at Luz; she seemed perfectly content as she ate.

117

Suddenly there were several loud knocks on the front door. Señor Ong rose and went into the *sala*. There was a silence. A man's voice said: "*Usted se llama Narciso Ong?*" All at once there followed a great deal of noise; feet scuffled and furniture scraped on the tile floor. Nicho's aunt jumped up and ran into the kitchen where she began to pray very loudly. In the *sala* there was grunting and wheezing, and then as the racket grew less intense, a man said: "*Bueno.* I have it. A hundred grams, at least, right in his pocket. That's all we needed, my friend. *Vamonos.*"

Nicho slid down from his chair and stood in the doorway. Two men in wet brown ponchos were pushing Señor Ong out the front door. But he did not seem to want to go. He twisted his head and saw Nicho, opened his mouth to speak to him. One of the men hit him in the side of the face with his fist. "Not in front of the boy," said Señor Ong, wriggling his jaw back and forth to see if it was all right. "Not in front of the boy," he said again thickly. The other man slammed the door shut. The *sala* was empty. There was no sound but his aunt's wailing voice in the kitchen, crying aloud to God. He turned to look at Luz, who was sitting perfectly still.

"Do you want to go home?" he said to her.

"Yes." She got up. His aunt came out of the kitchen wringing her hands. Going over to Luz she laid her hand briefly on the white hair, still muttering a prayer.

"*Adiós, niña.* Come back tomorrow," she said.

There was still a light rain falling. A few insects sang from the wet leaves as the two silent children passed along the way to the house where Luz lived. When they rapped on the door it was opened immediately. A tall thin girl stood there. Without speaking she seized Luz with one arm and pulled her violently inside, closing the door with the other.

When Nicho got home and went into the *sala*, his first thought was that Señor Ong had returned, but the next instant he felt that he was in the middle of a bad dream. Señor Ha was sitting there talking with his aunt. She looked up tearfully. "Go to bed," she commanded.

Señor Ha reached out from his chair as Nicho passed and caught his arm—caught it very tightly. "Ay!" said Nicho in spite of himself. "One moment," said Señor Ha, still looking at Nicho's aunt, and never for a second relaxing his grip. "Perhaps this one knows." And without turning his face toward Nicho he said: "The police have taken Señor Ong to prison. He will not come back here. He hid something in this house. Where is it?"

It seemed as though the hard fingers would cut through his skin. His aunt looked up at him hopefully. He felt suddenly very important.

"There," he said, pointing to the calendar.

Señor Ha rose and yanked the pretty girl down from the wall. In an instant he had the yellow envelope in his hand. As he examined its contents, he said: "Is there any more?"

"No," said Nicho, thinking of the envelope lying in the safety of his tree out there in the rainy night. Señor Ha began to twist his arm, but the thought of his secret made him feel strong; his pain and his hatred flowed into that feeling of strength. He stood stiffly and let Señor Ha hurt him. A moment later Señor Ha let go of him and gave him a violent push that sent him halfway across the room. "Go to bed," he said.

When Nicho had gone out and closed the door, Señor Ha turned to the aunt. "Tomorrow I shall come back with my clothes," he said. "It is not good to have a boy around the house doing nothing; he gets into trouble. From now on he will deliver it; there will be no one coming to the house."

"But if the police catch him . . ." she objected.

"There will be no trouble with them. It is all arranged. Fortunately I had nearly three thousand pesos on hand." He picked up his briefcase and went to the door. She looked after him with frank admiration and sighed deeply. "You won't stay tonight?" She said the words timidly, and they sounded strangely coquettish.

"No. The car is outside waiting for me. Tomorrow." He opened the door. Rising, she went and took his hand, pressing it warmly between her two hands. "Tomorrow," he repeated.

When the car had driven away and she could no longer hear it, she closed the door, turned off the light, and went out into the patio, where she got into a hammock and lay swinging gently back and forth.

"An intelligent man," she said to herself. "What good luck!" She stopped swinging a moment. "Good luck! Of course! Dionisio must bring her to the house again one day very soon."

The town went on being prosperous, the Indians kept coming down from the heights with money, the thick jungle along the way to Mapastenango was hacked away, the trail widened and improved. Nicho bought a packet of little envelopes. Far

down the river he found another hollow tree. Here he kept his
slowly increasing store of treasure; during the very first month
he picked up enough money on the side to buy Luz a lipstick
and a pair of dark glasses with red and green jewels all around
the rims.

the circular valley

The abandoned monastery stood on a slight eminence of land in the middle of a vast clearing. On all sides the ground sloped gently downward toward the tangled, hairy jungle that filled the circular valley, ringed about by sheer, black cliffs. There were a few trees in some of the courtyards, and the birds used them as meeting-places when they flew out of the rooms and corridors where they had their nests. Long ago bandits had taken whatever was removable out of the building. Soldiers had used it once as headquarters, had, like the bandits, built fires in the great windy rooms so that afterward they looked like ancient kitchens. And now that everything was gone from within, it seemed that never again would anyone come near the monastery. The vegetation had thrown up a protecting wall; the first story was soon quite hidden from view by small

122

trees which dripped vines to lasso the cornices of the windows. The meadows roundabout grew dank and lush; there was no path through them.

At the higher end of the circular valley a river fell off the cliffs into a great cauldron of vapor and thunder below; after this it slid along the base of the cliffs until it found a gap at the other end of the valley, where it hurried discreetly through with no rapids, no cascades—a great thick black rope of water moving swiftly downhill between the polished flanks of the canyon. Beyond the gap the land opened out and became smiling; a village nestled on the side hill just outside. In the days of the monastery it was there that the friars had got their provisions, since the Indians would not enter the circular valley. Centuries ago when the building had been constructed the Church had imported the workmen from another part of the country. These were traditional enemies of the tribes thereabouts, and had another language; there was no danger that the inhabitants would communicate with them as they worked at setting up the mighty walls. Indeed, the construction had taken so long that before the east wing was completed the workmen had all died, one by one. Thus it was the friars themselves who had closed off the end of the wing with blank walls, leaving it that way, unfinished and blind-looking, facing the black cliffs.

Generation after generation, the friars came, fresh-cheeked boys who grew thin and gray, and finally died, to be buried in the garden beyond the courtyard with the fountain. One day not long ago they had all left the monastery; no one knew where they had gone, and no one thought to ask. It was shortly after this that the bandits, and then the soldiers had come. And now, since the Indians do not change, still no one from the village went up through the gap to visit the monastery. The Atlájala lived there; the friars had not been able to kill it, had given up at last and gone away. No one was surprised, but the Atlájala gained in prestige by their departure. During the centuries the friars had been there in the monastery, the Indians had wondered why it allowed them to stay. Now, at last, it had driven them out. It always had lived there, they said, and would go on living there because the valley was its home, and it could never leave.

In the early morning the restless Atlájala would move through the halls of the monastery. The dark rooms sped past, one after the other. In a small patio, where eager young trees had pushed up the paving stones to reach the sun, it paused. The air was full of small sounds: the movements of butterflies, the falling to the ground of bits of leaves and flowers, the air following its myriad courses around the edges of things, the ants pursuing their endless labors in the hot dust. In the sun it waited, conscious of each gradation in sound and light and smell, living in the awareness of the slow, constant disintegration that attacked the morning and transformed it into afternoon. When evening came, it often slipped above the monastery roof and surveyed the darkening sky: the waterfall would roar distantly. Night after night, along the procession of years, it had hovered here above the valley, darting down to become a bat, a leopard, a moth for a few minutes or hours, returning to rest immobile in the center of the space enclosed by the cliffs. When the monastery had been built, it had taken to frequenting the rooms, where it had observed for the first time the meaningless gestures of human life.

And then one evening it had aimlessly become one of the young friars. This was a new sensation, strangely rich and complex, and at the same time unbearably stifling, as though every other possibility besides that of being enclosed in a tiny, isolated world of cause and effect had been removed forever. As the friar, it had gone and stood in the window, looking out at the sky, seeing for the first time, not the stars, but the space between and beyond them. Even at that moment it had felt the urge to leave, to step outside the little shell of anguish where it lodged for the moment, but a faint curiosity had impelled it to remain a little longer and partake a little further of the unaccustomed sensation. It held on; the friar raised his arms to the sky in an imploring gesture. For the first time the Atlájala sensed opposition, the thrill of a struggle. It was delicious to feel the young man striving to free himself of its presence, and it was immeasurably sweet to remain there. Then with a cry the friar had rushed to the other side of the room and seized a heavy leather whip hanging on the wall. Tearing off his clothing he had begun to carry out a ferocious self-beating. At the first blow of the lash the Atlájala had been on the point of letting go, but then it realized that the immediacy of that intriguing inner pain was only made more manifest by the impact of the blows from without, and so it stayed and felt the young man grow weak under his own lashing. When he had finished and said a prayer, he crawled to his pallet and fell asleep weeping, while the Atlájala slipped out obliquely and entered into a bird which passed the night sitting in a great tree on the edge of the jungle, listening intently to the night sounds, and uttering a scream from time to time.

Thereafter the Atlájala found it impossible to resist sliding inside the bodies of the friars; it visited one after the other, finding an astonishing variety of sensation in the process. Each was a separate world, a separate experience, because each had different reactions when he became conscious of the other being within him. One would sit and read or pray, one would go for a long troubled walk in the meadows, around and around the building, one would find a comrade and engage in an absurd but bitter quarrel, a few wept, some flagellated themselves or sought a friend to wield the lash for them. Always there was a rich profusion of perceptions for the Atlájala to enjoy, so that it no longer occurred to it to frequent the bodies of insects, birds and furred animals, nor even to leave the monastery and move in the air above. Once it almost got into difficulties when an old friar it was occupying suddenly fell back dead. That was a hazard it ran in the frequenting of men: they seemed not to know when they were doomed, or if they did know, they pretended with such strength not to know, that it amounted to the same thing. The other beings knew beforehand, save when it was a question of being seized unawares and devoured. And that the Atlájala was able to prevent: a bird in which it was staying was always avoided by the hawks and eagles.

When the friars left the monastery, and, following the government's orders, doffed their robes, dispersed and became workmen, the Atlájala was at a loss to know how to pass its days and nights. Now everything was as it had been before their arrival: there was no one but the creatures that always had lived in the circular valley. It tried a giant serpent, a deer, a bee: nothing had the savor it had grown to love. Everything was the same as before, but not for the Atlájala; it had known the existence of man, and now there were no men in the valley—only the abandoned building with its empty rooms to make man's absence more poignant.

Then one year bandits came, several hundred of them in one stormy afternoon. In delight it tried many of them as they sprawled about cleaning their guns and cursing, and it discovered still other facets of sensation: the hatred they felt for the world, the fear they had of the soldiers who were pursuing them, the strange gusts of desire that swept through them as they sprawled together drunk by the fire that smoldered in the center of the floor, and the insufferable pain of jealousy which the nightly orgies seem to awaken in some of them. But the bandits did not stay long. When they had left, the soldiers came in their wake. It felt very much the same way to be a soldier as to be a bandit. Missing were the strong fear and the hatred, but the rest was almost identical. Neither the bandits nor the soldiers appeared to be at all conscious of its presence in them; it could slip from one man to another without causing any change in their behavior. This surprised it, since its effect on the friars had been so definite, and it felt a certain disappointment at the impossibility of making its existence known to them.

Nevertheless, the Atlájala enjoyed both bandits and soldiers immensely, and was even more desolate when it was left alone once again. It would become one of the swallows that made their nests in the rocks beside the top of the waterfall. In the burning sunlight it would plunge again and again into the curtain of mist that rose from far below, sometimes uttering exultant cries. It would spend a day as a plant louse, crawling slowly along the under side of the leaves, living quietly in the huge green world down there which is forever hidden from the sky. Or at night, in the velvet body of a panther, it would know the pleasure of the kill. Once for a year it lived in an eel at the bottom of the pool below the waterfall, feeling the mud give slowly before it as it pushed ahead with its flat nose; that was a restful period, but afterward the desire to know again the mysterious life of man had returned—an obsession of which it was useless to try to rid itself. And now it moved restlessly through the ruined rooms, a mute presence, alone, and thirsting to be incarnate once again, but in man's flesh only. And with the building of highways through the country it was inevitable that people should come once again to the circular valley.

A man and a woman drove their automobile as far as a village down in a lower valley; hearing about the ruined monastery and the waterfall that dropped over the cliffs into the great amphitheatre, they determined to see these things. They came on burros as far as the village outside the gap, but there the

Indians they had hired to accompany them refused to go any farther, and so they continued alone, upward through the canyon and into the precinct of the Atlájala.

It was noon when they rode into the valley; the black ribs of the cliffs glistened like glass in the sun's blistering downward rays. They stopped the burros by a cluster of boulders at the edge of the sloping meadows. The man got down first, and reached up to help the woman off. She leaned forward, putting her hands on his face, and for a long moment they kissed. Then he lifted her to the ground and they climbed hand in hand up over the rocks. The Atlájala hovered near them, watching the woman closely: she was the first ever to have come into the valley. The two sat beneath a small tree on the grass, looking at one another, smiling. Out of habit, the Atlájala entered into the man. Immediately, instead of existing in the midst of the sunlit air, the bird calls and the plant odors, it was conscious only of the woman's beauty and her terrible imminence. The waterfall, the earth, and the sky itself receded, rushed into nothingness, and there were only the woman's smile and her arms and her odor. It was a world more suffocating and painful than the Atlájala had thought possible. Still, while the man spoke and the woman answered, it remained within.

"Leave him. He doesn't love you."

"He would kill me."

"But I love you. I need you with me."

"I can't. I'm afraid of him."

The man reached out to pull her to him; she drew back slightly, but her eyes grew large.

"We have today," she murmured, turning her face toward the yellow walls of the monastery.

The man embraced her fiercely, crushing her against him as though the act would save his life. "No, no, no. It can't go on like this," he said. "No."

The pain of his suffering was too intense; gently the Atlájala left the man and slipped into the woman. And now it would have believed itself to be housed in nothing, to be in its own spaceless self, so completely was it aware of the wandering wind, the small flutterings of the leaves, and the bright air that surrounded it. Yet there was a difference: each element was magnified in intensity, the whole sphere of being was immense, limitless. Now it understood what the man sought in the woman, and it knew that he suffered because he never would attain that sense of completion he sought. But the Atlájala, being one with the woman, had attained it, and being aware of possessing it, trembled with delight. The woman shuddered as her lips met those of the man. There on the grass in the shade of the tree their joy reached new heights; the Atlájala, knowing them both, formed a single channel between the secret springs of their desires. Throughout, it remained within the woman, and began vaguely to devise ways of keeping her, if not inside the valley, at least nearby, so that she might return.

In the afternoon, with dreamlike motions, they walked to the burros and mounted them, driving them through the deep meadow grass to the monastery. Inside the great courtyard they halted, looking hesitantly at the ancient arches in the sunlight, and at the darkness inside the doorways.

"Shall we go in?" said the woman.

"We must get back."

"I want to go in," she said. (The Atlájala exulted.) A thin gray snake slid along the ground into the bushes. They did not see it.

The man looked at her perplexedly. "It's late," he said.

But she jumped down from her burro by herself and walked beneath the arches into the long corridor within. (Never had the rooms seemed so real as now when the Atlájala was seeing them through her eyes.)

They explored all the rooms. Then the woman wanted to climb up into the tower, but the man took a determined stand.

"We must go back now," he said firmly, putting his hand on her shoulder.

"This is our only day together, and you think of nothing but getting back."

"But the time . . ."

"There is a moon. We won't lose the way."

He would not change his mind. "No."

"As you like," she said. "I'm going up. You can go back alone if you like."

The man laughed uneasily. "You're mad." He tried to kiss her.

She turned away and did not answer for a moment. Then she said: "You want me to leave my husband for you. You ask everything from me, but what do you do for me in return? You refuse even to climb up into a little tower with me to see the view. Go back alone. Go!"

She sobbed and rushed toward the dark stairwell. Calling after

131

her, he followed, but stumbled somewhere behind her. She was as sure of foot as if she had climbed the many stone steps a thousand times before, hurrying up through the darkness, around and around.

In the end she came out at the top and peered through the small apertures in the cracking walls. The beams which had supported the bell had rotted and fallen; the heavy bell lay on its side in the rubble, like a dead animal. The waterfall's sound was louder up here; the valley was nearly full of shadow. Below, the man called her name repeatedly. She did not answer. As she stood watching the shadow of the cliffs slowly overtake the farthest recesses of the valley and begin to climb the naked rocks to the east, an idea formed in her mind. It was not the kind of idea which she would have expected of herself, but it was there, growing and inescapable. When she felt it complete there inside her, she turned and went lightly back down. The man was sitting in the dark near the bottom of the stairs, groaning a little.

"What is it?" she said.

"I hurt my leg. Now are you ready to go or not?"

"Yes," she said simply. "I'm sorry you fell."

Without saying anything he rose and limped after her out into the courtyard where the burros stood. The cold mountain air was beginning to flow down from the tops of the cliffs. As they rode through the meadow she began to think of how she would broach the subject to him. (It must be done before they reached the gap. The Atlájala trembled.)

"Do you forgive me?" she asked him.

"Of course," he laughed.

"Do you love me?"

"More than anything in the world."

"Is that true?"

He glanced at her in the failing light, sitting erect on the jogging animal.

"Yow know it is," he said softly.

She hesitated.

"There is only one way, then," she said finally.

"But what?"

"I'm afraid of him. I won't go back to him. You go back. I'll stay in the village here." (Being that near, she would come each day to the monastery.) "When it is done, you will come and get me. Then we can go somewhere else. No one will find us."

The man's voice sounded strange. "I don't understand."

"You do understand. And that is the only way. Do it or not, as you like. It is the only way."

They trotted along for a while in silence. The canyon loomed ahead, black against the evening sky.

Then the man said, very clearly: "Never."

A moment later the trail led out into an open space high above the swift water below. The hollow sound of the river reached them faintly. The light in the sky was almost gone; in the dusk the landscape had taken on false contours. Everything was gray—the rocks, the bushes, the trail—and nothing had distance or scale. They slowed their pace.

His word still echoed in her ears.

"I won't go back to him!" she cried with sudden vehemence.

133

"You can go back and play cards with him as usual. Be his good friend the same as always. I won't go. I can't go on with both of you in the town." (The plan was not working; the Atlájala saw it had lost her, yet it still could help her.)

"You're very tired," he said softly.

He was right. Almost as he said the words, that unaccustomed exhilaration and lightness she had felt ever since noon seemed to leave her; she hung her head wearily, and said: "Yes, I am."

At the same moment the man uttered a sharp, terrible cry; she looked up in time to see his burro plunge from the edge of the trail into the grayness below. There was a silence, and then the faraway sound of many stones sliding downward. She could not move or stop the burro; she sat dumbly, letting it carry her along, an inert weight on its back.

For one final instant, as she reached the pass which was the edge of its realm, the Atlájala alighted tremulously within her. She raised her head and a tiny exultant shiver passed through her; then she let it fall forward once again.

Hanging in the dim air above the trail, the Atlájala watched her indistinct figure grow invisible in the gathering night. (If it had not been able to hold her there, still it had been able to help her.)

A moment later it was in the tower, listening to the spiders mend the webs that she had damaged. It would be a long, long time before it would bestir itself to enter into another being's awareness. A long, long time—perhaps forever.

the echo

Aileen pulled out her mirror; the vibration of the plane shook it so rapidly that she was unable to see whether her nose needed powder or not. There were only two other passengers and they were asleep. It was noon; the tropical sun shone violently down upon the wide silver wings and cast sharp reflections on the ceiling. Far below, the uniform green carpet of the jungle moved slowly by. She was sleepy, but she was also excited to be going to a new home. From her handbag she pulled a folded letter which she read again intently, as if to decipher a meaning that did not lie in the sequence of the words. It was in her mother's script:

"Aileen, Sweet—
"I must begin (and finish) this before supper. Prue has gone out for her shower, and that means that by the

time she has Luz (the cook) heat the water and can find José (the gardener) to carry it up on the roof to the tank, it will be about an hour. Add to that the time it takes her to do her actual bathing and to dress, and you can see I'll have just about time for a nice chat.

"Perhaps I should begin by saying that Prue and I are sublimely happy here. It is absolute heaven after Washington, as you can pretty well imagine. Prue, of course, never could stand the States, and I felt, after the trouble with your father, that I couldn't face anyone for a while. You know how much importance I have always attached to relaxation. And this is the ideal spot for that.

"Of course I did feel a little guilty about running off down here without seeing you. But I think the trip to Northampton would have sealed my doom. I honestly don't believe I could have stood it. And Prue was nervous about the State Department's passing some new law that would prevent citizens from leaving the U.S. because of the disturbed conditions, and so on. I also felt that the sooner we got down here to Jamonocal the more of a home we could make out of the old place, for you to spend your vacation in. And it *is* going to be beautiful. I won't drag out my reasons for not letting you know beforehand or it will sound apologetic, and I know I never have to apologize to you for anything. So I'll leave that and get on. I'm sure anyway that the eight months passed very quickly up there for you.

"We have had swarms of men working on the house ever since last October. Mr. Forbes happened to be in Barranquilla for a new American project in the interior, and I wanted to be sure of having him supervise the construction of the cantilever in the foundation. That man is really a prince. They don't come much finer. He was up again and again, and gave orders down to the last detail. I felt guilty about making him work so hard, but I honestly think he enjoyed himself with us girls. In any case it seemed silly, when one of the best architects in the U.S. was right here in Colombia and happened to be an old friend, not to use him when I needed him. Anyway, the old house is now the old wing and the new part, which is so exciting I can't wait for you to see it, is built right out over the gorge. I think there's not likely to be another house like it in the world, if I do say it myself. The terrace makes me think of an old cartoon in the *New Yorker* showing two men looking over the edge of the Grand Canyon, and one is saying to the other: 'Did you ever want to spit a mile, Bill? Now's your chance.'

"We are all installed. The weather has been wonderful, and if Luz could only learn a little more about what white people like to eat and how they like it served,

137

the setup would really be perfect. I know you will enjoy being here with Prue. She and you have many things in common, even if you do claim to 'remember not liking her much.' That was in Washington and you were, to put it mildly, at a difficult age. Now, as an adult (because you really are one by now), you'll be more understanding, I'm sure. She loves books, especially on philosophy and psychology and other things your poor mother just doesn't try to follow her in. She has rigged up a kiln and studio in the old guest house which you probably don't remember. She works at her ceramics out there all day, and I have all I can do keeping the house tidy and seeing that the marketing is done. We have a system by which Luz takes the list to her brother every afternoon, and he brings the things from town the following day. It just about keeps him fully busy getting up and down the mountain on his horse. The horse is a lazy old nag that has done nothing but plod back and forth between house and the valley all its life, so it doesn't know the meaning of the word speed. But after all, why hurry, down here?

"I think you will find everything to your liking, and I'm sure you won't require more than five minutes to see that Prue is a dear, and not at all 'peculiar,' as you wrote in your letter. Wire me as soon as you receive this, and let me know just what week you'll be finishing classes. Prue and I will meet you in Barranquilla. I have a list of things I want you to get me in New York. Will

wire it to you as soon as I hear. Prue's bath finished.
Must close.

Love,
Mother."

Aileen put the letter away, smiling a little, and watched
the wings diving in and out of the small thick clouds that lay
in the plane's way. There was a slight shock each time they
hit one, and the world outside became a blinding whiteness.
She fancied jumping out and walking on such solid softness,
like a character in an animated cartoon.

Her mother's letter had put her in mind of a much earlier
period in her life: the winter she had been taken to visit
Jamonocal. All she could recall in the way of incidents was that
she had been placed on a mule by one of the natives, and had
felt a painful horror that the animal would walk in the wrong
direction, away from the house toward the edge of the gorge.
She had no memory of the gorge. Probably she had never seen
it, although it was only a few paces from the house, through a
short but thick stretch of canebrake. However, she had a clear
memory of its presence, of the sensation of enormous void beyond and below that side of the house. And she recalled the
distant, hollow sound of water falling from a great height, a
constant, soft backdrop of sound that slipped into every moment of the day—between the conversations at mealtimes, in
the intervals of play in the garden, and at night between
dreams. She wondered if really it were possible to remember all
that from the time when she had been only five.

139

In Panama there was a plane change to be made. It was a clear green twilight, and she took a short walk beyond the airport. Parakeets were fighting in the upper branches of the trees; suddenly they became quiet. She turned back and went inside, where she sat reading until it was time to go aboard.

There was no one there to meet her when she arrived at Barranquilla in the early hours of the morning. She decided to go into town and take a room in the hotel. With her two valises she stepped outside and looked about for a cab. They had all gone to the town with passengers, but a man sitting on a packing case informed her that they would soon be coming back. Then suddenly he said, "You want two ladies?"

"What? No. What do you mean?"

"You want two ladies look for you this night?"

"Where are they?" said Aileen, understanding.

"They want a drink," he answered with an intimate grin.

"Where? Barranquilla?"

"No. Here." He pointed down the dark road.

"Where? Can I walk?"

"Sure. I go you."

"No! No thanks. You stay here. Thank you. I can go all right. Where is it? How far?"

"O.K."

"What is it? A bar? What's the name?"

"They got music. La Gloria. You go. You hear music. You look for two ladies. They drinking."

She went inside again and checked the bags with an airline employee who insisted on accompanying her. They strode in silence along the back road. The walls of vegetation on each side sheltered insects that made an occasional violent, dry noise like a wooden ratchet being whirled. Soon there was the sound of drums and trumpets playing Cuban dance music.

"La Gloria," said her escort triumphantly.

La Gloria was a brilliantly lighted mud hut with a thatch-covered veranda giving onto the road. The juke box was outside, where a few drunken Negroes sprawled.

"Are they here?" she said out loud, but to herself.

"La Gloria," he answered, pointing.

As they came opposite the front of the building, she caught a glimpse of a woman in blue jeans, and although instantaneously she knew it was Prue, her mind for some reason failed to accept the fact, and she continued to ask herself, "Are they here or not?"

She turned to go toward the veranda. The record had finished playing. The ditch lay in the dark between the road and the porch. She fell forward into it and heard herself cry out. The man behind her said, *"Cuidado!"* She lay there panting with fury and pain, and said, "Oh! My ankle!" There was an exclamation inside the bar. Her mother's voice cried, "That's Aileen!" Then the juke box began to scratch and roar again. The Negroes remained stationary. Someone helped her up. She was inside the bar in the raw electric glare.

"I'm all right," she said, when she had been eased into a chair.

"But darling, where've you been? We've been waiting for you since eight, and we'd just about given up. Poor Prue's ill."

141

"Nonsense, I'll recover," said Prue, still seated at the bar. "Been having a touch of the trots, that's all."

"But darling, are you all right? This is absurd, landing here this way."

She looked down at Aileen's ankle.

"Is it all right?"

Prue came over from the bar to shake her hand.

"A dramatic entrance, gal," she said.

Aileen sat there and smiled. She had a curious mental habit. As a child she had convinced herself that her head was transparent, that the thoughts there could be perceived immediately by others. Accordingly, when she found herself in uncomfortable situations, rather than risk the danger of being suspected of harboring uncomplimentary or rebellious thoughts, she had developed a system of refraining from thinking at all. For a while during her childhood this fear of having no mental privacy had been extended to anyone; even persons existing at a distance could have access to her mind. Now she felt open only to those present. And so it was that, finding herself face to face with Prue, she was conscious of no particular emotion save the familiar vague sense of boredom. There was not a thought in her head, and her face made the fact apparent.

Mornings were hard to believe. The primeval freshness, spilled down out of the jungle above the house, was held close to the earth by the mist. Outside and in, it was damp and smelled like a florist's shop, but the dampness was dispelled each day when the stinging sun burned through the thin cape of

142

moisture that clung to the mountain's back. Living there was like living sideways, with the land stretching up on one side and down on the other at the same angle. Only the gorge gave a feeling of perpendicularity; the vertical walls of rock on the opposite side of the great amphitheatre were a reminder that the center of gravity lay below and not obliquely to one side. Constant vapor rose from the invisible pool at the bottom, and the distant, indeterminate calling of water was like the sound of sleep itself.

For a few days Aileen lay in bed listening to the water and the birds, and to the nearby, unfamiliar, domestic sounds. Her mother and Prue both had breakfast in bed, and generally appeared just before the midday meal for a few minutes of conversation until Concha brought the invalid's lunch tray. In the afternoons she thumbed through old magazines and read at murder mysteries. Usually it began to rain about three; the sound at first would be like an augmentation of the waterfall in the distance, and then as its violence increased it came unmistakably nearer—a great roar all around the house that covered every other sound. The black clouds would close in tightly around the mountain, so that it seemed that night would soon arrive. She would ring a small bell for Concha to come and light the oil lamp on the table by the bed. Lying there looking at the wet banana leaves outside the window, with the rain's din everywhere, she felt completely comfortable for the precarious moment. There was no necessity to question the feeling, no need to think—only the subsiding of the rain, the triumphant emergence of the sun into the steaming twilight and an early dinner to look forward to. Each evening after dinner her mother came for a lengthy chat, usually about the servants. The first three nights Prue had come too, carrying a highball, but after that her mother came alone.

Aileen had asked to be put into the old part of the house, rather than into a more comfortable room in the new wing. Her window looked onto the garden, which was a small square of lawn with young banana trees on either side. At the far end was a fountain; behind it was the disordered terrain of the mountainside with its recently cut underbrush and charred stumps, and still further beyond was the high jungle whose frontier had been sliced in a straight line across the slopes many years ago to make the plantation. Here in her room she felt at least that the earth was somewhere beneath her.

When her ankle ceased to pain her, she began going downstairs for lunch, which was served out on the terrace at a table with a beach umbrella stuck in its center. Prue was regularly late in coming from her studio, and she arrived in her blue jeans, which were caked with clay, with smears of dirt across her face. Because Aileen could not bring herself to think what she really felt, which was that Prue was ungracious, ugly and something of an interloper, she remained emotionally unconscious of Prue's presence, which is to say that she was polite but bored, scarcely present in the mealtime conversations. Then, too, Aileen was definitely uncomfortable on the terrace. The emptiness was too near and the balustrade seemed altogether too low for safety. She liked the meals to be as brief as possible, with no unnecessary time spent sipping coffee afterward, but it never would have occurred to her to divulge her reasons. With Prue around she felt constrained to behave with the utmost decorum. Fortunately her ankle provided her with a convenient excuse to get back upstairs to her room.

She soon discovered a tiny patio next to the kitchen where heavy vines with sweet-smelling flowers grew up an arbor that had been placed at one side. The air was full of the humming of hundreds of bees that clung heavily to the petals and moved slowly about in the air. After lunch she would pull a deck chair into the arbor's shade and read until the rain began. It was a stifling, airless spot, but the sound of the bees covered that of the waterfall. One afternoon Prue followed her there and stood with her hands in her hip pockets looking at her.

"How can you take this heat?" she asked Aileen.

"Oh, I love it."

"You do?" She paused. "Tell me, do you really like it here, or do you think it's a bloody bore?"

"Why, I think it's absolutely wonderful."

"Mm. It is."

"Don't you like it?"

Prue yawned. "Oh, I'm all for it. But I keep busy. Wherever I can work, I get on, you know."

"Yes, I suppose so," said Aileen. Then she added, "Are you planning on staying long?"

"What the hell do you mean?" said Prue, leaning backward against the house, her hands still behind her. "I live here."

145

Aileen laughed shortly. To anyone but Prue it would have sounded like a merry, tinkling laugh, but Prue narrowed her eyes and thrust her jaw forward a bit.

"What's so funny?" she demanded.

"I think you're funny. You're so tied up in knots. You get upset so easily. Perhaps you work too hard out there in your little house."

Prue was looking at her with astonishment.

"God Almighty," she said finally, "your I.Q.'s showing, gal."

"Thank you," said Aileen with great seriousness. "Anyway, I think it's fine that you're happy here, and I hope you go on being happy."

"That's what I came to say to you."

"Then everything's fine."

"I can't make you out," said Prue, frowning.

"I don't know what you're talking about," replied Aileen, fingering the pages of her book impatiently. "It's the most pointless conversation I've ever had."

"That I *don't* think," Prue said, going into the kitchen.

The same evening, when her mother came for her usual after-dinner chat, she looked a little unhappy.

"You don't seem to be getting on very well with Prue," she said reproachfully, as she sat down at the foot of the bed.

"Why, we get on perfectly well. Oh. You're talking about this afternoon, probably."

"Yes, I am, probably. Really, Aileen. You simply can't be rude to a woman her age. She's my guest, and you're my guest, and you've got to be civil to each other. But she's always civil and I have a feeling you're not."

Aileen caught her breath and said, "I'm your guest . . ."

"I invited you here for your vacation and I want things pleasant, and I don't see the slightest reason why they shouldn't be."

Suddenly Aileen cried, "She's a maniac!"

Her mother rose and quickly left the room.

In the quiet days that followed, the incident was not mentioned by any of them. Aileen continued to haunt the little patio after lunch.

There came a morning sweeter than the rest, when the untouched early mist hung inside her bedroom, and the confusion of shrill bird cries came down with perfect clarity from the uncut forest. She dressed quickly and went out. There was a white radiance in the air that she had never seen before. She walked along the path that led by the native huts. There was life stirring within; babies were crying and captive parrots and songbirds laughed and sang. The path swung into a stretch of low trees that had been planted to shield the coffee bushes. It was still almost nocturnal in here; the air was streaked with chill, and the vegetable odors were like invisible festoons drooping from the branches as she walked through. A huge bright spider walked slowly across the path at her feet. She stood still and watched it until it had disappeared in the leaves at one side. She put her hand over her heart to feel how insistently it was beating. And she listened to its sound in her head for a moment, not wanting to break into its rhythm by starting to walk again. Then she began to walk ahead fast, following the path upward toward the lightest part of the sky. When it came out suddenly onto an eminence directly above the plantation, she could barely discern the cluster of roofs through the mist. But here the sound of the waterfall was stronger; she supposed she was near the gorge, although there was no sign of it. The path turned here and went along rough open ground upward. She climbed at a steady gait, breathing slowly and deeply, for perhaps half an hour, and was surprised to find that the jungle had been cut away on all sides in this portion of the mountainside. For a time she thought the sky was growing brighter, and that the sun was about to break through, but as the path leveled out and she was able to see for some distance ahead, she saw that the mist was even thicker up here than down below.

At certain points there was a steep declivity on each side of the path. It was impossible to see how deeply the land fell away. There were a few nearby plants and rocks, the highest fronds of a tree-fern a little beyond, and white emptiness after that. It was like going along the top of a wall high in the air. Then the path would make a wide turn and go sharply upward and she would see a solitary tree above her at one side.

Suddenly she came up against a row of huts. They were less well made than those down at the plantation, and smaller. The mist was full of woodsmoke; there was the smell of pigs. She stood still. A man was singing. Two small naked children came out of the door of one hut, looked at her a moment in terror,

148

and ran quickly back inside. She walked ahead. The singing came from behind the last hut. When she came opposite the hut, she saw that it was enclosed by a tangled but effective fence of barbed wire which left a runway about six feet wide all the way around. A young man appeared from the farther side of the closed-in space. His shirt and pants were tattered; the brown skin showed in many places. He was singing as he walked toward her, and he continued to sing, looking straight into her face with bright, questioning eyes. She smiled and said, *"Buenos dias."* He made a beckoning gesture, rather too dramatically. She stopped walking and stood still, looking hesitantly back at the other huts. The young man beckoned again and then stepped inside the hut. A moment later he came out, and still staring fascinatedly at her, made more summoning motions. Aileen stood perfectly quiet, not taking her eyes from his face. He walked slowly over to the fence and grasped the wire with both hands, his eyes growing wider as he pressed the barbs into his palms. Then he leaned across, thrusting his head toward her, his eyes fixing hers with incredible intensity. For several seconds they watched each other; then she stepped a little nearer, peering into his face and frowning. At that point with a cry he emptied his mouth of the water he had been holding in it, aiming with force at Aileen's face. Some of it struck her cheek, and the rest the front of her dress. His fingers unclenched themselves from around the wire, and straightening himself, he backed slowly into the hut, watching her face closely all the while.

She stood still an instant, her hand to her cheek. Then she

149

bent down, and picking up a large stone from the path she flung it with all her strength through the door. A terrible cry came from within; it was like nothing she had ever heard. Or yes, she thought as she began to run back past the other huts, it had the indignation and outraged innocence of a small baby, but it was also a grown man's cry. No one appeared as she passed the huts. Soon she was back in the silence of the empty mountainside, but she kept running, and she was astonished to find that she was sobbing as well. She sat down on a rock and calmed herself by watching some ants demolish a bush as they cut away squares of leaf and carried them away in their mouths. The sky was growing brighter now; the sun would soon be through. She went on. By the time she got back to the high spot above the plantation the mist had turned into long clouds that were rolling away down the mountainside into the ravines. She was horrified to see how near she stood to the ugly black edge of the gorge. And the house looked insane down there, leaning out over as if it were trying to see the bottom. Far below the house the vapor rose up from the pool. She followed the sheer sides of the opposite cliff upward with her eye, all the way to the top, a little above the spot where she stood. It made her feel ill, and she stumbled back down to the house with her hand to her forehead, paying no attention to the natives who greeted her from their doorways.

As she ran past the garden a voice called to her. She turned and saw Prue washing her hands in the fountain's basin. She stood still.

"You're up early. You must feel better," said Prue, drying her hands on her hair. "Your mother's been having a fit. Go in and see her."

Aileen stared at Prue a moment before she said, "I was going in. You don't have to tell me."

"Oh, I thought I did."

"You don't have to tell me anything. I think I can manage all right without your help."

"Help isn't exactly what I'd like to give you," said Prue, putting her hands into her pockets. "A swift kick in the teeth would be more like it. How do you think I like to see your mother worrying about you? First you're sick in bed, then you just disappear into the goddamn jungle. D'you think I like to have to keep talking about you, reassuring her every ten minutes? What the hell d'you think life is, one long coming-out party?"

Aileen stared harder, now with unmasked hatred. "I think," she said slowly, "that life is pretty awful. Here especially. And I think you should look once in the mirror and then jump off the terrace. And I think Mother should have her mind examined."

"I see," said Prue, with dire inflection. She lit a cigarette and strode off to her studio. Aileen went into the house and up to her room.

Less than an hour later, her mother knocked at her door. As she came into the room, Aileen could see she had been crying only a moment before.

"Aileen darling, I've got something to say to you," she began apologetically, "and it just breaks my heart to say it. But I've got to."

She stopped, as though waiting for encouragement.

"Mother, what is it?"

"I think you probably know."

"About Prue, I suppose. No?"

"It certainly is. I don't know how I can ever make it right with her. She told me what you said to her, and I must say I found it hard to believe. How could you?"

"You mean just now in the garden?"

"I don't know where you said it, but I do know this can't go on. So I'm just forced to say this. . . . You'll have to go. I can't be stirred up this way, and I can tell just how it'll be if you stay on."

"I'm not surprised at all," said Aileen, making a show of calm. "When do you want me to leave?"

"This is terribly painful . . ."

"Oh, stop! It's all right. I've had a vacation and I can get a lot of work done before the term starts. Today? Tomorrow?"

"I think the first of the week. I'll go to Barranquilla with you."

"Would you think I was silly if I had all my meals up here?"

"I think it's a perfect idea, darling, and we can have nice visits together, you and I, between meals."

Now, when the tension should have been over, somehow it was not. During the four nights before she was to leave, Aileen had endless excruciating dreams. She would wake up in the darkness too agonized even to move her hand. It was not fear; she could not recall the dreams. It was rather as if some newly discovered, innermost part of her being were in acute pain. Breath-

152

ing quickly, she would lie transfixed for long periods listening to the eternal sound of the waterfall, punctuated at great intervals by some slight, nearby nocturnal noise in the trees. Finally, when she had summoned sufficient energy to move, she would change her position in the bed, sigh profoundly, and relax enough to fall back into the ominous world of sleep.

When the final day came, there was a light tapping on her door just after dawn. She got up and unbolted it. Her mother was there, smiling thinly.

"May I come in?"

"Oh. Good morning. Of course. It's early, isn't it?"

Her mother walked across to the window and stood looking down at the misty garden.

"I'm not so well today," she said. "I'm afraid I can't take you to Barranquilla. I'm not up to getting onto a horse today. It's just too much, that three-hour trip to Jamonocal, and then the train and the boat all night. You'll just have to forgive me. I couldn't stand all three. But it won't matter, will it?" she went on, looking up at last. "We'll say good-bye here."

"But, Mother, how can I go alone?"

"Oh, José'll go all the way to Barranquilla with you and be back by Wednesday night. You don't think I'd let you go off by yourself?"

She began to laugh intensely, then stopped suddenly and looked pensive.

"I rather hate to be here two nights without him, but I don't see any other way to get you down there by tomorrow.

You can go shipside to Panama. There's usually a seat somewhere. Now, breakfast, breakfast . . ."

Patting Aileen's cheek, she hurried out and downstairs to the kitchen.

The birds' morning song was coming down from the forest; the mist lay ragged in the tops of the great trees up there. Aileen shifted her gaze to the garden at her feet. Suddenly she felt she could not leave; in a sense it was as if she were leaving love behind. She sat down on the bed. "But what is it?" she asked herself desperately. "Not Mother. Not the house. Not the jungle." Automatically she dressed and packed the remaining toilet articles in her overnight case. But the feeling was there, imperious and enveloping in its completeness.

She went downstairs. There was the sound of voices and the clatter of china in the kitchen. Concha and Luz were preparing her breakfast tray. She went out and watched them until everything was ready.

"*Ya se va la señorita?*" said Concha sadly.

She did not answer, but took the tray from her and carried it through the house, out onto the terrace, where she set it on the table. Everything on the terrace was wet with dew and moisture from the gorge. She turned the chair-cushion over and sat down to eat. The sound of the waterfall took her appetite away, but she thought, "This is the last time." She felt choked with emotions, but they were too disparate and confused for her to be able to identify any one of them as outstanding. As she sat there eating intently, she was suddenly aware that someone was watching her. She started up and saw Prue standing in the

154

doorway. She was wearing pajamas and a bathrobe, and in her hand she held a glass of water. She looked very sleepy.

"How are you?" she said, sipping her water.

Aileen stood up.

"We're all up bright and early this morning," Prue went on cheerily.

"I'm——leaving. I've got to go. Excuse me, it's late," mumbled Aileen, glancing about furtively.

"Oh, take your time, gal. You haven't said good-bye to your mother yet. And José is still saddling the nags. You've got a lot of grips with you."

"Excuse me," said Aileen, trying to slip past her through the doorway.

"Well, shake," Prue said, reaching for Aileen's hand.

"Get away!" cried Aileen, struggling to keep clear of her. "Don't touch me!" But Prue had succeeded in grasping one frantic arm. She held it fast.

"A dramatic entrance is enough. We don't have to have the same sort of exit. Say good-bye to me like a human being." She twisted the arm a bit, in spite of herself. Aileen leaned against the door and turned very white.

"Feel faint?" said Prue. She let go of her arm, and holding up her glass of water, flicked some of it into Aileen's face with her fingers.

The reaction was instantaneous. Aileen jumped at her with vicious suddenness, kicking, ripping and pounding all at once. The glass fell to the stone floor; Prue was caught off her guard. Mechanically, with rapid, birdlike fury, the girl hammered at the

155

woman's face and head, as she slowly impelled her away from the doorway and across the terrace.

From Prue's lips came several times the word "God." At first she did very little to defend herself; she seemed half asleep as she moved toward the outer edge beneath the onslaught. Then suddenly she threw herself to the floor. Aileen continued to kick her where she lay doubled over, trying to protect her face.

"Nobody! Nobody! Nobody! Nobody can do that to me!" she cried rhythmically as she kicked.

Her voice rose in pitch and volume; she stopped for an instant, and then, raising her head, she uttered the greatest scream of her life. It came back immediately from the black wall of rock across the gorge, straight through the noise of water. The sound of her own voice ended the episode for her, and she began to walk back across the terrace.

Concha and Luz stood frightened in the doorway; it was as if they had come to watch a terrible storm pass over the countryside. They stepped aside as Aileen walked through.

Outside the stable, José was whistling as he finished saddling the horses. The valises were already strapped on the burro.

Still in the midst of her deep dream, Aileen turned her head toward the house as they rode past. For a brief second, between the leaves, she saw the two figures of her mother and Prue standing side by side on the terrace, the wall of the gorge looming behind. Then the horses turned and began to descend the trail.

the scorpion

An old woman lived in a cave which her sons had hollowed out of a clay cliff near a spring before they went away to the town where many people live. She was neither happy nor unhappy to be there, because she knew that the end of life was near and that her sons would not be likely to return no matter what the season. In the town there are always many things to do, and they would be doing them, not caring to remember the time when they had lived in the hills looking after the old woman.

At the entrance to the cave at certain times of the year there was a curtain of water-drops through which the old woman had to pass to get inside. The water rolled down the bank from the plants above and dripped onto the clay below. So the old woman accustomed herself to sitting crouched in the cave for long periods of time in order to keep as dry as possible. Outside through the moving beads of water she saw the bare earth lighted by the gray sky, and sometimes large dry leaves went past, pushed by the wind that came from higher parts of the land. Inside where she was the light was pleasant and of a pink color from the clay all around.

A few people used to pass from time to time along the path not far away, and because there was a spring nearby, those travelers who knew that it existed but not just where it was would sometimes come near to the cave before they discovered that the spring was not there. The old woman would never call to them. She would merely watch them as they came near and suddenly saw her. Then she would go on watching as they turned back and went in other directions looking for the water to drink.

There were many things about this life that the old woman liked. She was no longer obliged to argue and fight with her sons to make them carry wood to the charcoal oven. She was free to move about at night and look for food. She could eat everything she found without having to share it. And she owed no one any debt of thanks for the things she had in her life.

One old man used to come from the village on his way down to the valley, and sit on a rock just distant enough from the cave for her to recognize him. She knew he was aware of her presence in the cave there, and although she probably did not know this, she disliked him for not giving some sign that he knew she was there. It seemed to her that he had an unfair advantage over her and was using it in an unpleasant way. She thought up many ideas for annoying him if he should ever come near enough, but he always passed by in the distance, pausing to sit down on the rock for some time, when he would often gaze straight at the cave. Then he would continue slowly on his way, and it always seemed to the old woman that he went more slowly after his rest than before it.

There were scorpions in the cave all year round, but above all during the days just before the plants began to let water drip through. The old woman had a huge bundle of rags, and with this she would brush the walls and ceiling clear of them, stamping quickly on them with her hard bare heel. Occasionally a small wild bird or animal strayed inside the entrance, but she was never quick enough to kill it, and she had given up trying.

One dark day she looked up to see one of her sons standing in the doorway. She could not remember which one it was, but she thought it was the one who had ridden the horse down the dry river bed and nearly been killed. She looked at his hand to see if it was out of shape. It was not that son.

He began to speak: "Is it you?"

"Yes."

"Are you well?"

"Yes."

"Is everything well?"

"Everything."

"You stayed here?"

"You can see."

"Yes."

There was a silence. The old woman looked around the cave and was displeased to see that the man in the doorway made it practically dark in there. She busied herself with trying to distinguish various objects: her stick, her gourd, her tin can, her length of rope. She was frowning with the effort.

The man was speaking again.

"Shall I come in?"

She did not reply.

He backed away from the entrance, brushing the water drops from his garments. He was on the point of saying something profane, thought the old woman, who, even though she did not know which one this was, remembered what he would do.

She decided to speak.

"What?" she said.

He leaned forward through the curtain of water and repeated his question.

"Shall I come in?"

"No."

"What's the matter with you?"

"Nothing."

Then she added: "There's no room."

He backed out again, wiping his head. The old woman thought he would probably go away, and she was not sure she wanted him to. However, there was nothing else he could do, she thought. She heard him sit down outside the cave, and then she smelled tobacco smoke. There was no sound but the dripping of water upon the clay.

A short while later she heard him get up. He stood outside the entrance again.

"I'm coming in," he said.

She did not reply.

He bent over and pushed inside. The cave was too low for him to stand up in it. He looked about and spat on the floor.

"Come on," he said.

"Where?"

"With me."

"Why?"

"Because you have to come."

She waited a little while, and then said suspiciously: "Where are you going?"

He pointed indifferently toward the valley, and said: "Down that way."

"In the town?"

"Farther."

"I won't go."

"You have to come."

"No."

He picked up her stick and held it out to her.

"Tomorrow," she said.

"Now."

"I must sleep," she said, settling back into her pile of rags.

"Good. I'll wait outside," he answered, and went out.

The old woman went to sleep immediately. She dreamed that the town was very large. It went on forever and its streets were filled with people in new clothes. The church had a high tower with several bells that rang all the time. She was in the streets all one day, surrounded by people. She was not sure whether they were all her sons or not. She asked some of them: "Are you

161

my sons?" They could not answer, but she thought that if they had been able to, they would have said: "Yes." Then when it was night she found a house with its door open. Inside there was a light and some women were seated in a corner. They rose when she went in, and said: "You have a room here." She did not want to see it, but they pushed her along until she was in it, and closed the door. She was a little girl and she was crying. The bells of the church were very loud outside, and she imagined they filled the sky. There was an open space in the wall high above her. She could see the stars through it, and they gave light to her room. From the reeds which formed the ceiling a scorpion came crawling. He came slowly down the wall toward her. She stopped crying and watched him. His tail curved up over his back and moved a little from side to side as he crawled. She looked quickly about for something to brush him down with. Since there was nothing in the room she used her hand. But her motions were slow, and the scorpion seized her finger with his pinchers, clinging there tightly although she waved her hand wildly about. Then she realized that he was not going to sting her. A great feeling of happiness went through her. She raised her finger to her lips to kiss the scorpion. The bells stopped ringing. Slowly in the peace which was beginning, the scorpion moved into her mouth. She felt his hard shell and his little clinging legs going across her lips and her tongue. He crawled slowly down her throat and was hers. She woke up and called out.

Her son answered: "What is it?"

"I'm ready."

"So soon?"

He stood outside as she came through the curtain of water, leaning on her stick. Then he began walking a few paces ahead of her toward the path.

"It will rain," said her son.

"Is it far?"

"Three days," he said, looking at her old legs.

She nodded. Then she noticed the old man sitting on the stone. He had an expression of deep surprise on his face, as if a miracle had just occurred. His mouth was open as he stared at the old woman. When they came opposite the rock he peered more intently than ever into her face. She pretended not to notice him. As they picked their way carefully downhill along the stony path, they heard the old man's thin voice behind them, carried by the wind.

"Good-bye."

"Who is that?" said her son.

"I don't know."

Her son looked back at her darkly.

"You're lying," he said.

the fourth day out from
santa cruz

Ramón signed on at Cádiz. The ship's first call was at Santa Cruz de Tenerife, a day and a half out. They put in at night, soon after dark. Floodlights around the harbor illumined the steep bare mountains and made them grass-green against the black sky. Ramón stood at the rail, watching. "It must have been raining here," he said to a member of the crew standing beside him. The man grunted, looking not at the green slopes unnaturally bright in the electric glare, but at the lights of the town ahead. "Very green," went on Ramón, a little less certainly; the man did not even grunt in reply.

As soon as the ship was anchored, scores of Hindu shopkeepers came aboard with laces and embroidered goods for the passengers who might not be going ashore. They stayed on the first-class deck, not bothering to go down below to third-class where Ramón was scullery boy in the passengers' *cocina*. The work so far did not upset him; he had held more exacting and tiring jobs in Cádiz. There was sufficient food, and although it was not very good, nevertheless it was better than what was taken out to the third-class passengers. It had never occurred to Ramón to want privacy in his living quarters, so that he was unmoved by the necessity of sharing a cabin with a dozen or so shipmates. Still, he had been acutely unhappy since leaving Cádiz. Except for the orders they gave him in the kitchen, the sailors behaved as if he did not exist. They covered his bunk with their dirty clothes, and lay on it, smoking, at night when he wanted to sleep. They failed to include him in any conversation, and so far no one had even made an allusion, however deprecatory, to his existence. For them it appeared that he simply was not present. To even the least egocentric man such a state of affairs can become intolerable. In his sixteen years Ramón had not been in a similar situation; he had been maltreated but not wholly disregarded.

Most of the crew stood at the prow smoking, pointing out bars to one another, as they scanned the waterfront. Partly out of perversity born of his grievance, and partly because he wanted to be by himself for a spell, Ramón walked to the stern and leaned heavily against the rail, looking down into the darkness below. He could hear an automobile horn being blown continuously as it drove along the waterfront. The hills behind backed up the sound, magnified it as they threw it across the water. To the other side was the dim roar of the sea's waves against the break-the fourth day out from santa cruz

water. He was a little homesick, and as he stood there he became angry as well. It was inadmissible that this state of affairs should continue. A day and a half was too long; he was determined to force a change immediately, and to his undisciplined young mind kept recurring the confused image of a fight—a large-scale struggle with the entire crew, in which he somehow finished as the sole victor.

It is pleasant to walk by the sea-wall of a foreign port at night, with the autumn wind gently pushing at your back. Ramón was in no hurry; he stopped before each café and listened to the guitars and shouting, without, however, allowing himself to be detained by the women who called to him from the darker doorways. Having had to clean up the galley after an extra meal had been served to sixty workmen who had just come aboard here at Santa Cruz, bound for South America, he had been the last to get off the ship, and so he was looking for his shipmates. At the Café del Teide he found several of them seated at a table sharing a bottle of rum. They saw him come in, but they gave no sign of recognition. There was no empty chair. He walked toward the table, slowed down a bit as he approached it, and then continued walking toward the back of the café. The man behind the bar called out to him: "You were looking for something?" Ramón turned around and sat down suddenly at a small table. The waiter came and served him, but he scarcely noticed what he was drinking. He was watching the table with the six men from his ship. Like one fascinated, he let his eyes follow each gesture: the filling of the little glasses, the

166

tossing down the liquor, the back of the hand wiping the mouth. And he listened to their words punctuated by loud laughter. Resentment began to swell in him; he felt that if he sat still any longer he would explode. Pushing back his chair, he jumped up and strode dramatically out into the street. No one noticed his exit.

He began to walk fast through the town, paying no attention to where he was going. His eyes fixed on an imaginary horizon, he went through the *plaza*, along the wide Paseo de Ronda, and into the tiny streets that lie behind the cathedral. The number of people in the streets increased as he walked away from the center of town, until when he had come to what seemed an outlying district, where the shops were mere stalls, he was forced to saunter along with the crowd. As he slowed down his gait, he felt less nervous. Gradually he took notice of the merchandise for sale, and of the people around him. It suddenly occurred to him that he would like to buy a large handkerchief. Outside certain booths there were wires strung up; from these hung, clipped by their corners, a great many of the squares of cloth, their bright colors showing in the flare of the carbide lamps. As Ramón stopped to choose one at the nearest booth he became aware that in the next booth a girl with a laughing face was also buying a bandana. He waited until she had picked out the one she wanted, and then he stepped quickly over to the shopkeeper and pointing down at the package he was making, said: "Have you another handkerchief exactly like that?" The girl paid no attention to him and put her change into her purse. "Yes," said the shopkeeper, reaching out over the counter to examine the bandanas. The girl picked up her little packet wrapped in newspaper, turned away, and walked along the street. "No, you haven't!" cried Ramón, and he hurried after her so as not to lose sight of her in the crowd. For some distance he trailed her along the thoroughfare, until she turned into a side street that led uphill. It smelled here of drains and there was very little light. He quickened his pace for fear she would go into one of the buildings before he had had the opportunity to talk to her. Somewhere in the back of his mind he hoped to persuade her to go with him to the Café del Teide. As he overtook her, he spoke quietly without turning his head: "Señorita." To his surprise she stopped walking and stood still on the pavement. Although she was very near to him, he could not see her face clearly.

"What do you want?"

"I wanted to talk to you."

"Why?"

He could not answer.

"I thought . . ." he stammered.

"What?"

There was a silence, and then as she laughed Ramón remembered her face: open and merry, but not a child's face. In spite of the confidence its recalled image inspired in him, he asked: "Why do you laugh?"

"Because I think you're crazy."

He touched her arm and said boldly: "You'll see if I'm crazy."

"I'll see nothing. You're a sailor. I live here"; she pointed to the opposite side of the street. "If my father sees you, you'll have to run all the way to your ship." Again she laughed. To Ramón her laugh was music, faintly disturbing.

"I don't want to bother you. I only wanted to talk to you," he said, timid again.

"Good. Now you've talked. *Adios.*" She began to walk on. So did Ramón, close beside her. She did not speak. A moment later, he remarked triumphantly: "You said you lived back there!"

"It was a lie," she said in a flat voice. "I always lie."

"Ah. You always lie," echoed Ramón with great seriousness.

They came to a street light at the foot of a high staircase. The sidewalk became a series of stone steps leading steeply upward between the houses. As they slowly ascended, the air changed. It smelled of wine, food cooking, and burning eucalyptus leaves. Up above the city here, life was more casual. People leaned over the balconies, sat in dark doorways chatting, stood in the streets like islands among the moving dogs and children.

The girl stopped and leaned against the side of a house. She was a little out of breath from the climb.

"Tired?" he asked.

Instead of replying she turned swiftly and darted inside the doorway beside her. For a few seconds Ramón was undecided whether or not to follow her. By the time he had tiptoed into the dimly lit passageway she had disappeared. He walked through into the courtyard. Some ragged boys who were running about stopped short and stared at him. A radio was playing guitar music above. He looked up. The building was four stories high; there were lights in almost all the windows.

On his way back to the waterfront a woman appeared from

169

the shadows of the little park by the cathedral and took his arm. He looked at her; she was being brazenly coy, with her head tilted at a crazy angle as she repeated: "I like sailors." He let her walk with him to the Café del Teide. Once inside, he was disappointed to see that his shipmates were gone. He bought the woman a *manzanilla* and walked out on her as she began to drink it. He had not said a word to her. Outside, the night seemed suddenly very warm. He came to the Blanco y Negro; a band was playing inside. Two or three of the men from the ship were on the dark dance floor, trying to instill a bit of life into the tired girls that hung to them. He did not even have a drink here, but hurried back to the ship. His bunk was piled with newspapers and bundles, but the cabin was empty, and he had several hours in the dark in which to brood and doze, before the others arrived. The boat sailed at dawn.

They skirted the island next day—not close enough to see the shore, but within sight of the great conical mountain, which was there all day beside them in the air, clear in distant outline. For two days the ship continued on a southwest course. The sea grew calm, a deep blue, and the sun blazed brighter in the sky. The crew had ceased gathering on the poopdeck, save in the early evening and at night, when they lay sprawled all over it, singing in raucous voices while the stars swayed back and forth over their heads.

For Ramón life continued the same. He could see no difference in the crew's attitude toward him. It still seemed to him that they lived without him. The magazines that had been bought at Santa Cruz were never passed around the cabin. Afternoons

170

when the men sat around the table in the third-class *comedor*, the stories that were recounted could never be interpreted by any gesture in their telling as being directed at a group that included him. And he certainly knew better than to attempt to tell any himself. He still waited for a stroke of luck that might impose him forcibly upon their consciousness.

In the middle of the fourth morning out from Santa Cruz he poked his head from the galley and noticed several of the men from his cabin gathered along the railing at the stern. The sun was blinding and hot, and he knew something must be keeping them there. He saw one man pointing aft. Casually he wandered out across the deck to within a few feet of the group, searching the sea and the horizon for some object—something besides the masses of red seaweed that constantly floated by on top of the dark water.

"It's getting nearer!"

"*Qué fuerza!*"

"It's worn out!"

"*Claro!*"

Ramón looked over their heads, and between them when they changed position from time to time. He saw nothing. He was almost ready to be convinced that the men were baiting him, in the hope of being able to amuse themselves when his curiosity should be aroused to the point of making him ask: "What is it?" And so he was determined to be quiet, to wait and see.

Suddenly he did see. It was a small yellow and brown bird flying crookedly after the boat, faltering as it repeatedly fell back toward the water between spurts of desperate energy.

171

"A thousand miles from land!"

"It's going to make it! Look! Here it comes!"

"No!"

"Next time."

At each wild attempt to reach the deck, the bird came closer to the men, and then, perhaps from fear of them, it fluttered down toward the boiling sea, missing the wake's maelstrom by an ever closer margin. And when it seemed that this time it surely would be churned under into the white chaos of air and water, it would surge feebly upward, its head turned resolutely toward the bright mass of the ship that moved always in front of it.

Ramón was fascinated. His first thought was to tell the men to step back a little from the rail so that the bird might have the courage to land. As he opened his mouth to suggest this, he thought better of it, and was immediately thankful for having remained quiet. He could imagine the ridicule that would have been directed at him later: in the cabin, at mealtime, evenings on the deck . . . Someone would have invented a shameful little ditty about Ramón and his bird. He stood watching, in a growing agony of suspense.

"Five pesetas it goes under!"

"Ten it makes it!"

Ramón wheeled about and ran lightly across to the galley. Almost immediately he came out again. In his arms he carried the ship's mascot, a heavy tomcat that blinked stupidly in the sudden glare of the sun. This time he walked directly back to the railing where the others stood. He set the animal down at their feet.

"What are you doing?" said one.

"Watch," said Ramón.

They were all quiet a moment. Ramón held the cat's flanks and head steady, waiting for it to catch sight of the fluttering bird. It was difficult to do. No matter how he directed its head it showed no sign of interest. Still they waited. As the bird came up to the level of the deck at a few feet from the boat, the cat's head suddenly twitched, and Ramón knew the contact had been made. He took his hands away. The cat stood perfectly still, the end of its tail moving slightly. It took a step closer to the edge, watching each movement of the bird's frantic efforts.

"Look at that!"

"He sees it."

"But the bird doesn't see him."

"If it touches the boat, the ten pesetas still go."

The bird rose in the air, flew faster for a moment until it was straight above their heads. They looked upward into the flaming sun, trying to shade their eyes. It flew still farther forward, until, if it had dropped, it would have landed a few feet ahead of them on the deck. The cat, staring up into the air, ran quickly across the deck so that it was directly below the bird, which slowly let itself drop until it seemed that they could reach out and take it. The cat made a futile spring into the air. They all cried out, but the bird was too high. Suddenly it rose much higher; then it stopped flying. Swiftly they passed beneath it as it remained poised an instant in the air. When they had turned their heads back it was a tiny yellow thing falling

173

slowly downward, and almost as quickly they lost sight of it.

At the noonday meal they talked about it. After some argument the bets were paid. One of the oilers went to his cabin and brought out a bottle of cognac and a set of little glasses which he put in front of him and filled, one after the other.

"Have some?" he said to Ramón.

Ramón took a glass, and the oiler passed the rest around to the others.

pages from cold point

Our civilization is doomed to a short life: its component parts are too heterogeneous. I personally am content to see everything in the process of decay. The bigger the bombs, the quicker it will be done. Life is visually too hideous for one to make the attempt to preserve it. Let it go. Perhaps some day another form of life will come along. Either way, it is of no consequence. At the same time, I am still a part of life, and I am bound by this to protect myself to whatever extent I am able. And so I am here. Here in the Islands vegetation still has the upper hand, and man has to fight even to make his presence seen at all. It is beautiful here, the trade winds blow all year, and I suspect that bombs are extremely unlikely to be wasted on this unfrequented side of the island, if indeed on any part of it.

I was loath to give up the house after Hope's death. But it was the obvious move to make. My university career always having been an utter farce (since I believe no reason inducing a man to "teach" can possibly be a valid one), I was elated by the idea of resigning, and as soon as her affairs had been settled and the money properly invested, I lost no time in doing so.

I think that week was the first time since childhood that I had managed to recapture the feeling of there being a content in existence. I went from one pleasant house to the next, making my adieux to the English quacks, the Philosophy fakirs, and so on—even to those colleagues with whom I was merely on speaking terms. I watched the envy in their faces when I announced my departure by Pan American on Saturday morning; and the greatest pleasure I felt in all this was in being able to answer, "Nothing," when I was asked, as invariably I was, what I intended to do.

When I was a boy people used to refer to Charles as "Big Brother C.", although he is only a scant year older than I. To me now he is merely "Fat Brother C.", a successful lawyer. His thick, red face and hands, his back-slapping joviality, and his fathomless hypocritical prudery, these are the qualities which make him truly repulsive to me. There is also the fact that he once looked not unlike the way Racky does now. And after all, he still is my big brother, and disapproves openly of everything I do. The loathing I feel for him is so strong that for years I have not been able to swallow a morsel of food or a drop of liquid in his presence without making a prodigious effort. No one knows this but me—certainly not Charles, who would be the last one I should tell about it. He came up on the late train two nights before I left. He got quickly to the point—as soon as he was settled with a highball.

"So you're off for the wilds," he said, sitting forward in his chair like a salesman.

"If you can call it the wilds," I replied. "Certainly it's not wild like Mitichi." (He has a lodge in northern Quebec.) "I consider it really civilized."

He drank and smacked his lips together stiffly, bringing the glass down hard on his knee.

"And Racky. You're taking him along?"

"Of course."

"Out of school. Away. So he'll see nobody but you. You think that's good."

I looked at him. "I do," I said.

"By God, if I could stop you legally, I would!" he cried, jumping up and putting his glass on the mantel. I was trembling inwardly with excitement, but I merely sat and watched him. He went on. "You're not fit to have custody of the kid!" he shouted. He shot a stern glance at me over his spectacles.

"You think not?" I said gently.

Again he looked at me sharply. "D'ye think I've forgotten?"

I was understandably eager to get him out of the house as soon as I could. As I piled and sorted letters and magazines on the desk, I said: "Is that all you came to tell me? I have a good deal to do tomorrow and I must get some sleep. I probably shan't see you at breakfast. Agnes'll see that you eat in time to make the early train."

All he said was: "God! Wake up! Get wise to yourself! You're not fooling anybody, you know."

That kind of talk is typical of Charles. His mind is slow and obtuse; he constantly imagines that everyone he meets is playing some private game of deception with him. He is so utterly incapable of following the functioning of even a moderately evolved intellect that he finds the will to secretiveness and duplicity everywhere.

"I haven't time to listen to that sort of nonsense," I said, preparing to leave the room.

But he shouted, "You don't want to listen! No! Of course not! You just want to do what you want to do. You just want to go on off down there and live as you've a mind to, and to hell with the consequences!" At this point I heard Racky coming downstairs. C. obviously heard nothing, and he raved on. "But just remember, I've got your number all right, and if there's any trouble with the boy I'll know who's to blame."

I hurried across the room and opened the door so he could see that Racky was there in the hallway. That stopped his tirade. It was hard to know whether Racky had heard any of it or not. Although he is not a quiet young person, he is the soul of discretion, and it is almost never possible to know any more about what goes on inside his head than he intends one to know.

I was annoyed that C. should have been bellowing at me in my own house. To be sure, he is the only one from whom I would accept such behavior, but then, no father likes to have his son see him take criticism meekly. Racky simply stood there in his bathrobe, his angelic face quite devoid of expression, saying:

"Tell Uncle Charley good night for me, will you? I forgot."

I said I would, and quickly shut the door. When I thought Racky was back upstairs in his room, I bade Charles good night. I have never been able to get out of his presence fast enough. The effect he has on me dates from an early period of our lives, from days I dislike to recall.

Racky is a wonderful boy. After we arrived, when we found it impossible to secure a proper house near any town where he might have the company of English boys and girls his own age, he showed no sign of chagrin, although he must have been disappointed. Instead, as we went out of the renting office into the glare of the street, he grinned and said: "Well, I guess we'll have to get bikes, that's all."

The few available houses near what Charles would have called "civilization" turned out to be so ugly and so impossibly confining in atmosphere that we decided immediately on Cold Point, even though it was across the island and quite isolated on its seaside cliff. It was beyond a doubt one of the most desirable properties on the island, and Racky was as enthusiastic about its splendors as I.

"You'll get tired of being alone out there, just with me," I said to him as we walked back to the hotel.

"Aw, I'll get along all right. When do we look for the bikes?"

At his insistence we bought two the next morning. I was sure I should not make much use of mine, but I reflected that an extra bicycle might be convenient to have around the house. It turned out that the servants all had their own bicycles, without

179

which they would not have been able to get to and from the village of Orange Walk, eight miles down the shore. So for a while I was forced to get astride mine each morning before breakfast and pedal madly along beside Racky for a half hour. We would ride through the cool early air, under the towering silk-cotton trees near the house, and out to the great curve in the shoreline where the waving palms bend landward in the stiff breeze that always blows there. Then we would make a wide turn and race back to the house, loudly discussing the degrees of our desires for the various items of breakfast we knew were awaiting us there on the terrace. Back home we would eat in the wind, looking out over the Caribbean, and talk about the news in yesterday's local paper, brought to us by Isiah each morning from Orange Walk. Then Racky would disappear for the whole morning on his bicycle, riding furiously along the road in one direction or the other until he had discovered an unfamiliar strip of sand along the shore that he could consider a new beach. At lunch he would describe it in detail to me, along with a recounting of all the physical hazards involved in hiding the bicycle in among the trees, so that natives passing along the road on foot would not spot it, or in climbing down unscalable cliffs that turned out to be much higher than they had appeared at first sight, or in measuring the depth of the water preparatory to diving from the rocks, or in judging the efficacy of the reef in barring sharks and barracuda. There is never any element of bragadoccio in Racky's relating of his exploits—only the joyous excitement he derives from telling how he satisfies his inexhaustible curiosity. And his mind shows its alertness in all directions at once. I do not mean to say that I expect him to be an "intellectual." That is no affair of mine, nor do I have any particular interest in whether he turns out to be a thinking man or not. I know he will always have a certain boldness of manner and a great purity of spirit in judging values. The former will prevent his becoming what I call a "victim": he never will be brutalized by realities. And his unerring sense of balance in ethical considerations will shield him from the paralyzing effects of present-day materialism.

For a boy of sixteen Racky has an extraordinary innocence of vision. I do not say this as a doting father, although God knows I can never even think of the boy without that familiar overwhelming sensation of delight and gratitude for being vouchsafed the privilege of sharing my life with him. What he takes so completely as a matter of course, our daily life here together, is a source of never-ending wonder to me; and I reflect upon it a good part of each day, just sitting here being conscious of my great good fortune in having him all to myself, beyond the reach of prying eyes and malicious tongues. (I suppose I am really thinking of C. when I write that.) And I believe that a part of the charm of sharing Racky's life with him consists precisely in his taking it all so utterly for granted. I have never asked him whether he likes being here—it is so patent that he does, very much. I think if he were to turn to me one day and tell me how happy he is here, that somehow, perhaps, the spell might be broken. Yet if he were to be thoughtless and inconsiderate, or even unkind to me, I feel that I should be able only to love him the more for it.

I have reread that last sentence. What does it mean? And why should I even imagine it could mean anything more than it says?

Still, much as I may try, I can never believe in the gratuitous, isolated fact. What I must mean is that I feel that Racky already has been in some way inconsiderate. But in what way? Surely I cannot resent his bicycle treks; I cannot expect him to want to stay and sit talking with me all day. And I never worry about his being in danger; I know he is more capable than most adults of taking care of himself, and that he is no more likely than any native to come to harm crawling over the cliffs or swimming in the bays. At the same time there is no doubt in my mind that something about our existence annoys me. I must resent some detail in the pattern, whatever that pattern may be. Perhaps it is just his youth, and I am envious of the lithe body, the smooth skin, the animal energy and grace.

For a long time this morning I sat looking out to sea, trying to solve that small puzzle. Two white herons came and perched on a dead stump east of the garden. They stayed a long time there without stirring. I would turn my head away and accustom my eyes to the bright sea-horizon, then I would look suddenly at them to see if they had shifted position, but they would always be in the same attitude. I tried to imagine the black stump without them—a purely vegetable landscape—but it was impossible. All the while I was slowly forcing myself to accept a ridiculous explanation of my annoyance with Racky. It had made itself manifest to me only yesterday, when instead of appearing for lunch, he sent a young colored boy from Orange

Walk to say that he would be lunching in the village. I could not help noticing that the boy was riding Racky's bicycle. I had been waiting lunch a good half hour for him, and I had Gloria serve immediately as the boy rode off, back to the village. I was curious to know in what sort of place and with whom Racky could be eating, since Orange Walk, as far as I know, is inhabited exclusively by Negroes, and I was sure Gloria would be able to shed some light on the matter, but I could scarcely ask her. However, as she brought on the dessert, I said: "Who was that boy that brought the message from Mister Racky?"

She shrugged her shoulders. "A young lad of Orange Walk. He's named Wilmot."

When Racky returned at dusk, flushed from his exertion (for he never rides casually), I watched him closely. His behavior struck my already suspicious eye as being one of false heartiness and a rather forced good humor. He went to his room early and read for quite a while before turning off his light. I took a long walk in the almost day-bright moonlight, listening to the songs of the night insects in the trees. And I sat for a while in the dark on the stone railing of the bridge across Black River. (It is really only a brook that rushes down over the rocks from the mountain a few miles inland, to the beach near the house.) In the night it always sounds louder and more important than it does in the daytime. The music of the water over the stones relaxed my nerves, although why I had need of such a thing I find it difficult to understand, unless I was really upset by Racky's not having come home for lunch. But if that were true it would be absurd, and moreover, dangerous—just the sort of the thing the parent of an adolescent has to beware of and fight against, unless he is indifferent to the prospect of losing the trust and affection of his offspring permanently. Racky must stay out whenever he likes, with whom he likes, and for as long as he likes, and I must not think twice about it, much less mention it to him, or in any way give the impression of prying. Lack of confidence on the part of a parent is the one unforgivable sin.

Although we still take our morning dip together on arising, it is three weeks since we have been for the early spin. One morning I found that Racky had jumped onto his bicycle in his wet trunks while I was still swimming, and gone by himself, and since then there has been an unspoken agreement between us that such is to be the procedure; he will go alone. Perhaps I held him back; he likes to ride so fast.

Young Peter, the smiling gardener from Saint Ives Cove, is Racky's special friend. It is amusing to see them together among the bushes, crouched over an ant-hill or rushing about trying to catch a lizard, almost of an age the two, yet so disparate—Racky with his tan skin looking almost white in contrast to the glistening black of the other. Today I know I shall be alone for lunch, since it is Peter's day off. On such days they usually go together on their bicycles into Saint Ives Cove, where Peter keeps a small rowboat. They fish along the coast there, but they have never returned with anything so far.

Meanwhile I am here alone, sitting on the rocks in the sun, from time to time climbing down to cool myself in the water, always conscious of the house behind me under the high palms, like a large glass boat filled with orchids and lilies. The servants are clean and quiet, and the work seems to be accomplished almost automatically. The good, black servants are another blessing of the islands; the British, born here in this paradise, have no conception of how fortunate they are. In fact, they do nothing but complain. One must have lived in the United States to appreciate the wonder of this place. Still, even here ideas are changing each day. Soon the people will decide that they want their land to be a part of today's monstrous world, and once that happens, it will be all over. As soon as you have that desire, you are infected with the deadly virus, and you begin to show the symptoms of the disease. You live in terms of time and money, and you think in terms of society and progress. Then all that is left for you is to kill the other people who think the same way, along with a good many of those who do not, since that is the final manifestation of the malady. Here for the moment at any rate, one has a feeling of staticity—existence ceases to be like those last few seconds in the hour-glass when what is left of the sand suddenly begins to rush through to the bottom all at once. For the moment, it seems suspended. And if it seems, it is. Each wave at my feet, each bird-call in the forest at my back, does *not* carry me one step nearer the final disaster. The disaster is certain, but it will suddenly have happened, that is all. Until then, time stays still.

I am upset by a letter in this morning's mail: the Royal Bank of Canada requests that I call in person at its central office to sign the deposit slips and other papers for a sum that was cabled from the bank in Boston. Since the central office is on the other side of the island, fifty miles away, I shall have to spend the night over there and return the following day. There is no point in taking Racky along. The sight of "civilization" might awaken a longing for it in him; one never knows. I am sure it would have in me when I was his age. And if that should once start, he would merely be unhappy, since there is nothing for him but to stay here with me, at least for the next two years, when I hope to renew the lease, or, if things in New York pick up, buy the place. I am sending word by Isiah when he goes home into Orange Walk this evening, to have the McCoigh car call for me at seven-thirty tomorrow morning. It is an enormous old open Packard, and Isiah can save the ride out to work here by piling his bicycle into the back and riding with McCoigh.

The trip across the island was beautiful, and would have been highly enjoyable if my imagination had not played me a strange trick at the very outset. We stopped in Orange Walk for gasoline, and while that was being seen to, I got out and went to the corner store for some cigarettes. Since it was not yet eight o'clock, the store was still closed, and I hurried up the side street to the other little shop which I thought might be open. It was, and I bought my cigarettes. On the way back to the corner I noticed a large black woman leaning with her arms on the gate in front of her tiny house, staring into the street. As I passed by her, she looked straight into my face and said something with the strange accent of the island. It was said in what seemed an unfriendly tone, and ostensibly was directed at me, but I had no notion what it was. I got back into the car and the driver started it. The sound of the words had stayed in my head, however, as a bright shape outlined by darkness is likely to stay in the mind's eye, in such a way that when one shuts one's eyes one can see the exact contour of the shape. The car was already roaring up the hill toward the overland road when I suddenly reheard the very words. And they were: "Keep your boy at home, mahn." I sat perfectly rigid for a moment as the open countryside rushed past. Why should I think she had said that? Immediately I decided that I was giving an arbitrary sense to a phrase I could not have understood even if I had been paying strict attention. And then I wondered why my subconscious should have chosen that sense, since now that I whispered the words over to myself they failed to connect with any anxiety to which my mind might have been disposed. Actually I have never given a thought to Racky's wanderings about Orange Walk. I can find no such preoccupation no matter how I put the question to myself. Then, could she really have said those words? All the way through the mountains I pondered the question, even though it was obviously a waste of energy. And soon I could no longer hear the sound of her voice in my memory: I had played the record over too many times, and worn it out.

Here in the hotel a gala dance is in progress. The abominable orchestra, comprising two saxophones and one sour violin, is playing directly under my window in the garden, and the serious-looking couples slide about on the waxed concrete floor of the terrace, in the light of strings of paper lanterns. I suppose it is meant to look Japanese.

At this moment I wonder what Racky is doing there in the house with only Peter and Ernest the watchman to keep him company. I wonder if he is asleep. The house, which I am accustomed to think of as smiling and benevolent in its airiness, could just as well be in the most sinister and remote regions of the globe, now that I am here. Sitting here with the absurd orchestra bleating downstairs, I picture it to myself, and it strikes me as terribly vulnerable in its isolation. In my mind's eye I see the moonlit point with its tall palms waving restlessly in the wind, its dark cliffs licked by the waves below. Suddenly, although I struggle against the sensation, I am inexpressibly glad to be away from the house, helpless there, far on its point of land, in the silence of the night. Then I remember that the night is seldom silent. There is the loud sea at the base of the rocks, the droning of the thousands of insects, the occasional cries of the night birds—all the familiar noises that make sleep so sound. And Racky is there surrounded by them as usual, not even hearing them. But I feel profoundly guilty for having left him, unutterably tender and sad at the thought of him, lying there alone in the house with the two Negroes the only human beings within miles. If I keep thinking of Cold Point I shall be more and more nervous.

I am not going to bed yet. They are all screaming with laughter down there, the idiots; I could never sleep anyway. The bar is still open. Fortunately it is on the street side of the hotel. For once I need a few drinks.

Much later, but I feel no better; I may be a little drunk. The dance is over and it is quiet in the garden, but the room is too hot.

As I was falling asleep last night, all dressed, and with the overhead light shining sordidly in my face, I heard the black woman's voice again, more clearly even than I did in the car yesterday. For some reason this morning there is no doubt in my mind that the words I heard are the words she said. I accept that and go on from there. Suppose she did tell me to keep Racky home. It could only mean that she, or someone else in Orange Walk, has had a childish altercation with him; although I must say it is hard to conceive of Racky's entering into any sort of argument or feud with those people. To set my mind at rest (for I do seem to be taking the whole thing with great seriousness), I am going to stop in the village this afternoon before going home, and try to see the woman. I am extremely curious to know what she could have meant.

I had not been conscious until this evening when I came back to Cold Point how powerful they are, all those physical elements that go to make up its atmosphere: the sea and wind-sounds that isolate the house from the road, the brilliancy of the water, sky and sun, the bright colors and strong odors of the flowers, the feeling of space both outside and within the house. One naturally accepts these things when one is living here. This afternoon when I returned I was conscious of them all over again, of their existence and their strength. All of them together are like a powerful drug; coming back made me feel as though I had been disintoxicated and were returning to the scene of my former indulgences. Now at eleven it is as if I had never been absent an hour. Everything is the same as always, even to the dry palm branch that scrapes against the window screen by my night table. And indeed, it is only thirty-six hours since I was here; but I always expect my absence from a place to bring about irremediable changes.

Strangely enough, now that I think of it, I feel that something *has* changed since I left yesterday morning, and that is the general attitude of the servants—their collective aura, so to speak. I noticed that difference immediately upon arriving back, but was unable to define it. Now I see it clearly. The network of common understanding which slowly spreads itself through a well-run household has been destroyed. Each person is by himself now. No unfriendliness, however, that I can see. They all behave with the utmost courtesy, excepting possibly Peter, who struck me as looking unaccustomedly glum when I encountered him in the kitchen after dinner. I meant to ask Racky if he had noticed it, but I forgot and he went to bed early.

In Orange Walk I made a brief stop on the pretext to McCoigh that I wanted to see the seamstress in the side street. I walked up and back in front of the house where I had seen the woman, but there was no sign of anyone.

As for my absence, Racky seems to have been perfectly content, having spent most of the day swimming off the rocks below the terrace. The insect sounds are at their height now, the breeze is cooler than usual, and I shall take advantage of these favorable conditions to get a good long night's rest.

Today has been one of the most difficult days of my life. I arose early, we had breakfast at the regular time, and Racky went off in the direction of Saint Ives Cove. I lay in the sun on the terrace for a while, listening to the noises of the household's regime. Peter was all over the property, collecting dead leaves and fallen blossoms in a huge basket and carrying them off to the compost heap. He appeared to be in an even fouler humor than last night. When he came near to me at one point on his way to another part of the garden I called to him. He set the basket down and stood looking at me; then he walked across the grass toward me slowly—reluctantly, it seemed to me.

"Peter, is everything all right with you?"

"Yes, sir."

"No trouble at home?"

"Oh, no, sir."

"Good."

"Yes, sir."

He went back to his work. But his face belied his words. Not only did he seem to be in a decidedly unpleasant temper; out here in the sunlight he looked positively ill. However, it was not my concern, if he refused to admit it.

When the heavy heat of the sun reached the unbearable point for me, I got out of my chair and went down the side of the cliff along the series of steps cut there into the rock. A level platform is below, and a diving board, for the water is deep. At each side, the rocks spread out and the waves break over them, but by the platform the wall of rock is vertical and the water merely hits against it below the springboard. The place is a tiny amphitheatre, quite cut off in sound and sight from the house. There too I like to lie in the sun; when I climb out of the water I often remove my trunks and lie stark naked on the springboard. I regularly make fun of Racky because he is embarrassed to do the same. Occasionally he will do it, but never without being coaxed. I was spread out there without a stitch on, being lulled by the slapping of the water, when an unfamiliar voice very close to me said: "Mister Norton?"

I jumped with nervousness, nearly fell off the springboard, and sat up, reaching at the same time, but in vain, for my trunks, which were lying on the rock practically at the feet of a middle-aged mulatto gentleman. He was in a white duck suit, and wore a high collar with a black tie, and it seemed to me that he was eyeing me with a certain degree of horror.

My next reaction was one of anger at being trespassed upon in this way. I rose and got the trunks, however, donning them calmly and saying nothing more meaningful than: "I didn't hear you come down the steps."

"Shall we go up?" said my caller. As he led the way, I had a definite premonition that he was here on an unpleasant errand. On the terrace we sat down, and he offered me an American cigarette which I did not accept.

"This is a delightful spot," he said, glancing out to sea and then at the end of his cigarette, which was only partially aglow. He puffed at it.

I said, "Yes," waiting for him to go on; presently he did.

"I am from the constabulary of this parish. The police, you see." And seeing my face, "This is a friendly call. But still it must be taken as a warning, Mister Norton. It is very serious. If anyone else comes to you about this it will mean trouble for you, heavy trouble. That's why I want to see you privately this way and warn you personally. You see."

I could not believe I was hearing his words. At length I said faintly: "But what about?"

"This is not an official call. You must not be upset. I have taken it upon myself to speak to you because I want to save you deep trouble."

"But I *am* upset!" I cried, finding my voice at last. "How can I help being upset, when I don't know what you're talking about?"

He moved his chair close to mine, and spoke in a very low voice.

"I have waited until the young man was away from the house so we could talk in private. You see, it is about him."

Somehow that did not surprise me. I nodded.

"I will tell you very briefly. The people here are simple country folk. They make trouble easily. Right now they are all talking about the young man you have living here with you. He is your son, I hear." His inflection here was sceptical.

"Certainly he's my son."

His expression did not change, but his voice grew indignant. "Whoever he is, that is a bad young man."

"What do you mean?" I cried, but he cut in hotly: "He may be your son; he may not be. I don't care who he is. That is not my affair. But he is bad through and through. We don't have such things going on here, sir. The people in Orange Walk and Saint Ives Cove are very cross now. You don't know what these folk do when they are aroused."

I thought it my turn to interrupt. "Please tell me why you say my son is bad. What has he done?" Perhaps the earnestness in my voice reached him, for his face assumed a gentler aspect. He leaned still closer to me and almost whispered.

"He has no shame. He does what he pleases with all the young boys, and the men too, and gives them a shilling so they won't tell about it. But they talk. Of course they talk. Every man for twenty miles up and down the coast knows about it. And the women too, they know about it." There was a silence.

I had felt myself preparing to get to my feet for the last few seconds because I wanted to go into my room and be alone, to get away from that scandalized stage whisper. I think I mumbled "Good morning" or "Thank you," as I turned away and began walking toward the house. But he was still beside me, still whispering like an eager conspirator into my ear: "Keep him home, Mister Norton. Or send him away to school, if he is your son. But make him stay out of these towns. For his own sake."

I shook hands with him and went to lie on my bed. From there I heard his car door slam, heard him drive off. I was painfully trying to formulate an opening sentence to use in speaking to Racky about this, feeling that the opening sentence

194

would define my stand. The attempt was merely a sort of therapeutic action, to avoid thinking about the thing itself. Every attitude seemed impossible. There was no way to broach the subject. I suddenly realized that I should never be able to speak to him directly about it. With the advent of this news he had become another person—an adult, mysterious and formidable. To be sure, it did occur to me that the mulatto's story might not be true, but automatically I rejected the doubt. It was as if I wanted to believe it, almost as if I had already known it, and he had merely confirmed it.

Racky returned at midday, panting and grinning. The inevitable comb appeared and was used on the sweaty, unruly locks. Sitting down to lunch, he exclaimed: "Gosh! Did I find a swell beach this morning! But what a job to get to it!" I tried to look unconcerned as I met his gaze; it was as if our positions had been reversed, and I were hoping to stem his rebuke. He prattled on about thorns and vines and his machete. Throughout the meal I kept telling myself: "Now is the moment. You must say something." But all I said was: "More salad? Or do you want dessert now?" So the lunch passed and nothing happened. After I had finished my coffee I went into my bedroom and looked at myself in the large mirror. I saw my eyes trying to give their reflected brothers a little courage. As I stood there I heard a commotion in the other wing of the house: voices, bumpings, the sound of a scuffle. Above the noise came Gloria's sharp voice, imperious and excited: "No, mahn! Don't strike him!" And louder: "Peter, mahn, no!"

I went quickly toward the kitchen, where the trouble seemed

to be, but on the way I was run into by Racky, who staggered into the hallway with his hands in front of his face.

"What is it, Racky?" I cried.

He pushed past me into the living room without moving his hands away from his face; I turned and followed him. From there he went into his own room, leaving the door open behind him. I heard him in his bathroom running the water. I was undecided what to do. Suddenly Peter appeared in the hall doorway, his hat in his hand. When he raised his head, I was surprised to see that his cheek was bleeding. In his eyes was a strange, confused expression of transient fear and deep hostility. He looked down agan.

"May I please talk with you, sir?"

"What was all the racket? What's been happening?"

"May I talk with you outside, sir?" He said it doggedly, still not looking up.

In view of the circumstances, I humored him. We walked slowly up the cinder road to the main highway, across the bridge, and through the forest while he told me his story. I said nothing.

At the end he said: "I never wanted to, sir, even the first time, but after the first time I was afraid, and Mister Racky was after me every day."

I stood still, and finally said: "If you had only told me this the first time it happened, it would have been much better for everyone."

He turned his hat in his hands, studying it intently. "Yes, sir. But I didn't know what everyone was saying about him in

Orange Walk until today. You know I always go to the beach at Saint Ives Cove with Mister Racky on my free days. If I had known what they were all saying I wouldn't have been afraid, sir. And I wanted to keep on working here. I needed the money." Then he repeated what he had already said three times. "Mister Racky said you'd see about it that I was put in the jail. I'm a year older than Mister Racky, sir."

"I know, I know," I said impatiently; and deciding that severity was what Peter expected of me at this point I added: "You had better get your things together and go home. You can't work here any longer, you know."

The hostility in his face assumed terrifying proportions as he said: "If you killed me I would not work any more at Cold Point, sir."

I turned and walked briskly back to the house, leaving him standing there in the road. It seems he returned at dusk, a little while ago, and got his belongings.

In his room Racky was reading. He had stuck some adhesive tape on his chin and over his cheekbone.

"I've dismissed Peter," I announced. "He hit you, didn't he?"

He glanced up. His left eye was swollen, but not yet black.

"He sure did. But I landed him one, too. And I guess I deserved it anyway."

I rested against the table. "Why?" I asked nonchalantly.

"Oh, I had something on him from a long time back that he was afraid I'd tell you."

"And just now you threatened to tell me?"

197

"Oh, no! He said he was going to quit the job here, and I kidded him about being yellow."

"Why did he want to quit? I thought he liked the job."

"Well, he did, I guess, but he didn't like me." Racky's candid gaze betrayed a shade of pique. I still leaned against the table. I persisted. "But I thought you two got on fine together. You seemed to."

"Nah. He was just scared of losing his job. I had something on him. He was a good guy, though; I liked him all right." He paused. "Has he gone yet?" A strange quaver crept into his voice as he said the last words, and I understood that for the first time Racky's heretofore impeccable histrionics were not quite equal to the occasion. He was very much upset at losing Peter.

"Yes, he's gone," I said shortly. "He's not coming back, either." And as Racky, hearing the unaccustomed inflection in my voice, looked up at me suddenly with faint astonishment in his young eyes, I realized that this was the moment to press on, to say: "What did you have on him?" But as if he had arrived at the same spot in my mind a fraction of a second earlier, he proceeded to snatch away my advantage by jumping up, bursting into loud song, and pulling off all his clothes simultaneously. As he stood before me naked, singing at the top of his lungs, and stepped into his swimming trunks, I was conscious that again I should be incapable of saying to him what I must say.

He was in and out of the house all afternoon: some of the time he read in his room, and most of the time he was down on the diving board. It is strange behavior for him; if I could only know what is in his mind. As evening approached, my problem took on a purely obsessive character. I walked to and fro in my room, always pausing at one end to look out the window over the sea, and at the other end to glance at my face in the mirror. As if that could help me! Then I took a drink. And another. I thought I might be able to do it at dinner, when I felt fortified by the whisky. But no. Soon he will have gone to bed. It is not that I expect to confront him with any accusations. That I know I never can do. But I must find a way to keep him from his wanderings, and I must offer a reason to give him, so that he will never suspect that I know.

We fear for the future of our offspring. It is ludicrous, but only a little more palpably so than anything else in life. A length of time has passed; days which I am content to have known, even if now they are over. I think that this period was what I had always been waiting for life to offer, the recompense I had unconsciously but firmly expected, in return for having been held so closely in the grip of existence all these years.

That evening seems long ago only because I have recalled its details so many times that they have taken on the color of legend. Actually my problem already had been solved for me then, but I did not know it. Because I could not perceive the pattern, I foolishly imagined that I must cudgel my brains to find the right words with which to approach Racky. But it was he who came to me. That same evening, as I was about to go out for a solitary stroll which I thought might help me hit upon a formula, he appeared at my door.

"Going for a walk?" he asked, seeing the stick in my hand.

The prospect of making an exit immediately after speaking with him made things seem simpler. "Yes," I said, "but I'd like to have a word with you first."

"Sure. What?" I did not look at him because I did not want to see the watchful light I was sure was playing in his eyes at this moment. As I spoke I tapped with my stick along the designs made by the tiles in the floor. "Racky, would you like to go back to school?"

"Are you kidding? You know I hate school."

I glanced up at him. "No, I'm not kidding. Don't look so horrified. You'd probably enjoy being with a bunch of fellows your own age." (That was not one of the arguments I had meant to use.)

"I might like to be with guys my own age, but I don't want to have to be in school to do it. I've had school enough."

I went to the door and said lamely: "I thought I'd get your reactions."

He laughed. "No, thanks."

"That doesn't mean you're not going," I said over my shoulder as I went out.

On my walk I pounded the highway's asphalt with my stick, stood on the bridge having dramatic visions which involved such eventualities as our moving back to the States, Racky's having a bad spill on his bicycle and being paralyzed for some months, and even the possibility of my letting events take their course, which would doubtless mean my having to visit him now and then in the governmental prison with gifts of food, if it meant nothing more tragic and violent. "But none of these things will happen," I said to myself, and I knew I was wasting precious time; he must not return to Orange Walk tomorrow.

I went back toward the point at a snail's pace. There was no moon and very little breeze. As I approached the house, trying to tread lightly on the cinders so as not to awaken the watchful Ernest and have to explain to him that it was only I, I saw that there were no lights in Racky's room. The house was dark save for the dim lamp on my night table. Instead of going in, I skirted the entire building, colliding with bushes and getting my face sticky with spider webs, and went to sit a while on the terrace where there seemed to be a breath of air. The sound of the sea was far out on the reef, where the breakers sighed. Here below, there were only slight watery chugs and gurgles now and then. It was unusually low tide. I smoked three cigarettes mechanically, having ceased even to think, and then, my mouth tasting bitter from the smoke, I went inside.

My room was airless. I flung my clothes onto a chair and looked at the night table to see if the carafe of water was there. Then my mouth opened. The top sheet of my bed had been stripped back to the foot. There on the far side of the bed, dark against the whiteness of the lower sheet, lay Racky asleep on his side, and naked.

I stood looking at him for a long time, probably holding my breath, for I remember feeling a little dizzy at one point. I was whispering to myself, as my eyes followed the curve of his arm, shoulder, back, thigh, leg: "A child. A child." Destiny, when one perceives it clearly from very near, has no qualities at all. The recognition of it and the consciousness of the vision's clarity leave no room on the mind's horizon. Finally I turned off the light and softly lay down. The night was absolutely black.

He lay perfectly quiet until dawn. I shall never know whether or not he was really asleep all that time. Of course he couldn't have been, and yet he lay so still. Warm and firm, but still as death. The darkness and silence were heavy around us. As the birds began to sing, I sank into a soft, enveloping slumber; when I awoke in the sunlight later, he was gone.

I found him down by the water, cavorting alone on the springboard; for the first time he had discarded his trunks without my suggesting it. All day we stayed together around the terrace and on the rocks, talking, swimming, reading, and just lying flat in the hot sun. Nor did he return to his room when night came. Instead after the servants were asleep, we brought three bottles of champagne in and set the pail on the night table.

Thus it came about that I was able to touch on the delicate subject that still preoccupied me, and profiting by the new understanding between us, I made my request in the easiest, most natural fashion.

"Racky, would you do me a tremendous favor if I asked you?"

He lay on his back, his hands beneath his head. It seemed to me his regard was circumspect, wanting in candor.

"I guess so," he said. "What is it?"

"Will you stay around the house for a few days—a week, say? Just to please me? We can take some rides together, as far as you like. Would you do that for me?"

"Sure thing," he said, smiling.

I was temporizing, but I was desperate.

Perhaps a week later—(it is only when one is not fully happy that one is meticulous about time, so that it may have been more or less)—we were having breakfast. Isiah stood by, in the shade, waiting to pour us more coffee.

"I noticed you had a letter from Uncle Charley the other day," said Racky. "Don't you think we ought to invite him down?"

My heart began to beat with great force.

"Here? He'd hate it here," I said casually. "Besides, there's no room. Where would he sleep?" Even as I heard myself saying the words, I knew that they were the wrong ones, that I was not really participating in the conversation. Again I felt the fascination of complete helplessness that comes when one is suddenly a conscious on-looker at the shaping of one's fate.

"In my room," said Racky. "It's empty."

I could see more of the pattern at that moment than I had ever suspected existed. "Nonsense," I said. "This is not the sort of place for Uncle Charley."

Racky appeared to be hitting on an excellent idea. "Maybe if I wrote and invited him," he suggested, motioning to Isiah for more coffee.

"Nonsense," I said again, watching still more of the pattern reveal itself, like a photographic print becoming constantly clearer in a tray of developing solution.

Isiah filled Racky's cup and returned to the shade. Racky drank slowly, pretending to be savoring the coffee.

"Well, it won't do any harm to try. He'd appreciate the invitation," he said speculatively.

For some reason, at this juncture I knew what to say, and as I said it, I knew what I was going to do.

"I thought we might fly over to Havana for a few days next week."

He looked guardedly interested, and then he broke into a wide grin. "Swell!" he cried. "Why wait till next week?"

The next morning the servants called "Good-bye" to us as we drove up the cinder road in the McCoigh car. We took off from the airport at six that evening. Racky was in high spirits; he kept the stewardess engaged in conversation all the way to Camagüey.

He was delighted also with Havana. Sitting in the bar at the Nacional, we continued to discuss the possibility of having C. pay us a visit at the island. It was not without difficulty that I eventually managed to persuade Racky that writing him would be inadvisable.

We decided to look for an apartment right there in Vedado for Racky. He did not seem to want to come back here to Cold Point. We also decided that living in Havana he would need a larger income than I. I am already having the greater part of

Hope's estate transferred to his name in the form of a trust fund which I shall administer until he is of age. It was his mother's money, after all.

We bought a new convertible, and he drove me out to Rancho Boyeros in it when I took my plane. A Cuban named Claudio with very white teeth, whom Racky had met in the pool that morning, sat between us.

We were waiting in front of the landing field. An official finally unhooked the chain to let the passengers through. "If you get fed up, come to Havana," said Racky, pinching my arm.

The two of them stood together behind the rope, waving to me, their shirts flapping in the wind as the plane started to move.

The wind blows by my head; between each wave there are thousands of tiny licking and chopping sounds as the water hurries out of the crevices and holes; and a part-floating, part-submerged feeling of being in the water haunts my mind even as the hot sun burns my face. I sit here and I read, and I wait for the pleasant feeling of repletion that follows a good meal, to turn slowly, as the hours pass along, into the even more delightful, slightly stirring sensation deep within, which accompanies the awakening of the appetite.

I am perfectly happy here in reality, because I still believe that nothing very drastic is likely to befall this part of the island in the near future.

you are not i

You are not I. No one but me could possibly be. I know that, and I know where I have been and what I have done ever since yesterday when I walked out the gate during the train wreck. Everyone was so excited that no one noticed me. I became completely unimportant as soon as it was a question of cut people and smashed cars down there on the tracks. We girls all went running down the bank when we heard the noise, and we landed against the cyclone fence like a lot of monkeys. Mrs. Werth was chewing on her crucifix and crying her eyes out. I suppose it hurt her lips. Or maybe she thought one of her daughters was on the train down there. It was really a bad accident; anyone could see that. The spring rains had dissolved the earth that kept the ties firm, and so the rails had spread a little and the train had gone into the ditch. But how everyone could get so excited I still fail to understand.

I always hated the trains, hated to see them go by down there, hated to see them disappear way off up the valley toward the next town. It made me angry to think of all those people moving from one town to another, without any right to. Whoever said to them: "You may go and buy your ticket and make the trip this morning to Reading. You will go past twenty-three stations, over forty bridges, through three tunnels, and still keep going, if you want to, even after you get to Reading"? No one. I know that. I know there is no chief who says things like that to people. But it makes it pleasanter for me when I imagine such a person does exist. Perhaps it would be only a tremendous voice speaking over a public-address system set up in all the main streets.

When I saw the train down there helpless on its side like an old worm knocked off a plant, I began to laugh. But I held on to the fence very hard when the people started to climb out the windows bleeding.

I was up in the courtyard, and there was the paper wrapper off a box of Cheese Tid Bits lying on the bench. Then I was at the main gate, and it was open. A black car was outside at the curb, and a man was sitting in front smoking. I thought of speaking to him and asking him if he knew who I was, but I decided not to. It was a sunny morning full of sweet air and birds. I followed the road around the hill, down to the tracks. Then I walked up the tracks feeling excited. The dining car looked strange lying on its side with the window glass all broken and some of the cloth shades drawn down. A robin kept whistling in a tree above. "Of course," I said to myself. "This is just in man's world. If something real should happen, they would stop singing." I walked up and down along the cinder bed beside the track, looking at the people lying in the bushes. Men were beginning to carry them up toward the front end of the train where the road crosses the tracks. There was a woman in a white uniform, and I tried to keep from passing close to her.

I decided to go down a wide path that led through the blackberry bushes, and in a small clearing I found an old stove with a lot of dirty bandages and handkerchiefs in the rubbish around the base of it. Underneath everything was a pile of stones. I found several round ones and some others. The earth here was very soft and moist. When I got back to the train there seemed to be a lot more people running around. I walked close to the ones who were lying side by side on the cinders, and looked at their faces. One was a girl and her mouth was open. I dropped one of the stones in and went on. A fat man also had his mouth open. I put in a sharp stone that looked like a piece of coal. It occurred to me that I might not have enough stones for them all, and the cinders were too small. There was one old woman walking up and down wiping her hands on her skirt very quickly, over and over again. She had on a long black silk dress with a design of blue mouths stamped all over it. Perhaps they were supposed to be leaves but they were formed like mouths. She looked crazy to me and I kept clear of her. Suddenly I noticed a hand with rings on the fingers sticking out from under a lot of bent pieces of metal. I tugged at the metal and saw a face. It was a woman and her mouth was closed. I tried to open it so I could get a stone in. A man grabbed me by the shoulder and pulled at me. He looked angry. "What are you doing?" he yelled. "Are you crazy?" I began to cry and said she was my sister. She did look a little like her, and I sobbed and kept saying: "She's dead. She's dead." The man stopped looking so angry and pushed me along toward the head of the train, holding my arm tightly with one hand. I tried to jerk away from him. At the same time I decided not to say anything more except "She's dead" once in a while. "That's all right," the man said. When we got to the front end of the train he made me sit down on the grass embankment alongside a lot of other people. Some of them were crying, so I stopped and watched them.

It seemed to me that life outside was like life inside. There was always somebody to stop people from doing what they wanted to do. I smiled when I thought that this was just the opposite of what I had felt when I was still inside. Perhaps what we want to do is wrong, but why should they always be the ones to decide? I began to consider this as I sat there pulling the little new blades of grass out of the ground. And I thought that for once I would decide what was right, and do it.

It was not very long before several ambulances drove up. They were for us, the row of people sitting on the bank, as well as for the ones lying around on stretchers and overcoats. I don't know why, since the people weren't in pain. Or perhaps they were. When a great many people are in pain together they aren't so likely to make a noise about it, probably because no one listens. Of course I was in no pain at all. I could have told anyone that if I had been asked. But no one asked me. What they did ask me was my address, and I gave my sister's address because it is only a half hour's drive. Besides, I stayed with her for quite a while before I went away, but that was years ago, I think. We all drove off together, some lying down inside the ambulances, and the rest of us sitting on an uncomfortable bench in one that had no bed. The woman next to me must have been a foreigner; she was moaning like a baby, and there was not a drop of blood on her that I could see, anywhere. I looked her all over very carefully on the way, but she seemed to resent it, and turned her face the other way, still crying. When we got to the hospital we were all taken in and examined. About me they just said: "Shock," and asked me again where I lived. I gave them the same address as before, and soon they took me out again and put me into the front seat of a sort of station wagon, between the driver and another man, an attendant, I suppose. They both spoke to me about the weather, but I knew enough not to let myself be trapped that easily. I know how the simplest subject can suddenly twist around and choke you when you think you're quite safe. "She's dead," I said once, when we were halfway between the two towns. "Maybe not, maybe not," said the driver, as if he were talking to a child. I kept my head down most of the time, but I managed to count the gas stations as we went along.

When we arrived at my sister's house the driver got out and rang the bell. I had forgotten that the street was so ugly. The houses were built one against the other, all alike, with only a narrow cement walk between. And each one was a few feet lower than the other, so that the long row of them looked like an enormous flight of stairs. The children were evidently allowed to run wild over all the front yards, and there was no grass anywhere in sight, only mud.

My sister came to the door. The driver and she spoke a few words, and then I saw her look very worried very suddenly. She came out to the car and leaned in. She had new glasses, thicker than the others. She did not seem to be looking at me. Instead she said to the driver: "Are you *sure* she's all right?"

"Absolutely," he answered. "I wouldn't be telling you if she wasn't. She's just been examined all over up at the hospital. It's just shock. A good rest will fix her up fine." The attendant got out, to help me out and up the steps, although I could have gone perfectly well by myself. I saw my sister looking at me out of the corner of her eye the same as she used to. When I was on the porch I heard her whisper to the attendant: "She don't look well yet to *me*." He patted her arm and said: "She'll be fine. Just don't let her get excited."

"That's what they always said," she complained, "but she just *does*."

The attendant got into the car. "She ain't hurt at *all*, lady." He slammed the door.

"Hurt!" exclaimed my sister, watching the car. It drove off and she stood following it with her eyes until it got to the top of the hill and turned. I was still looking down at the porch floor because I wasn't sure yet what was going to happen. I often feel that something is about to happen, and when I do, I stay perfectly still and let it go ahead. There's no use wondering about it or trying to stop it. At this time I had no particular feeling that a special event was about to come out, but I did feel that I would be more likely to do the right thing if I waited and let my sister act first. She stood where she was, in her apron, breaking off the tips of the pussywillow stems that stuck out of the bush beside her. She still refused to look at me. Finally she grunted: "Might as well go on inside. It's cold out here." I opened the door and walked in.

Right away I saw she had had the whole thing rebuilt, only backward. There was always a hall and a living room, except that the hall used to be on the left-hand side of the living room and now it was on the right. That made me wonder why I had failed to notice that the front door was now at the right end of the porch. She had even switched the stairs and fireplace around into each other's places. The furniture was the same, but each piece had been put into the position exactly opposite to the way it had been before. I decided to say nothing and let her do the explaining if she felt like it. It occurred to me that it must have cost her every cent she had in the bank, and still it looked exactly the same as it had when she began. I kept my mouth shut, but I could not help looking around with a good deal of curiosity to see if she had carried out the reversal in every detail.

I went into the living room. The three big chairs around the center table were still wrapped in old sheets, and the floor lamp by the pianola had the same torn cellophane cover on its shade. I began to laugh, everything looked so comical backward. I saw her grab the fringe of the portiere and look at me hard. I went on laughing.

The radio next door was playing an organ selection. Suddenly my sister said: "Sit down, Ethel. I've got something to do. I'll be right back." She went into the kitchen through the hall and I heard the back door open.

I knew already where she was going. She was afraid of me, and she wanted Mrs. Jelinek to come over. Sure enough, in a minute they both came in, and my sister walked right into the living room this time. She looked angry now, but she had nothing to say. Mrs. Jelinek is sloppy and fat. She shook hands with me and said: "Well, well, old-timer!" I decided not to talk to her either because I distrust her, so I turned around and lifted the lid of the pianola. I tried to push down some keys, but the catch was on and they were all stiff and wouldn't move. I closed the lid and went over to see out the window. A little girl was wheeling a doll carriage along the sidewalk down the hill; she kept looking back at the tracks the wheels made when they left a wet part of the pavement and went onto a dry patch. I was determined not to let Mrs. Jelinek gain any advantage over me, so I kept quiet. I sat down in the rocker by the window and began to hum.

Before long they started to talk to each other in low voices, but of course I heard everything they said. Mrs. Jelinek said: "I thought they was keeping her." My sister said: "I don't know. So did I. But the man kept telling me she was all right. Huh! She's just the same." "Why, sure," said Mrs. Jelinek. They were quiet a minute.

"Well, I'm not going to put up with it!" said my sister suddenly. "I'm going to tell Dr. Dunn what I think of him."

"Call the Home," urged Mrs. Jelinek.

"I certainly am," my sister answered. "You stay here. I'll see if Kate's in." She meant Mrs. Schultz, who lives on the

213

other side and has a telephone. I did not even look up when she went out. I had made a big decision, and that was to stay right in the house and under no condition let myself be taken back there. I knew it would be difficult, but I had a plan I knew would work if I used all my will power. I have great will power.

The first important thing to do was to go on keeping quiet, not to speak a word that might break the spell I was starting to work. I knew I would have to concentrate deeply, but that is easy for me. I knew it was going to be a battle between my sister and me, but I was confident that my force of character and superior education had fitted me for just such a battle, and that I could win it. All I had to do was to keep insisting inside myself, and things would happen the way I willed it. I said this to myself as I rocked. Mrs. Jelinek stood in the hall doorway with her arms folded, mostly looking out the front door. By now life seemed much clearer and more purposeful than it had in a long, long time. This way I would have what I wanted. "No one can stop you," I thought.

It was a quarter of an hour before my sister came back. When she walked in she had both Mrs. Schultz and Mrs. Schultz's brother with her, and all three of them looked a little frightened. I knew exactly what had happened even before she told Mrs. Jelinek. She had called the Home and complained to Dr. Dunn that I had been released, and he had been very much excited and told her to hold on to me by all means because I had not been discharged at all but had somehow *got out*. I was a little shocked to hear it put that way, but now that I thought of it, I had to admit to myself that that was just what I had done.

214

I got up when Mrs. Schultz's brother came in, and glared at him hard.

"Take it easy, now, Miss Ethel," he said, and his voice sounded nervous. I bowed low to him: at least he was polite.

" 'Lo, Steve," said Mrs. Jelinek.

I watched every move they made. I would have died rather than let the spell be broken. I felt I could hold it together only by a great effort. Mrs. Schultz's brother was scratching the side of his nose, and his other hand twitched in his pants pocket. I knew he would give me no trouble. Mrs. Schultz and Mrs. Jelinek would not go any further than my sister told them to. And she herself was terrified of me, for although I had never done her any harm, she had always been convinced that some day I would. It may be that she knew now what I was about to do to her, but I doubt it, or she would have run away from the house.

"When they coming?" asked Mrs. Jelinek.

"Soon's they can get here," said Mrs. Schultz.

They all stood in the doorway.

"I see they rescued the flood victims, you remember last night on the radio?" said Mrs. Schultz's brother.

Nobody answered. I was concentrating on my plan, and it took all my strength, so I sat down again.

"She'll be all right," said Mrs. Schultz's brother. He lit a cigarette and leaned back against the banisters.

The house was very ugly, but I already was getting ideas for making it look better. I have excellent taste in decoration. I tried not to think of those things, and said over and over inside my head: "Make it work."

215

Mrs. Jelinek finally sat down on the couch by the door, pulled her skirts around her legs and coughed. She still looked red in the face and serious. I could have laughed out loud when I thought of what they were really waiting to see if they had only known it.

I heard a car door slam outside. I looked out. Two of the men from the Home were coming up the walk. Somebody else was sitting at the wheel, waiting. My sister went quickly to the front door and opened it. One of the men said: "Where is she?" They both came in and stood a second looking at me and grinning.

"Well, hel-*lo!*" said one. The other turned and said to my sister: "No trouble?" She shook her head. "It's a wonder you couldn't be more careful," she said angrily. "They get out like that, how do *you* know what they're going to do?"

The man grunted and came over to me. "Wanna come with us? I know somebody who's waiting to see you."

I got up and walked slowly across the room, looking at the rug all the way, with one of the men on each side of me. When I got to the doorway beside my sister I pulled my hand out of the pocket of my coat and looked at it. I had one of my stones in my hand. It was very easy. Before either of them could stop me I reached out and stuffed the stone into her mouth. She screamed just before I touched her, and just afterward her lips were bleeding. But the whole thing took a very long time. Everybody was standing perfectly still. Next, the two men had hold of my arms very tight and I was looking around the room at the walls. I felt that my front teeth were broken. I could taste blood on my lips. I thought I was going to faint. I wanted to put my hand to my mouth, but they held my arms. "This is the turning point," I thought.

I shut my eyes very hard. When I opened them everything was different and I knew I had won. For a moment I could not see very clearly, but even during that moment I saw myself sitting on the divan with my hands in front of my mouth. As my vision cleared, I saw that the men were holding my sister's arms, and that she was putting up a terrific struggle. I buried my face in my hands and did not look up again. While they were getting her out the front door, they managed to knock over the umbrella stand and smash it. It hurt her ankle and she kicked pieces of porcelain back into the hall. I was delighted. They dragged her along the walk to the car, and one man sat on each side of her in the back. She was yelling and showing her teeth, but as they left the city limits she stopped, and began to cry. All the same, she was really counting the service stations along the road on the way back to the Home, and she found there was one more of them than she had thought. When they came to the grade crossing near the spot where the train accident had happened, she looked out, but the car was over the track before she realized she was looking out the wrong side.

Driving in through the gate, she really broke down. They kept promising her ice cream for dinner, but she knew better than to believe them. As she walked through the main door between the two men she stopped on the threshold, took out one of the stones from her coat pocket and put it into her mouth. She tried to swallow it, but it choked her, and they rushed her down the hall into a little waiting room and made her give it up. The strange thing, now that I think about it, was that no one realized she was not I.

They put her to bed, and by morning she no longer felt like crying: she was too tired.

It's the middle of the afternoon and raining torrents. She is sitting on her bed (the very one I used to have) in the Home, writing all this down on paper. She never would have thought of doing that up until yesterday, but now she thinks she has become me, and so she does everything I used to do.

The house is very quiet. I am still in the living room, sitting on the divan. I could walk upstairs and look into her bedroom if I wanted to. But it is such a long time since I have been up there, and I no longer know how the rooms are arranged. So I prefer to stay down here. If I look up I can see the square window of colored glass over the stairs. Purple and orange, an hourglass design, only the light never comes in very much because the house next door is so close. Besides, the rain is coming down hard here, too.

how many midnights

How many midnights, she wondered, had she raised the shade, opened the big window, and leaned out to gaze across the gently stirring city toward the highest towers? Over there behind a certain unmistakable group of them was his building, and at the very top of the building was his apartment, six flights up. In the summer she would look out over the rooftops at some length and sigh, and during the hottest weeks she moved her bed over, directly under the window. Then she would turn off all the lights and sit on the bed combing her hair in the glowing dimness of the city night, or sometimes even by moonlight, which of course was perfect. In the winter however she had to content herself with a moment of looking and a flash of imagining before she bounded across the room into bed.

It was winter now. She was walking crosstown, east, along one of the late Forties. This part of town always had seemed vaguely mysterious to her because of its specially constructed buildings that did not quite touch the pavement. All the buildings just north of the Grand Central were built that way, to absorb the shock, Van had told her; and there were long stretches of grill-work in the sidewalks through which, particularly at night, one could see another world beneath: railway tracks and sometimes a slowly moving train. When it snowed, as it was doing now, the snow filtered down through the grills and covered the ties; then they were even more apparent.

Van worked here in this neighborhood: he was manager of a large bookshop and lending library on Madison Avenue. And he lived in the neighborhood as well, only farther over east, between Third and Second Avenues. His place was not ideal, either as to actual physical comfort or as to locality (since the immediate district was clearly a slum), but with her help he had made it livable, and she used to tell him: "New York and Paris are like that: no clear demarcation of neighborhoods."

In any case, they already had signed a sublease for a place near Gramercy Park which was to be free the first of March. This was of prime importance because they planned to marry on Valentine's Day. They were by no means sentimental souls, either one of them, and for that very reason it seemed to June a little daring to announce to their friends during cocktails: "It's to be Valentine's Day."

Her father, who always was to be counted on to do the thoughtful thing, was staking them to two weeks in Bermuda. "God knows why," Van said. "He hates my guts."

"I don't know how you can say a thing like that about Dad," objected June. "He's never been anything but the essence of politeness with you."

"That's right," said Van, but impenitently.

She crossed Lexington Avenue. The entire sky looked as though it were being illumined from above by gray-violet neons. The tops of the buildings were lost in the cloud made by the falling snow. And the harbor sounds, instead of coming from the river ahead, came from above, as if the tugs were making their careful way around the tips of the towers. "This is the way New York was meant to be," she thought—not the crowded fire-escape, open-hydrant, sumac-leaved summer. Just this quiet, damp, neutral weather when the water seemed all around. She stood still a moment in the middle of the block, listening to the fog horns; there was a whole perspective of them. In the remotest background was a very faint, smothered one that said: "Mmmmm! Mmmmm!" "It must be on the Sound," she thought. She started to walk again.

In her coat pocket she had the keys, because this was to be a special night. Not that there had been any overt reference to that: there was no need for it. It had been implicit in their conversation yesterday afternoon when she had stopped in at the bookshop to see him. They had stood a few minutes talking in the back of the store among the desks, and then he had slipped her the keys. That was surely the most exciting single thing that ever had happened between them—the passage of the keys from his hand to hers. By the gesture he gave up what she knew was most dear to him: his privacy. She did not want him to think that she was in any way unaware of this, and she said in a low voice: "You can trust me with them, I think," laughing immediately afterward so that her remark should not sound ridiculous. He had kissed her and they had gone out for ten minutes to have coffee.

Sitting at the counter he had told how he had caught a man stealing books the night before. (The bookshop was open at night; because of the location it seemed they did almost as much business in the evening as they did during the day.) Van had just finished arranging a display of new books in one of the show windows, and was standing outside in the street looking in. He had noticed a man wearing a long overcoat, standing by the technical books. "I had my eye on him from the beginning. It's a type, you know. You get to spot them. He looked at me right through the window. I suppose he thought I was just another man in the street. I had on *my* overcoat, too." And the man had taken a quick glance around the store to be sure that no one was watching him, had reached up, snatched down a book and dropped it inside his coat. Van had gone quickly to the corner, tapped the traffic policeman on the shoulder and said: "Would you mind coming into my store for a minute? I want you to arrest a man." They had caught him, and when they had opened his coat they found he already had taken three books.

Van always said: "You see some funny things in a bookshop," and often they were really funny. But this story struck June as remotely sinister rather than amusing. Not because it had to do with a theft, certainly. It was not the first case of booklifting he had related to her. Perhaps it was because more than anything else she hated being watched behind her back, and involuntarily she put herself in the place of the thief, with whom she felt that Van had not been quite fair. It seemed to her that he might have gone in and said to him: "I've been watching you. I've seen everything you've been doing. Now, I give you one last chance. Put back whatever you've taken and get the hell out, and don't come back in here." To spring on the man out of the dark after spying on him did seem a little unfair. But she knew she was being absurd. Van could never be unfair with anyone; this was his way of handling the affair, and it was typical of him: he never would argue. She never knew even when he was angry with her until after it was all over, and he told her, smiling: "Gee, I was burned up last Friday."

She crossed Third Avenue. Up to now the snow had been melting as fast as it fell, but the air was getting colder, and the sidewalk began to show silver. The keys jingled in her coat pocket; she pulled off her glove and felt for them. They also were cold. When she had left her house, she had said to her parents: "I'm going out with Van. I'll probably be rather late." They had merely said: "Yes." But she thought she had intercepted a look of mutual understanding between them. It was all right: in ten more days they would be married. She had climbed up the six steep flights of stairs on a good many evenings during the past two years, just to spend an hour or so with him, but never, she reflected with an obscure sort of pride, had anything ever occurred between them which was not what her parents would call "honorable."

She had arrived at the apartment house; it had a gray-stone

façade and a good deal of wrought iron around the entrance
door. A woman who looked like a West Indian of some sort came
out. Noticing that June was carrying a potted plant under her
arm, she held the door partially open for her. June thanked her
and went in. It was a rubber plant she had bought for Van's
apartment. He was inclined to be indifferent about flowers, and,
she feared, about decoration in general. She always had hoped to
develop aesthetic appreciation in him, and she considered that
she had made remarkable progress during the past year. Practically all the adornments in his apartment were objects either of her
buying or her choosing.

She knew just how many steps there were to each flight of
stairs: nineteen for the first and fifteen for the others. The halls
were tiled in black and white, like a bathroom, and tonight, to
add to that impression, the stairs and floors were thoroughly
wet with the melting snow people had tracked in; the air
smelled of wet doormats, wet rubbers, wet clothing. On the
third floor a huge perambulator of black leatherette nearly
blocked the passageway between the stairs. She frowned at it
and thought of the fire regulations.

Because she did not want to be out of breath she mounted the
stairs slowly. Not that Van would be there when she arrived—it
was still too early—but being out of breath always created in her
a false kind of excitement which she particularly wanted to
avoid tonight. She turned the key in the lock and stepped inside. It gave her a strange sensation to push open the door all by
herself and stand there in the hall alone, smelling the special odor
of the place: an amalgam in which she imagined she detected

furniture polish, shaving cream and woodsmoke. Woodsmoke there surely was, because he had a fireplace. It was she who had persuaded him to have it installed. And it had not been nearly so expensive to build as he had imagined it was going to be, because since this was the top floor the chimney had only to be built up through the roof. Many times he had said to her: "That was one sensible idea you had," as though the others had not been just as good! They had cut down the legs of all the living-room furniture so that it nestled nearer the floor and made the room seem spacious; they had painted each wall a different shade of gray, adding the occasional wall brackets of ivy; they had bought the big glass coffee table. All these things had made the place pleasanter, and they had all been her ideas.

She shut the door and went into the kitchen. It was a little chilly in the apartment; she lit the gas oven. Then she unwrapped the wet brown paper from around the rubber plant, and set the pot upright on the table. The plant leaned somewhat to one side. She tried to make it stand straight, but it would not. The ice-box motor was purring. She took out two trays of ice and dumped the cubes into a bowl. Reaching up to the top shelf of the cabinet she brought down an almost full bottle of Johnny Walker, and set it, along with two highball glasses, onto the big lacquer tray. The room suddenly seemed terribly close; she turned off the oven. Then she scurried about looking for newspapers with which to lay a fire. There were only a few, but she found some old magazines in the kitchen. She rolled the newspapers into thin little logs and set them at various angles across the andirons. Underneath she pushed crumpled pages of the maga-

225

zines, and on top she put what kindling wood there was. The logs she decided to leave until the kindling already was burning. When the fire was laid, but not lighted, she looked out the window. The snow was coming down thicker than it had been when she came in. She drew the heavy woolen curtains; they covered one entire wall, and they too had been her idea. Van had wanted to have Venetian blinds made. She had tried to make him see how hideous they would be, but although he had agreed that the black-and-white curtains were smart, he never would admit that Venetian blinds were ugly. "Maybe you're right, for this room," he said. "For every room in the world," she had wanted to declare, but she decided against it, since after all, he had given in.

It wasn't that Van had really bad taste. He had an innate sensitivity and a true intelligence which became manifest whenever he talked about the books he had read (and he read a good many during odd moments at the bookshop). But his aesthetic sense had never been fully awakened. Naturally she never mentioned it—she merely made small suggestions which he was free to take or to leave as he saw fit. And usually, if she let her little hints fall at strategic moments, he would take them.

On the mantel were two enormous plaster candelabra covered with angels; she had brought them herself all the way from Matamoros Izúcar in Mexico. Actually she had packed six of them, and all had broken except these two which did not quite match, one of them being somewhat taller than the other. (These were among the few things about which Van was still a bit recalcitrant: he could not be sure he liked them, even yet.)

Each one held six candles. She went to a drawer in the desk and got out a dozen long yellow tapers. Often she brought him a dozen at a time. "Where am I supposed to put the damned things?" he would complain. She got a knife from the kitchen and began to scrape the bottoms of the candles to make them fit the holders. "In the middle of this operation he's going to arrive," she said to herself. She wanted the place to be perfect before he got there. Nervously she tossed the paraffine scrapings into the fireplace. She had a feeling that he would not just come up; it would be more like him to ring from the vestibule downstairs. At least, she hoped he would do that. The time it would take him to get up the six flights might make a great difference in the way the room would look. She fitted the last candle into the bright holder and sighed with relief. They were slow-burning ones; she decided to light them now before returning the candelabra to the mantel. Up there they looked beautiful. She stepped back to admire their splendor, and for a moment watched the slowly moving interplay of shadows on the wall. She switched off the electric lights in the room. With the fireplace aglow the effect would be breathtaking.

Impetuously she determined to do a very daring thing. It might possibly annoy Van when he first saw it, but she would do it anyway. She rushed to the other side of the room and feverishly began to push the divan across the floor toward the fireplace. It would be so snug to be right in front of the blaze, especially with the snow outside. The cushions fell off and a caster got entangled with the long wool of the goatskin rug she had given him for his birthday. She got the rug out of the way

227

and continued to manipulate the divan. It looked absurd out there in the middle of the room, and she swung one end around so that it lay at right angles to the fireplace, against the wall. After she had piled the cushions back she stepped aside to observe it, and decided to leave it there. Then the other pieces had to be arranged. The whole room was in disorder at this point.

"I know he's going to open that door this minute," she thought. She turned the overhead light back on and quickly began to shift chairs, lamps and tables. The last piece to be moved was a small commode that she had once helped him sandpaper. As she carried it across the room its one little drawer slid out and fell on the floor. All the letters Van had received in the past months were there, lying in a fairly compact heap at her feet. "Damnation!" she said aloud, and as she said it, the hideous metallic sound of the buzzer in the kitchen echoed through the apartment. She let go of the commode and rushed out to press the button that opened the door downstairs onto the street. Then, without pressing it, she ran back into the living room and knelt on the floor, quickly gathering up the letters and dumping them into the drawer. But they had been piled carefully into that small space before the accident, and now they were not; as a result the drawer was overfull and would not close. Again she spoke aloud. "Oh, my God!" she said. And she said that because for no reason at all it had occurred to her that Van might think she had been reading his correspondence. The main thing now was to get the commode over into the corner; then she might be able to force the drawer shut. As she lifted it, the buzzer pealed again, with insistence. She ran into the kitchen, and this time pressed the answer button with all her might. Swiftly she hurried back and carried the commode into the corner. Then she tried to close the drawer and found it an impossibility. In a burst of inspiration she turned the little piece of furniture around so that the drawer opened toward the wall. She stepped to the fireplace and touched a match to the paper logs. By now he would got only about to the fourth floor; there were three more.

She turned off the light once again, went into the hall and looked at herself briefly in the mirror, put out the light there, and moved toward the entrance door. With her hand on the knob, she held her breath, and found that her heart was beating much too fast. It was just what she had not wanted. She had hoped to have him step into a little world of absolute calm. And now because of that absurd drawer she was upset. Or perhaps it was the dragging around of all that furniture. She opened the door a crack and listened. A second later she stepped out into the hall, and again she listened. She walked to the stairs. "Van?" she called, and immediately she was furious with herself.

A man's voice answered from two floors below. "Riley?" he yelled.

"What?" she cried.

"I'm looking for Riley."

"You've rung the wrong bell," she shouted, enunciating the words very distinctly in spite of her raised voice.

She went in and shut the door, holding onto the knob and leaning her forehead against the panel for a moment. Now her heart was beating even more violently. She returned to the commode in the corner. "I might as well fix it once and for all right now," she thought. Otherwise her mind would be on it every instant. She turned it around, took out all the letters and carefully replaced them in four equal piles. Even then the drawer shut with difficulty, but it did close. When that was done, she went to the window and pulled back the curtain. It seemed to be growing much colder. The wind had risen; it was blowing from the east. The sky was no longer violet. It was black. She could see the snow swirling past the street lamp below. She wondered if it were going to turn into a blizzard. Tomorrow was Sunday; she simply would stay on. There would be a terrible moment in the morning, of course, when her parents arose and found she had not come in, but she would not be there to see it, and she could make it up with them later. And what an ideal little vacation it would make: a night and day up there in the snow, isolated from everything, shut away from everyone but Van. As she watched the street, she gradually became convinced that the storm would last all night. She looked back into the room. It gave her keen pleasure to contrast its glow with the hostile night outside. She let the curtain fall and went to the fireplace. The kindling was at the height of its blazing and there was no more; she piled two small logs on top of it. Soon they were crackling with such energy that she thought it wise to put the screen across in front of them. She sat on the divan looking at her legs in the blended firelight and candleglow. Smiling, she leaned back against the cushions. Her heart was no longer racing. She felt almost calm. The wind whined outside; to her it was inevitably a melancholy sound. Even tonight.

Suddenly she decided that it would be inexcusable not to let her parents know she was staying the night. She went into the bedroom and lay on the bed, resting the telephone on her stomach. It moved ridiculously while she dialed. Her mother, not her father, answered. "Thank God," she said to herself, and she let her head fall back upon the pillows. Her mother had been asleep; she did not sound too pleased to have been called to the telephone. "You're all right, I hope," she said. They spoke of the storm. "Yes, it's awful out," said June. "Oh, no, I'm at Van's. We have a fire. I'm going to stay. All night." There was a short silence. "Well, I think you're very foolish," she heard her mother say. And she went on. June let her talk a bit. Then she interrupted, letting a note of impatience sound in her voice. "I can't very well discuss it now. You understand." Her mother's voice was shrill. "No, I *don't* understand!" she cried. She was taking it more seriously than June had expected. "I can't talk now," said June. "I'll see you tomorrow." She said good night and hung up, lying perfectly still for a moment. Then she lifted the telephone and set it on the night table, but still she did not move. When she had heard herself say: "We have a fire," a feeling of dread had seized her. It was as if in giving voice to the pretense she thereby became conscious of it. Van had not yet arrived; why then had she taken care to speak as though he had? She could only have been trying to reassure herself. Again her heart had begun to beat heavily. And finally she did what she had been trying not even to think of doing ever since she had arrived: she looked at her watch.

It was a little after midnight. There was absolutely no doubt about it; already he was quite late. He no longer could arrive without going into explanations. Something must have happened, and it only could be something bad. "Ridiculous!" she cried in anger, jumping up and going out into the kitchen. The ice cubes had melted a good deal; she poured the cold water into the sink between her spread fingers, and shook the cubes around in the bowl petulantly, trying to stem the resentment she felt rising up inside her. "It will be interesting to know what his excuse will be," she said to herself. She decided that when he arrived her only possible behavior would be to pretend not to have noticed his lateness.

She dropped some of the ice cubes into one of the glasses, poured in some Scotch, stirred it, and went into the living room with it. The fire was burning triumphantly; the whole room danced in flamelight. She sat on the couch and downed her drink, a little too quickly for a young woman completely at her ease, which was what she was trying to be. When she had finished the last drop, she forced herself to sit without moving for ten minutes by her watch. Then she went out and made herself another drink, a little stronger. This one she drank walking thoughtfully around and around the center of the room. She was fighting against an absurd impulse to put on her coat and go into the street to look for him. "Old woman," she said to herself. Old people always had that reaction—they always expected tragedies. As she came to the end of her second drink she succeeded in convincing herself that the mathematical probabilities of Van's having met with his first serious accident on this particular evening were extremely slight. This moral certitude engendered a feeling of light-heartedness, which expressed itself in the desire for a third drink. She had only just begun this one when an even sharper anguish seized her. If it was not likely that he had had an accident, it was utterly unthinkable that he should have let some unforeseen work detain him until this late; he would have telephoned her anyway. It was even more inconceivable that their rendezvous should have slipped his mind. The final, remaining possibility therefore was that he had deliberately avoided it, which of course was absurd. She tossed another log onto the fire. Again she went to the window and peered between the curtains down into the empty street. The wind had become a gale. She felt each blast against her face through the closed window. Listening for sounds of traffic, she heard none; even the boats seemed to have been silenced. Only the rushing of the wind was left—that and the occasional faint hissing of the fine snow against the glass. She burst into tears; she did not know whether it was out of self-pity, anger and humiliation, loneliness, or just plain nervousness.

As she stood there in the window with the tears covering her sight, it occurred to her how ironic it would be if he should come and find her like this: slightly drunk, sobbing, with her make-up surely in a state of complete ruin. A sound behind her ended her weeping instantly. She let go of the curtain and turned to face the room: through her tears she could see nothing but quivering webs of light. She squeezed her lids tightly together: one of the logs had broken in two. The smaller half lay on the hearth smoking. She went over and kicked it into the fire. Then she tiptoed into the hall to the entrance door and slipped the chain on. As soon as she had done that she was terrified. It was nothing less than a symbol of fear—she realized it as she looked at the brass links stretching across from jamb to door. But once having put it up, she did not have the courage to take it down again.

Still on tiptoe, she returned to the living room and lay on the divan, burying her face in the cushions. She was not crying any longer—she felt too empty and frightened to do anything but lie quite still. But after a while she sat up and looked slowly about the room. The candles had burned down half way; she looked at them, at the ivy trailing down from the little pots on the wall, at the white goatskin by her feet, at the striped curtains. They were all hers. "Van, Van," she said under her breath. Unsteadily she rose and made her way to the bathroom. The glaring light hurt her eyes. Hanging on the inside of the door was Van's old flannel bathrobe. It was too big for her, but she got into it and rolled the sleeves back, turning up the collar and pulling the belt tightly about her waist. In the living room she lay down again on the divan among the cushions. From time to time she rubbed her cheek against the wool of the sleeve under her face. She stared into the fire.

Van was in the room. It was daylight out—a strange gray dawn. She sat up, feeling light-headed. "Van," she said. He was moving slowly across the floor toward the window. And the curtains had been drawn back. There was the rectangle of dim white sky, with Van going toward it. She called to him again. If he heard her he paid no attention. She sat back, watching. Now and then he shook his head slowly from side to side; the gesture made her feel like crying again, but not for herself this time. It was quite natural that he should be there, shuffling slowly across the room in the pale early light, shaking his head from one side to the other. Suddenly she said to herself that he was looking for something, that he might find it, and she began to shiver sitting up there in the cold. "He *has* found it," she thought, "but he's pretending he hasn't because he knows I'm watching him." And even as the idea formed itself in her mind she saw him reach up and swing himself through the window. She screamed, jumped down from the couch and ran across the room. When she got to the window there was nothing to see but the vast gray panorama of a city at dawn, spitefully clear in every tiniest detail. She stood there looking out, seeing for miles up and down the empty streets. It was a foreign city.

The sputtering of a candle as it went out roused her. Several of them had already burned out. The shadows on the ceiling were wavering like bats. The room was cold and the curtains across the closed window moved inward with the force of the wind. She lay perfectly still. In the fireplace she heard the powdery, faintly metallic sound of a cooling ember as it fell. For a long time she remained unmoving. Then she sprang up, turned on all the lights, went into the bedroom and stood for a moment looking at the telephone. The sight of it calmed her a little. She took off the bathrobe and opened the closet door to hang it up. She knew his luggage by heart; his small overnight valise was missing. Slowly her mouth opened. She did not think to put her hand over it.

She slipped on her coat and unhooked the chain on the entrance door. The hall outside was full of scurrying draughts.

235

Down the six flights she ran, one after the other, until she was at the front door. The snow had drifted high, completely covering the steps. She went out. It was bitter cold in the wind, but only a stray flake fell now and then. She stood there. The street did not tell her what to do. She began to wade through the deep snow, eastward. A taxi, moving cautiously down Second Avenue, its chains clanking rhythmically, met her at the corner. She hailed it, got in.

"Take me to the river," she said, pointing.

"What street?"

"Any street that goes down all the way."

Almost immediately they were there. She got out, paid the driver, walked slowly to the end of the pavement, and stood watching. The dawn was really breaking now, but it was very different from the one she had seen through the window. The wind took her breath away, the water out there was alive. Against the winter sky across the river there were factories. The lights of a small craft moved further down in midstream. She clenched her fists. A terrible anguish had taken possession of her. She was trembling, but she did not feel the cold. Abruptly she turned around. The driver was standing in the street blowing into his cupped hands. And he was looking at her intently.

"You're not waiting for me, are you?" she said. (Was that her voice?)

"Yes, *Ma'am*," he said with force.

"I didn't tell you to." (With her whole life falling to pieces before her, how was it that her voice rang with such asperity, such hard self-assurance?)

"That's right." He put his gloves back on. "Take your time," he said.

She turned her back on him and watched the changing water. Suddenly she felt ridiculous. She went over to the cab, got in, and gave her home address.

The doorman was asleep when she rang, and even after she was inside she had to wait nearly five minutes for the elevator boy to bring the car up from the basement. She tiptoed through the apartment to her room, shutting the door behind her. When she had undressed she opened the big window without looking out, and got into bed. The cold wind blew through the room.

a thousand days for mokhtar

Mokhtar lived in a room not far from his shop, overlooking the sea. There was a tiny window in the wall above his sleeping-mattress, through which, if he stood on tiptoe, he could see the waves pounding against the rocks of the breakwater far below. The sound came up, too, especially on nights when the Casbah was wrapped in rain and its narrow streets served only for the passage of unexpected gusts of wind. On these nights the sound of the waves was all around, even though he kept the window shut. Throughout the year there were many such nights, and it was precisely at such times that he did not feel like going home to be alone in his little room. He had been by himself ten years now, ever since his wife had died; his solitude never weighed on him when the weather was clear and the stars shone in the sky. But a rainy night put him in mind of the happy hours of his life, when in just such nocturnal wind and storm he and his great-eyed bride would pull the heavy blinds shut and live quietly in each other's company until dawn. These things he could not think about; he would go to the Café Ghazel and play dominoes hour after hour with anyone who came along, rather than return to his room.

Little by little the other men who sat regularly in the café had come to count on Mokhtar's appearance. "It's beginning to rain: Si Mokhtar will be along soon. Save him the mat next to you." And he never disappointed them. He was pleasant and quiet; the latter quality made him a welcome addition to a game, since the café's habitués considered each other far too talkative.

Sitting in the Café Ghazel tonight Mokhtar was unaccountably uneasy. He was disturbed by the bonelike sound of the dominoes as they were shuffled on the tables. The metallic scraping of the old phonograph in the inner room bothered him, and he looked up with an unreasoning annoyance at each new arrival who came in through the door, heralded by blasts of wet wind. Often he glanced out the window beside him at the vast blackness of the sea lying below at the foot of the city. On the other side of the glass, just at the edge of the cliff, a few tall stalks of bamboo caught the light from inside, stood out white against the blackness beyond, bending painfully before the gale.

"They'll break," murmured Mokhtar.

"What?" said Mohammed Slaoui.

Mokhtar laughed, but said nothing. As the evening continued, his discomfort increased. In the inner room they had stopped the

239

phonograph and were singing a strident song. Some of the men around him joined in the noise. He could no longer hear the wind. As that round of dominoes came to an end, he rose precipitately and said: "Good night," not caring how strange his sudden departure might seem to the others.

Outside in the street it was scarcely raining at all, but the wind raged upward from the shore below, bringing with it the bloodlike smell of the sea; the crashing waves seemed very near, almost at his feet. He looked down as he walked along. At each mound of garbage there were cats; they ran across in front of him constantly from one pile to another. As Mokhtar reached his door and pulled out his key, he had the feeling that he was about to perform an irrevocable act, that stepping inside would be a gesture of finality.

"What is happening?" he asked himself. "Am I going to die?" He would not be afraid of that; still, he would like to know it a few moments in advance, if possible. He flexed his arms and legs before opening the door: there was no pain anywhere, everything appeared to be in good condition. "It's my head," he decided. But his head felt clear, his thoughts moved forward in orderly fashion. Nevertheless, these discoveries did not reassure him; he knew something was wrong. He bolted the door behind him and began to mount the stairs in the dark. More clearly than anything else at the moment he sensed that this conviction of having entered into a new region of his life was only in the nature of a warning. "Don't go on," he was being told. "Doing what?" he asked himself as he undressed. He had no secrets, no involvements, no plans for the future, no responsibilities. He merely lived. He could not heed the warning because he could not understand it. And yet there was no doubt that it was there in his room, and it made itself most strongly felt when he lay down. The wind shook the blinds. The rain had begun to fall again; it showered violently on the panes of glass over the corridor, and rattled down the drainpipe from the roof. And the unappeased roaring of the waves went on, down at the base of the ramparts. He considered the sadness, the coldness of the damp blanket; he touched the straw-covered wall with his finger. In the black night he groaned: "Al-lah!" and fell asleep.

But even in sleep he went on worrying; his dreams were a chaotic, relentless continuation of his waking state. The same accent of implicit warning was present in the sequences of streets and shops which unrolled before his eyes. He was at the entrance to the public market. A great many people were inside, where they had gone to get out of the rain. Although it was mid-morning, the day was so dark that all the stalls were blazing with electric lights. "If only she could have seen this," he said to himself, thinking of how much pleasure it would have given his wife. "Poor girl, in her day it was always dark here." And Mokhtar wondered if really he had the right to go on living and watching the world change, without her. Each month the world had changed a little more, had gone a little further away from what it had been when she had known it.

"Also, since she is not here to eat it, what am I doing buying meat?" He was standing before the stall of his friend Abdallah ben Bouchta, looking at the cuts that were displayed on the slab of white marble in front of him. And all at once he was em-

241

broiled in a quarrel with Bouchta. He felt himself seizing the old man by the throat; he felt his fingers pressing with increasing force: he was choking Bouchta and he was glad to be doing it. The violence of the act was a fulfillment and a relief. Bouchta's face grew black, he fell, and his glazed eyes stared like the eyes in a sheep's head served on a platter for the feast of Aïd el Kébir.

Mokhtar awoke, horrified. The wind was still blowing, carrying with it, above the town, wisps of the voice of the muezzin who at that moment was calling from the Jaamâa es Seghira. But the warnings had ceased, and this was comforting enough to make more sleep possible.

The morning was gray and cheerless. Mokhtar rose at the usual hour, made his daily visit to the great mosque for a few moments of prayer and a thorough wash, and proceeded through the rain to his shop. There were few people in the streets. The memory of his dream weighed upon him, saddening him even more than the prospect of a day of infrequent sales. As the morning progressed he thought often of his old friend; he was consumed with the desire to pass by the market, just to assure himself that Bouchta was there as always. There was no reason why he should not be, but once Mokhtar had seen him with his own eyes he would be content.

A little before noon he boarded up the front of his shop and set out for the market. When his eyes became accustomed to the dim inner light of the building, the first person he saw was Bouchta standing behind the counter in his stall, chopping and slicing the meat the same as any other day. Feeling immensely relieved, Mokhtar wandered over to the counter and spoke to him. Perhaps the note of excessive cordiality in his voice surprised Bouchta, for he glanced up with a startled expression in his face, and seeing Mokhtar, said shortly: "*Sbalkheir.*" Then he resumed hacking at a piece of meat for a customer. His rather unfriendly look was lost on Mokhtar, who was so pleased to see him there that he was momentarily unable to perceive anything but that one fact. However, when Bouchta, on completing the sale, turned to him and said abruptly: "I'm busy this morning," Mokhtar stared at him, and again felt his fear stir within him.

"Yes, Sidi?" he said pleasantly.

Bouchta glared. "Twenty-two douro would be a more welcome offering than your foolish smile," he said.

Mokhtar looked confused. "Twenty-two douro, Sidi?"

"Yes. The twenty-two douro you never paid me for the lamb's head at last Aïd el Kébir."

Mokhtar felt the blood leap upward in him like a fire. "I paid you for that the following month."

"*Abaden!* Never!" cried Bouchta excitedly. "I have eyes and a head too! I remember what happens! You can't take advantage of me the way you did of poor old Tahiri. I'm not that old yet!" And he began to call out unpleasant epithets, brandishing his cleaver.

People had stopped in their tracks and were following the conversation with interest. As Mokhtar's anger mounted, he suddenly heard, among the names that Bouchta was calling him, one which offended him more than the rest. He reached across the counter and seized Bouchta's *djellaba* in his two hands,

243

pulling on the heavy woolen fabric until it seemed that it would surely be ripped off the old man's back.

"Let go of me!" shouted Bouchta. The people were crowding in to see whatever violence might result. "Let go of me!" he kept screaming, his face growing steadily redder.

At this point the scene was so much like his dream that Mokhtar, even while he was enjoying his own anger and the sight of Bouchta as he became the victim of such a senseless rage, was suddenly very much frightened. He let go of the *djellaba* with one hand, and turning to the onlookers said loudly: "Last night I dreamed that I came here and killed this man, who is my friend. I do not want to kill him. I am not going to kill him. Look carefully. I am not hurting him."

Bouchta's fury was reaching grotesque proportions. With one hand he was trying to pry Mokhtar's fingers from his garment, and with the other, which held the cleaver, he was making crazy gyrations in the air. All the while he jumped quickly up and down, crying: "Let go! Let go! *Khlass!*"

"At any moment he is going to hit me with the cleaver," thought Mokhtar, and so he seized the wrist that held it, pulling Bouchta against the counter. For a moment they struggled and panted, while the slabs of meat slid about under their arms and fell heavily onto the wet floor. Bouchta was strong, but he was old. Suddenly he relaxed his grasp on the cleaver and Mokhtar felt his muscles cease to push. The crowd murmured. Mokhtar let go of both the wrist and the *djellaba*, and looked up. Bouchta's face was an impossible color, like the sides of meat that hung behind him. His mouth opened and his head slowly

244

tilted upward as if he were looking at the ceiling of the market. Then, as if someone had pushed him from behind, he fell forward onto the marble counter and lay still, his nose in a shallow puddle of pinkish water. Mokhtar knew he was dead, and he was a little triumphant as he shouted to everyone: "I dreamed it! I dreamed it! I told you! Did I kill him? Did I touch him? You saw!" The crowd agreed, nodding.

"Get the police!" cried Mokhtar. "I want everyone to be my witness." A few people moved away quietly, not wishing to be involved. But most of them stayed, quite ready to give the authorities their version of the strange phenomenon.

In court the Cadi proved to be unsympathetic. Mokhtar was bewildered by his lack of friendliness. The witnesses had told the story exactly as it had happened; obviously they all were convinced of Mokhtar's innocence.

"I have heard from the witnesses what happened in the market," said the Qadi impatiently, "and from those same witnesses I know you are an evil man. It is impossible for the mind of an upright man to bring forth an evil dream. Bouchta died as a result of your dream." And as Mokhtar attempted to interrupt: "I know what you are going to say, but you are a fool, Mokhtar. You blame the wind, the night, your long solitude. Good. For a thousand days in our prison here you will not hear the wind, you will not know whether it is night or day, and you will never lack the companionship of your fellow-prisoners."

The Qadi's sentence shocked the inhabitants of the town, who found it of an unprecedented severity. But Mokhtar, once he had been locked up, was persuaded of its wisdom. For one thing, he was not unhappy to be in prison, where each night, when he had begun to dream that he was back in his lonely room, he could awaken to hear on all sides of him the comforting snores of the other prisoners. His mind no longer dwelled upon the earlier happy hours of his life, because the present hours were happy ones as well. And then, the very first day there, he had suddenly remembered with perfect clarity that, although he had intended to do so, he never had paid Bouchta the twenty-two douro for the lamb's head, after all.

tea on the mountain

The mail that morning had brought her a large advance from her publishers. At least, it looked large to her there in the International Zone where life was cheap. She had opened the letter at a table of the sidewalk café opposite the Spanish post office. The emotion she felt at seeing the figures on the check had made her unexpectedly generous to the beggars that constantly filed past. Then the excitement had worn off, and she felt momentarily depressed. The streets and the sky seemed brighter and stronger than she. She had of necessity made very few friends in the town, and although she worked steadily every day at her novel, she had to admit that sometimes she was lonely. Driss came by, wearing a spotless mauve *djellaba* over his shoulders and a new fez on his head.

"*Bon jour, mademoiselle*," he said, making an exaggerated bow.

He had been paying her assiduous attention for several months, but so far she had been successful in putting him off without losing his friendship; he made a good escort in the evenings. This morning she greeted him warmly, let him pay her check, and moved off up the street with him, conscious of the comment her action had caused among the other Arabs sitting in the café.

They turned into the rue du Télégraphe Anglais, and walked slowly down the hill. She decided she was trying to work up an appetite for lunch; in the noonday heat it was often difficult to be hungry. Driss had been Europeanized to the point of insisting on apéritifs before his meals; however, instead of having two Dubonnets, for instance, he would take a Gentiane, a Byrrh, a Pernod and an Amer Picon. Then he usually went to sleep and put off eating until later. They stopped at the café facing the Marshan Road, and sat down next to a table occupied by several students from the Lycée Français, who were drinking *limonades* and glancing over their notebooks. Driss wheeled around suddenly and began a casual conversation. Soon they both moved over to the students' table.

She was presented to each student in turn; they solemnly acknowledged her *"Enchantée,"* but remained seated while doing so. Only one, named Mjid, rose from his chair and quickly sat down again, looking worried. He was the one she immediately wanted to get to know, perhaps because he was more serious and soft-eyed, yet at the same time seemed more eager and violent than any of the others. He spoke his stilted theatre-French swiftly, with less accent than his schoolmates, and he punctuated his sentences with precise, tender smiles instead of the correct or expected inflections. Beside him sat Ghazi, plump and Negroid.

She saw right away that Mjid and Ghazi were close friends. They replied to her questions and flattery as one man, Ghazi preferring, however, to leave the important phrases to Mjid. He had an impediment in his speech, and he appeared to think more slowly. Within a few minutes she had learned that they had been going to school together for twelve years, and had always been in the same form. This seemed strange to her, inasmuch as Ghazi's lack of precocity became more and more noticeable as she watched him. Mjid noticed the surprise in her face, and he added:

"Ghazi is very intelligent, you know. His father is the high judge of the native court of the International Zone. You will go to his home one day and see for yourself."

"Oh, but of course I believe you," she cried, understanding now why Ghazi had experienced no difficulty in life so far, in spite of his obvious slow-wittedness.

"I have a very beautiful house indeed," added Ghazi. "Would you like to come and live in it? You are always welcome. That's the way we Tanjaoui are."

"Thank you. Perhaps some day I shall. At any rate, I thank you a thousand times. You are too kind."

"And my father," interposed Mjid suavely but firmly, "the poor man, he is dead. Now it's my brother who commands."

"But, alas, Mjid, your brother is tubercular," sighed Ghazi.

Mjid was scandalized. He began a vehement conversation

249

with Ghazi in Arabic, in the course of which he upset his empty *limonade* bottle. It rolled onto the sidewalk and into the gutter, where an urchin tried to make off with it, but was stopped by the waiter. He brought the bottle to the table, carefully wiped it with his apron, and set it down.

"Dirty Jew dog!" screamed the little boy from the middle of the street.

Mjid heard this epithet even in the middle of his tirade. Turning in his chair, he called to the child: "Go home. You'll be beaten this evening."

"Is it your brother?" she asked with interest.

Since Mjid did not answer her, but seemed not even to have heard her, she looked at the urchin again and saw his ragged clothing. She was apologetic.

"Oh, I'm sorry," she began. "I hadn't looked at him. I see now . . ."

Mjid said, without looking at her: "You would not need to look at that child to know he was not of my family. You heard him speak. . . ."

"A neighbor's child. A poor little thing," interrupted Ghazi.

Mjid seemed lost in wonder for a moment. Then he turned and explained slowly to her: "One word we can't hear is tuberculosis. Any other word, syphillis, leprosy, even pneumonia, we can listen to, but not that word. And Ghazi knows that. He wants you to think we have Paris morals here. There I know everyone says that word everywhere, on the boulevards, in the cafés, in Montparnasse, in the Dôme—" he grew excited as he listed these points of interest— "in the Moulin Rouge, in

Sacré Coeur, in the Louvre. Some day I shall go myself. My brother has been. That's where he got sick."

During this time Driss, whose feeling of ownership of the American lady was so complete that he was not worried by any conversation she might have with what he considered schoolboys, was talking haughtily to the other students. They were all pimply and bespectacled. He was telling them about the football games he had seen in Malaga. They had never been across to Spain, and they listened, gravely sipped their *limonade*, and spat on the floor like Spaniards.

"Since I can't invite you to my home, because we have sickness there, I want you to make a picnic with me tomorrow," announced Mjid. Ghazi made some inaudible objection which his friend silenced with a glance, whereupon Ghazi decided to beam, and followed the plans with interest.

"We shall hire a carriage, and take some ham to my country villa," continued Mjid, his eyes shining with excitement. Ghazi started to look about apprehensively at the other men seated on the terrace; then he got up and went inside.

When he returned he objected: "You have no sense, Mjid. You say 'ham' right out loud when you know some friends of my father might be here. It would be very bad for me. Not everyone is free as you are."

Mjid was penitent for an instant. He stretched out his leg, pulling aside his silk *gandoura*. "Do you like my garters?" he asked her suddenly.

She was startled. "They're quite good ones," she began.

"Let me see yours," he demanded.

She glanced down at her slacks. She had espadrilles on her feet, and wore no socks. "I'm sorry," she said. "I haven't any."

Mjid looked uncomfortable, and she guessed that it was more for having discovered, in front of the others, a flaw in her apparel, than for having caused her possible embarrassment. He cast a contrite glance at Ghazi, as if to excuse himself for having encouraged a foreign lady who was obviously not of the right sort. She felt that some gesture on her part was called for. Pulling out several hundred francs, which was all the money in her purse, she laid it on the table, and went on searching in her handbag for her mirror. Mjid's eyes softened. He turned with a certain triumph to Ghazi, and permitting himself a slight display of exaltation, patted his friend's cheek three times.

"So it's set!" he exclaimed. "Tomorrow at noon we meet here at the Café du Télégraphe Anglais. I shall have hired a carriage at eleven-thirty at the market. You, dear mademoiselle," turning to her, "will have gone at ten-thirty to the English grocery and bought the food. Be sure to get Jambon Olida, because it's the best."

"The best ham," murmured Ghazi, looking up and down the street a bit uneasily.

"And buy one bottle of wine."

"Mjid, you know this can get back to my father," Ghazi began.

Mjid had had enough interference. He turned to her. "If you like, mademoiselle, we can go alone."

She glanced at Ghazi; his cowlike eyes had veiled with actual tears.

Mjid continued. "It'll be very beautiful up there on the mountain with just us two. We'll take a walk along the top of the mountain to the rose gardens. There's a breeze from the sea all afternoon. At dusk we'll be back at the farm. We'll have tea and rest." He stopped at this point, which he considered crucial.

Ghazi was pretending to read his social correspondence textbook, with his *chechia* tilted over his eyebrows so as to hide his hopelessly troubled face. Mjid smiled tenderly.

"We'll go all three," he said softly.

Ghazi simply said: "Mjid is bad."

Driss was now roaring drunk. The other students were impressed and awed. Some of the bearded men in the café looked over at the table with open disapproval in their faces. She saw that they regarded her as a symbol of corruption. Consulting her fancy little enamel watch, which everyone at the table had to examine and study closely before she could put it back into its case, she announced that she was hungry.

"Will you eat with us?" Ghazi inquired anxiously. It was clear he had read that an invitation should be extended on such occasions; it was equally clear that he was in terror lest she accept.

She declined and rose. The glare of the street and the commotion of the passers-by had tired her. She took her leave of all the students while Driss was inside the café, and went down to the restaurant on the beach where she generally had lunch.

There while she ate, looking out at the water, she thought: "That was amusing, but it was just enough," and she decided not to go on the picnic.

She did not even wait until the next day to stock up with provisions at the English grocery. She bought three bottles of ordinary red wine, two cans of Jambon Olida, several kinds of Huntley and Palmer's biscuits, a bottle of stuffed olives and five hundred grams of chocolates full of liqueurs. The English lady made a splendid parcel for her.

At noon next day she was drinking an *orgeat* at the Café du Télégraphe Anglais. A carriage drove up, drawn by two horses loaded down with sleighbells. Behind the driver, shielded from the sun by the beige canopy of the victoria, sat Ghazi and Mjid, looking serious and pleasant. They got down to help her in. As they drove off up the hill, Mjid inspected the parcel approvingly and whispered: "The wine?"

"All inside," she said.

The locusts made a great noise from the dusty cliffs beside the road as they came to the edge of town. "Our nightingales," smiled Mjid. "Here is a ring for you. Let me see your hand."

She was startled, held out her left hand.

"No, no! The right!" he cried. The ring was of massive silver; it fitted her index finger. She was immensely pleased.

"But you are too nice. What can I give you?" She tried to look pained and helpless.

"The pleasure of having a true European friend," said Mjid gravely.

"But I'm American," she objected.

254

"All the better."

Ghazi was looking silently toward the distant Riffian mountains. Prophetically he raised his arm with its silk sleeve blowing in the hot wind, and pointed across the cracked mud fields.

"Down that way," he said softly, "there is a village where all the people are mad. I rode there once with one of my father's assistants. It's the water they drink."

The carriage lurched. They were climbing. Below them the sea began to spread out, a poster blue. The tops of the mountains across the water in Spain rose above the haze. Mjid started to sing. Ghazi covered his ears with his fat dimpled hands.

The summer villa was inhabited by a family with a large number of children. After dismissing the carriage driver and instructing him not to return, since he wanted to walk back down, Mjid took his guests on a tour of inspection of the grounds. There were a good many wells; Ghazi had certainly seen these countless times before, but he stopped as if in amazement at each well as they inspected it, and whispered: "Think of it!"

On a rocky elevation above the farm stood a great olive tree. There they spread the food, and ate slowly. The Berber woman in charge of the farm had given them several loaves of native bread, and olives and oranges. Ghazi wanted Mjid to decline this food.

"A real European picnic is what we should have."

But she insisted they take the oranges.

The opening of the ham was observed in religious silence. It was no time before both cans were consumed. Then they attacked the wine.

255

"If my father could see us," said Ghazi, draining a tin cup of it. "Ham and wine!"

Mjid drank a cup, making a grimace of distaste. He lay back, his arms folded behind his head. "Now that I've finished, I can tell you that I don't like wine, and everyone knows that ham is filthy. But I hate our severe conventions."

She suspected that he had rehearsed the little speech.

Ghazi was continuing to drink the wine. He finished a bottle all by himself, and excusing himself to his companions, took off his *gandoura*. Soon he was asleep.

"You see?" whispered Mjid. He took her hand and pulled her to her feet. "Now we can go to the rose garden." He led her along the ledge, and down a path away from the villa. It was very narrow; thorny bushes scraped their arms as they squeezed through.

"In America we call walking like this going Indian fashion," she remarked.

"Ah, yes?" said Mjid. "I'm going to tell you about Ghazi. One of his father's women was a Senegalese slave, poor thing. She made Ghazi and six other brothers for her husband, and they all look like Negroes."

"Don't you consider Negroes as good as you?" she asked.

"It's not a question of being as good, but of being as beautiful," he answered firmly.

They had come out into a clearing on the hillside. He stopped and looked closely at her. He pulled his shirt off over his head. His body was white.

"My brother has blond hair," he said with pride. Then con-

256

fusedly he put the shirt back on and laid his arm about her shoulder. "You are beautiful because you have blue eyes. But even some of us have blue eyes. In any case, you are *magnificent!*" He started ahead again, singing a song in Spanish.

> *"Es pa' mi la màs bonita,*
> *La mujer que yo màs quiero . . ."*

They came to a cactus fence, with a small gate of twisted barbed wire. A yellow puppy rushed up to the gate and barked delightedly.

"Don't be afraid," said Mjid, although she had given no sign of fear. "You are my sister. He never bites the family." Continuing down a dusty path between stunted palms which were quite dried-up and yellow, they came presently to a primitive bower made of bamboo stalks. In the center was a tiny bench beside a wall, and around the edges several dessicated rose plants grew out of the parched earth. From these he picked two bright red roses, placing one in her hair and the other under his *chechia*, so that it fell like a lock of hair over his forehead. The thick growth of thorny vines climbing over the trellises cast a shadow on the bench. They sat awhile in silence in the shade.

Mjid seemed lost in thought. Finally he took her hand. "I'm thinking," he said in a whisper. "When one is far away from the town, in one's own garden, far from everyone, sitting where it is quiet, one always thinks. Or one plays music," he added.

Suddenly she was conscious of the silence of the afternoon. Far in the distance she heard the forlorn crow of a cock. It

257

made her feel that the sun would soon set, that all creation was on the brink of a great and final sunset. She abandoned herself to sadness, which crept over her like a chill.

Mjid jumped up. "If Ghazi wakes!" he cried. He pulled her arm impatiently. "Come, we'll take a walk!" They hurried down the path, through the gate, and across a bare stony plateau toward the edge of the mountain.

"There's a little valley nearby where the brother of the caretaker lives. We can go there and get some water."

"Way down there?" she said, although she was encouraged by the possibility of escaping from Ghazi for the afternoon. Her mood of sadness had not left her. They were running downhill, leaping from one rock to the next. Her rose fell off and she had to hold it in her hand.

The caretaker's brother was cross-eyed. He gave them some foul-smelling water in an earthen jug.

"Is it from the well?" she inquired under her breath to Mjid.

His face darkened with displeasure. "When you're offered something to drink, even if it's poison, you should drink it and thank the man who offers it."

"Ah," she said. "So it is poison. I thought so."

Mjid seized the jug from the ground between them, and taking it to the edge of the cliff, flung it down with elegant anger. The cross-eyed man protested, and then he laughed. Mjid did not look at him, but walked into the house and began a conversation with some of the Berber women inside, leaving her to face the peasant alone and stammer her dozen words of Arabic with him. The afternoon sun was hot, and the idea of some water to drink had completely filled her mind. She sat down perversely with her back to the view and played with pebbles, feeling utterly useless and absurd. The cross-eyed man continued to laugh at intervals, as if it provided an acceptable substitute for conversation.

When Mjid finally came out, all his ill-humor had vanished. He put out his hand to help her up, and said: "Come, we'll climb back up and have tea at the farm. I have my own room there. I decorated it myself. You'll look at it and tell me if you have as pleasant a room in your house in America for drinking tea." They set off, up the mountain.

The woman at the villa was obsequious. She fanned the charcoal fire and fetched water from the well. The children were playing a mysterious, quiet game at a far end of the enclosure. Mjid led her into the house, through several dim rooms, and finally into one that seemed the last in the series. It was cooler, and a bit darker than the others.

"You'll see," said Mjid, clapping his hands twice. Nothing happened. He called peevishly. Presently the woman entered. She smoothed the mattresses on the floor, and opened the blinds of the one small window, which gave onto the sea. Then she lit several candles which she stuck onto the tile floor, and went out.

His guest stepped to the window. "Can you ever hear the sea here?"

"Certainly not. It's about six kilometers away."

"But it looks as though you could drop a stone into it," she objected, hearing the false inflection of her voice; she was not

259

interested in the conversation, she had the feeling that everything had somehow gone wrong.

"What am I doing here? I have no business here. I said I
wouldn't come." The idea of such a picnic had so completely
coincided with some unconscious desire she had harbored for
many years. To be free, out-of-doors, with some young man she
did not know—*could* not know—that was probably the important part of the dream. For if she could not know him, he could
not know her. She swung the little blind shut and hooked it. A
second later she opened it again and looked out at the vast expanse of water growing dim in the twilight.

Mjid was watching her. "You are crazy," he said at last de-
spairingly. "You find yourself here in this beautiful room. You
are my guest. You should be happy. Ghazi has already left to go
to town. A friend came by with a horse and he got a ride in.
You could lie down, sing, drink tea, you could be happy with
me . . ." He stopped, and she saw that he was deeply upset.

"What's the matter? What's the matter?" she said very quickly.

He sighed dramatically; perhaps it was a genuine sigh. She
thought: "There is nothing wrong. It should have been a man,
not a boy, that's all." It did not occur to her to ask herself:
"But would I have come if it had been a man?" She looked at
him tenderly, and decided that his face was probably the most
intense and beautiful she had ever seen. She murmured a word
without quite knowing what it was.

"What?" he said.

She repeated it: "Incredible."

He smiled inscrutably.

They were interrupted by the sound of the woman's bare feet slapping the floor. She had a tremendous tray bearing the teapot and its accessories.

While he made the tea, Mjid kept glancing at her as if to assure himself that she was still there. She sat perfectly still on one of the mattresses, waiting.

"You know," he said slowly, "If I could earn money I'd go away tomorrow to wherever I could earn it. I finish school this year anyway, and my brother hasn't the money to send me to a Medersa at Fez. But even if he had it, I wouldn't go. I always stay away from school. Only my brother gets very angry."

"What do you do instead? Go bathing?"

He laughed scornfully, sampled the tea, poured it back into the pot, and sat up on his haunches. "In another minute it will be ready. Bathing? Ah, my friend, it has to be something important for me to risk my brother's anger. I make love those days, all day long!"

"Really? You mean all day?" She was thoughtful.

"All day and most of the night. Oh, I can tell you it's marvelous, magnificent. I have a little room," he crawled over to her and put his hand on her knee, looking up into her face with an eagerness born of faith. "A room my family knows nothing about, in the Casbah. And my little friend is twelve. She is like the sun, soft, beautiful, lovely. Here, take your tea." He sipped from his glass noisily, smacking his lips.

"All day long," she reflected aloud, settling back against the cushions.

"Oh, yes. But I'll tell you a secret. You have to eat as much

261

as you can. But that's not so hard. You're that much hungrier."

"Yes, of course," she said. A little gust of wind blew along the floor and the candles flickered.

"How good it is to have tea and then lie down to rest!" he exclaimed, pouring her more tea and stretching out beside her on the mattress. She made a move as if to spring up, then lay still.

He went on. "It's curious that I never met you last year."

"I wasn't in town very much. Only evenings. And then I was at the beach. I lived on the mountain."

He sat up. "On this mountain here? And I never saw you! Oh, what bad luck!"

She described the house, and since he insisted, told him the rent she had paid. He was ferociously indignant. "For that miserable house that hasn't even a good well? You had to send your Mohammed down the road for water! I know all about that house. My poor friend, you were robbed! If I ever see that dirty bandit I'll smash his face. I'll demand the money you paid him, and we'll make a trip together." He paused. "I mean, I'll give it to you of course, and you can decide what you want to do with it."

As he finished speaking he held up her handbag, opened it, and took out her fountain pen. "It's a beautiful one," he murmured. "Do you have many?"

"It's the only one."

"Magnificent!" He tossed it back in and laid the bag on the floor.

Settling against the pillows he ruminated. "Perhaps some day

262

I shall go to America, and then you can invite me to your house for tea. Each year we'll come back to Morocco and see our friends and bring back cinema stars and presents from New York."

What he was saying seemed so ridiculous to her that she did not bother to answer. She wanted to ask him about the twelve-year-old girl, but she could find no excuse for introducing the subject again.

"You're not happy?" He squeezed her arm.

She raised herself to listen. With the passing of the day the countryside had attained complete silence. From the distance she could hear a faint but clear voice singing. She looked at Mjid.

"The *muezzin?* You can hear it from here?"

"Of course. It's not so far to the Marshan. What good is a country house where you can't hear the *muezzin?* You might as well live in the Sahara."

"Sh. I want to listen."

"It's a good voice, isn't it? They have the strongest voices in the world."

"It always makes me sad."

"Because you're not of the faith."

She reflected a minute and said: "I think that's true." She was about to add: "But your faith says women have no souls." Instead she rose from the mattress and smoothed her hair. The *muezzin* had ceased. She felt quite chilled. "This is over," she said to herself. They stumbled down the dark road into town, saying very little on the way.

He took her to her small hotel. The cable she had vaguely expected for weeks was there. They climbed the stairs to her room, the concierge looking suspiciously after them. Once in the room, she opened the envelope. Mjid had thrown himself onto the bed.

"I'm leaving for Paris tomorrow."

His face darkened, and he shut his eyes for an instant. "You must go away? All right. Let me give you my address." He pulled out his wallet, searched for a piece of paper, and finding none, took a calling card someone had given him, and carefully wrote.

"Fuente Nueva," he said slowly as he formed the letters. "It's my little room. I'll look every day to see if there's a letter."

She had a swift vision of him, reading a letter in a window flooded with sunshine, above the city's terraced roofs, and behind him, in the darkness of the room, with a face wise beyond its years, a complacent child waiting.

He gave her the card. Underneath the address he had written the word "Incredible," enclosed in quotation marks and under-lined twice. She glanced quickly to see his face, but it betrayed nothing.

Below them the town was blue, the bay almost black.

"The lighthouse," said Mjid.

"It's flashing," she observed.

He turned and walked to the door. "Good-bye," he said. "You will come back." He left the door open and went down the stairs. She stood perfectly still and finally moved her head up and down a few times, as if thoughtfully answering a question. Through the open window in the hallway she heard his rapid footsteps on the gravel in the garden. They grew fainter.

She looked at the bed; at the edge, ready to fall to the floor, was the white card where she had tossed it. She wanted more than anything to lie down and rest. Instead, she went downstairs into the cramped little salon and sat in the corner looking at old copies of *L'Illustration*. It was almost an hour before dinner would be served.

by the water

The melting snow dripped from the balconies. People hurried through the little street that always smelled of frying fish. Now and then a stork swooped low, dragging his sticklike legs below him. The small gramophones scraped day and night behind the walls of the shop where young Amar worked and lived. There were few spots in the city where the snow was ever cleared away, and this was not one of them. So it gathered all through the winter months, piling up in front of the shop doors.

But now it was late winter; the sun was warmer. Spring was on the way, to confuse the heart and melt the snow. Amar, being alone in the world, decided it was time to visit a neighboring city where his father had once told him some cousins lived.

Early in the morning he went to the bus station. It was still

266

dark, and the empty bus came in while he was drinking hot coffee. The road wound through the mountains all the way.

When he arrived in the other city it was already dark. Here the snow was even deeper in the streets, and it was colder. Because he had not wanted to, Amar had not foreseen this, and it annoyed him to be forced to wrap his burnous closely about him as he left the bus station. It was an unfriendly town; he could tell that immediately. Men walked with their heads bent forward, and if they brushed against a passer-by they did not so much as look up. Excepting the principal street, which had an arc-light every few meters, there seemed to be no other illumination, and the alleys that led off on either side lay in utter blackness; the white-clad figures that turned into them disappeared straightway.

"A bad town," said Amar under his breath. He felt proud to be coming from a better and larger city, but his pleasure was mingled with anxiety about the night to be passed in this inimical place. He abandoned the idea of trying to find his cousins before morning, and set about looking for a fondouk or a bath where he might sleep until daybreak.

Only a short distance ahead the street-lighting system terminated. Beyond, the street appeared to descend sharply and lose itself in darkness. The snow was uniformly deep here, and not cleared away in patches as it had been nearer the bus station. He puckered his lips and blew his breath ahead of him in little clouds of steam. As he passed over into the unlighted district he heard a few languid notes being strummed on an oud. The music came from a doorway on his left. He paused and listened.

Someone approached the doorway from the other direction and inquired, apparently of the man with the oud, if it was "too late."

"No," the musician answered, and he played several more notes.

Amar went over to the door.

"Is there still time?" he said.

"Yes."

He stepped inside the door. There was no light, but he could feel warm air blowing upon his face from the corridor to the right. He walked ahead, letting his hand run along the damp wall beside him. Soon he came into a large dimly lit room with a tile floor. Here and there, at various angles, figures lay asleep, wrapped in gray blankets. In a far corner a group of men, partially dressed, sat about a burning brazier, drinking tea and talking in low tones. Amar slowly approached them, taking care not to step on the sleepers.

The air was oppressively warm and moist.

"Where is the bath?" said Amar.

"Down there," answered one of the men in the group, without even looking up. He indicated the dark corner to his left. And, indeed, now that Amar considered it, it seemed to him that a warm current of air came up from that part of the room. He went in the direction of the dark corner, undressed, and leaving his clothes in a neat pile on a piece of straw matting, walked toward the warmth. He was thinking of the misfortune he had encountered in arriving in this town at nightfall, and he wondered if his clothes would be molested during his absence.

He wore his money in a leather pouch which hung on a string about his neck. Feeling vaguely of the purse under his chin, he turned around to look once again at his clothing. No one seemed to have noticed him as he undressed. He went on. It would not do to seem too distrustful. He would be embroiled immediately in a quarrel which could only end badly for him.

A little boy rushed out of the darkness toward him, calling: "Follow me, Sidi, I shall lead you to the bath." He was extremely dirty and ragged, and looked rather more like a midget than a child. Leading the way, he chattered as they went down the slippery, warm steps in the dark. "You will call for Brahim when you want your tea? You're a stranger. You have much money. . . ."

Amar cut him short. "You'll get your coins when you come to wake me in the morning. Not tonight."

"But, Sidi! I'm not allowed in the big room. I stay in the doorway and show gentlemen down to the bath. Then I go back to the doorway. I can't wake you."

"I'll sleep near the doorway. It's warmer there, in any case."

"Lazrag will be angry and terrible things will happen. I'll never get home again, or if I do I might be a bird so my parents will not know me. That's what Lazrag does when he gets angry."

"Lazrag?"

"It is his place here. You'll see him. He never goes out. If he did the sun would burn him in one second, like a straw in the fire. He would fall down in the street burned black the minute he stepped out of the door. He was born down here in the grotto."

Amar was not paying strict attention to the boy's babble.

269

They were descending a wet stone ramp, putting one foot before the other slowly in the dark, and feeling the rough wall carefully as they went. There was the sound of splashing water and voices ahead.

"This is a strange *hammam*," said Amar. "Is there a pool full of water?"

"A pool! You've never heard of Lazrag's grotto? It goes on forever, and it's made of deep warm water."

As the boy spoke, they came out onto a stone balcony a few meters above the beginning of a very large pool, lighted beneath where they stood by two bare electric bulbs, and stretching away through the dimness into utter dark beyond. Parts of the roof hung down, "Like gray icicles," thought Amar, as he looked about in wonder. But it was very warm down here. A slight pall of steam lay above the surface of the water, rising constantly in wisps toward the rocky ceiling. A man dripping with water ran past them and dove in. Several more were swimming about in the brighter region near the lights, never straying beyond into the gloom. The plunging and shouting echoed violently beneath the low ceiling.

Amar was not a good swimmer. He turned to ask the boy: "Is it deep?" but he had already disappeared back up the ramp. He stepped backward and leaned against the rock wall. There was a low chair to his right, and in the murky light it seemed to him that a small figure was close beside it. He watched the bathers for a few minutes. Those standing at the edge of the water soaped themselves assiduously; those in the water swam to and fro in a short radius below the lights. Suddenly a deep voice

spoke close beside him. He looked down as he heard it say: "Who
are you?"

The creature's head was large; its body was small and it had no
legs or arms. The lower part of the trunk ended in two flipper-
like pieces of flesh. From the shoulders grew short pincers. It was
a man, and it was looking up at him from the floor where it
rested.

"Who are you?" it said again, and its tone was unmistakably
hostile.

Amar hesitated. "I came to bathe and sleep," he said at
last.

"Who gave you permission?"

"The man at the entrance."

"Get out. I don't know you."

Amar was filled with anger. He looked down with scorn at the
little being, and stepped away from it to join the men washing
themselves by the water's edge. But more swiftly than he
moved, it managed to throw itself along the floor until it was
in front of him, when it raised itself again and spoke.

"You think you can bathe when I tell you to get out?" It
laughed shortly, a thin sound, but deep in pitch. Then it moved
closer and pushed its head against Amar's legs. He drew back his
foot and kicked the head, not very hard, but with enough
firmness to send the body off balance. The thing rolled over in
silence, making efforts with its neck to keep from reaching the
edge of the platform. The men all looked up. An expression of
fear was on their faces. As the little creature went over the
edge it yelled. The splash was like that of a large stone. Two

men already in the water swam quickly to the spot. The others
started up after Amar, shouting: "He hit Lazrag!"

Bewildered and frightened, Amar turned and ran back to the
ramp. In the blackness he stumbled upward. Part of the wall
scraped his bare thigh. The voices behind him grew louder and
more excited.

He reached the room where he had left his clothing. Nothing
had changed. The men still sat by the brazier talking. Quickly
he snatched the pile of garments, and struggling into his
burnous, he ran to the door that led into the street, the rest
of his clothes tucked under his arm. The man in the doorway
with the oud looked at him with a startled face and called after
him. Amar ran up the street barelegged toward the center of
the town. He wanted to be where there were some bright
lights. The few people walking in the street paid him no attention. When he got to the bus station it was closed. He went
into a small park opposite, where the iron bandstand stood deep
in snow. There on a cold stone bench he sat and dressed himself
as unostentatiously as possible, using his burnous as a screen. He
was shivering, reflecting bitterly upon his poor luck, and wishing he had not left his own town, when a small figure approached
him in the half-light.

"Sidi," it said, "come with me. Lazrag is hunting for you."

"Where to?" said Amar, recognizing the urchin from the bath.

"My grandfather's."

The boy began to run, motioning to him to follow. They
went through alleys and tunnels, into the most congested part
of the town. The boy did not bother to look back, but Amar

did. They finally paused before a small door at the side of a narrow passageway. The boy knocked vigorously. From within came a cracked voice calling: *"Chkoun?"*

"Annah! Brahim!" cried the boy.

With great deliberation the old man swung the door open and stood looking at Amar.

"Come in," he finally said; and shutting the door behind them he led them through the courtyard filled with goats into an inner room where a feeble light was flickering. He peered sternly into Amar's face.

"He wants to stay here tonight," explained the boy.

"Does he think this is a *fondouk?"*

"He has money," said Brahim hopefully.

"Money!" the old man cried with scorn. "That's what you learn in the *hammam!* How to steal money! How to take money from men's purses! Now you bring them here! What do you want me to do? Kill him and get his purse for you? Is he too clever for you? You can't get it by yourself? Is that it?" The old man's voice had risen to a scream and he gestured in his mounting excitement. He sat down on a cushion with difficulty and was silent a moment.

"Money," he said again, finally. "Let him go to a *fondouk* or a bath. Why aren't you at the *hammam?"* He looked suspiciously at his grandson.

The boy clutched at his friend's sleeve. "Come," he said, pulling him out into the courtyard.

"Take him to the *hammam!"* yelled the old man. "Let him spend his money there!"

Together they went back into the dark streets.

"Lazrag is looking for you," said the boy. "Twenty men will be going through the town to catch you and take you back to him. He is very angry and he will change you into a bird."

"Where are we going now?" asked Amar gruffly. He was cold and very tired, and although he did not really believe the boy's story, he wished he were out of the unfriendly town.

"We must walk as far as we can from here. All night. In the morning we'll be far away in the mountains, and they won't find us. We can go to your city."

Amar did not answer. He was pleased that the boy wanted to stay with him, but he did not think it fitting to say so. They followed one crooked street downhill until all the houses had been left behind and they were in the open country. The path led down a narrow valley presently, and joined the highway at one end of a small bridge. Here the snow was packed down by the passage of vehicles, and they found it much easier to walk along.

When they had been going down the road for perhaps an hour in the increasing cold, a great truck came rolling by. It stopped just ahead and the driver, an Arab, offered them a ride on top. They climbed up and made a nest of some empty sacks. The boy was very happy to be rushing through the air in the dark night. Mountains and stars whirled by above his head and the truck made a powerful roaring noise as it traveled along the empty highway.

"Lazrag has found us and changed us both into birds," he cried

274

when he could no longer keep his delight to himself. "No one will ever know us again."

Amar grunted and went to sleep. But the boy watched the sky and the trees and the cliffs for a long time before he closed his eyes.

Some time before morning the truck stopped by a spring for water.

In the stillness the boy awoke. A cock crowed in the distance, and then he heard the driver pouring water. The cock crowed again, a sad, thin arc of sound away in the cold murk of the plain. It was not yet dawn. He buried himself deeper in the pile of sacks and rags, and felt the warmth of Amar as he slept.

When daylight came they were in another part of the land. There was no snow. Instead, the almond trees were in flower on the hillsides as they sped past. The road went on unwinding as it dropped lower and lower, until suddenly it came out of the hills upon a spot below which lay a great glittering emptiness. Amar and the boy watched it and said to each other that it must be the sea, shining in the morning light.

The spring wind pushed the foam from the waves along the beach; it rippled Amar's and the boy's garments landward as they walked by the edge of the water. Finally they found a sheltered spot between rocks, and undressed, leaving the clothes on the sand. The boy was afraid to go into the water, and found enough excitement in letting the waves break about his legs, but Amar tried to drag him out further.

"No, no!"

"Come," Amar urged him.

Amar looked down. Approaching him sideways was an enormous crab which had crawled out from a dark place in the rocks. He leapt back in terror, lost his balance, and fell heavily, striking his head against one of the great boulders. The boy stood perfectly still watching the animal make its cautious way toward Amar through the tips of the breaking waves. Amar lay without moving, rivulets of water and sand running down his face. As the crab reached his feet, the boy bounded into the air, and in a voice made hoarse by desperation, screamed: "Lazrag!"

The crab scuttled swiftly behind the rock and disappeared. The boy's face became radiant. He rushed to Amar, lifted his head above a newly breaking wave, and slapped his cheeks excitedly.

"Amar! I made him go away!" he shouted. "I saved you!"

If he did not move, the pain was not too great. So Amar lay still, feeling the warm sunlight, the soft water washing over him, and the cool, sweet wind that came in from the sea. He also felt the boy trembling in his effort to hold his head above the waves, and he heard him saying many times over: "I saved you, Amar."

After a long time he answered: "Yes."

the delicate prey

There were three Filala who sold leather in Tabelbala—two brothers and the young son of their sister. The two older merchants were serious, bearded men who liked to engage in complicated theological discussions during the slow passage of the hot hours in their *hanoute* near the market-place; the youth naturally occupied himself almost exclusively with the black-skinned girls in the small *quartier réservé*. There was one who seemed more desirable than the others, so that he was a little sorry when the older men announced that soon they would all leave for Tessalit. But nearly every town has its *quartier*, and Driss was reasonably certain of being able to have any lovely resident of any *quartier*, whatever her present emotional entanglements; thus his chagrin at hearing of the projected departure was short-lived.

The three Filala waited for the cold weather before starting out for Tessalit. Because they wanted to get there quickly they chose the westernmost trail, which is also the one leading through the most remote regions, contiguous to the lands of the plundering Reguibat tribes. It was a long time since the uncouth mountain men had swept down from the *hammada* upon a caravan; most people were of the opinion that since the war of the Sarrho they had lost the greater part of their arms and ammunition, and, more important still, their spirit. And a tiny group of three men and their camels could scarcely awaken the envy of the Reguibat, traditionally rich with loot from all Rio de Oro and Mauretania.

Their friends in Tabelbala, most of them other Filali leather merchants, walked beside them sadly as far as the edge of the town; then they bade them farewell, and watched them mount their camels to ride off slowly toward the bright horizon.

"If you meet any Reguibat, keep them ahead of you!" they called.

The danger lay principally in the territory they would reach only three or four days' journey from Tabelbala; after a week the edge of the land haunted by the Reguibat would be left entirely behind. The weather was cool save at midday. They took turns sitting guard at night; when Driss stayed awake he brought out a small flute whose piercing notes made the older uncle frown with annoyance, so that he asked him to go and sit at some distance from the sleeping-blankets. All night he sat playing whatever sad songs he could call to mind; the bright ones in his opinion belonged to the *quartier*, where one was never alone.

When the uncles kept watch, they sat quietly, staring ahead of them into the night. There were just the three of them.

And then one day a solitary figure appeared, moving toward them across the lifeless plain from the west. One man on a camel; there was no sign of any others, although they scanned the wasteland in every direction. They stopped for a while; he altered his course slightly. They went ahead; he changed it again. There was no doubt that he wanted to speak with them.

"Let him come," grumbled the older uncle, glaring about the empty horizon once more. "We each have a gun."

Driss laughed. To him it seemed absurd even to admit the possibility of trouble from one lone man.

When finally the figure arrived within calling distance, it hailed them in a voice like a muezzin's: *"S'l'm aleikoum!"* They halted, but did not dismount, and waited for the man to draw nearer. Soon he called again; this time the older uncle replied, but the distance was still too great for his voice to carry, and the man did not hear his greeting. Presently he was close enough for them to see that he did not wear Reguiba attire. They muttered to one another: "He comes from the north, not the west." And they all felt glad. However, even when he came up beside them they remained on the camels, bowing solemnly from where they sat, and always searching in the new face and in the garments below it for some false note which might reveal

279

the possible truth—that the man was a scout for the Reguibat, who would be waiting up on the *hammada* only a few hours distant, or even now moving parallel to the trail, closing in upon them in such a manner that they would not arrive at a point within visibility until after dusk.

Certainly the stranger himself was no Reguiba; he was quick and jolly, with light skin and very little beard. It occurred to Driss that he did not like his small, active eyes which seemed to take in everything and give out nothing, but this passing reaction became only a part of the general initial distrust, all of which was dissipated when they learned that the man was a Moungari. Moungar is a holy place in that part of the world, and its few residents are treated with respect by the pilgrims who go to visit the ruined shrine nearby.

The newcomer took no pains to hide the fear he had felt at being alone in the region, or the pleasure it gave him to be now with three other men. They all dismounted and made tea to seal their friendship, the Moungari furnishing the charcoal.

During the third round of glasses he made the suggestion that since he was going more or less in their direction he accompany them as far as Taoudeni. His bright black eyes darting from one Filali to the other, he explained that he was an excellent shot, that he was certain he could supply them all with some good gazelle meat en route, or at least an *aoudad*. The Filala considered; the oldest finally said: "Agreed." Even if the Moungari turned out to have not quite the hunting prowess he claimed for himself, there would be four of them on the voyage instead of three.

Two mornings later, in the mighty silence of the rising sun, the Moungari pointed at the low hills that lay beside them to the east: "*Timma.* I know this land. Wait here. If you hear me shoot, then come, because that will mean there are gazelles."

The Moungari went off on foot, climbing up between the boulders and disappearing behind the nearest crest. "He trusts us," thought the Filala. "He has left his *mehari,* his blankets, his packs." They said nothing, but each knew that the others were thinking the same as he, and they all felt warmly toward the stranger. They sat waiting in the early morning chill while the camels grumbled.

It seemed unlikely that there would prove to be any gazelles in the region, but if there should be any, and the Moungari were as good a hunter as he claimed to be, then there was a chance they would have a *mechoui* of gazelle that evening, and that would be very fine.

Slowly the sun mounted in the hard blue sky. One camel lumbered up and went off, hoping to find a dead thistle or a bush between the rocks, something left over from a year when rain might have fallen. When it had disappeared, Driss went in search of it and drove it back to the others, shouting: "*Hut!*"

He sat down. Suddenly there came a shot, a long empty interval, and then another shot. The sounds were fairly distant, but perfectly clear in the absolute silence. The older brother said: "I shall go. Who knows? There may be many gazelles."

He clambered up the rocks, his gun in his hand, and was gone.

Again they waited. When the shots sounded this time, they came from two guns.

281

"Perhaps they have killed one!" Driss cried.

"*Yemkin*. With Allah's aid," replied his uncle, rising and taking up his gun. "I want to try my hand at this."

Driss was disappointed: he had hoped to go himself. If only he had got up a moment ago, it might have been possible, but even so it was likely that he would have been left behind to watch the *mehara*. In any case, now it was too late; his uncle had spoken.

"Good."

His uncle went off singing a song from Tafilalet: it was about date-palms and hidden smiles. For several minutes Driss heard snatches of the song, as the melody reached the high notes. Then the sound was lost in the enveloping silence.

He waited. The sun began to be very hot. He covered his head with his burnous. The camels looked at each other stupidly, craning their necks, baring their brown and yellow teeth. He thought of playing his flute, but it did not seem the right moment: he was too restless, too eager to be up there with his gun, crouching behind the rocks, stalking the delicate prey. He thought of Tessalit and wondered what it would be like. Full of blacks and Touareg, certainly more lively than Tabelbala, because of the road that passed through it. There was a shot. He waited for others, but no more came this time. Again he imagined himself there among the boulders, taking aim at a fleeing beast. He pulled the trigger, the animal fell. Others appeared, and he got them all. In the dark the travelers sat around the fire gorging themselves with the rich roasted flesh, their faces gleaming with grease. Everyone was happy, and even the Moungari admitted that the young Filali was the best hunter of them all.

In the advancing heat he dozed, his mind playing over a landscape made of soft thighs and small hard breasts rising like sand dunes; wisps of song floated like clouds in the sky, and the air was thick with the taste of fat gazelle meat.

He sat up and looked around quickly. The camels lay with their necks stretched along the ground in front of them. Nothing had changed. He stood up, uneasily scanned the stony landscape. While he had slept, a hostile presence had entered into his consciousness. Translating into thought what he already sensed, he cried out. Since first he had seen those small, active eyes he had felt mistrust of their owner, but the fact that his uncles had accepted him had pushed suspicion away into the dark of his mind. Now, unleashed in his slumber, it had bounded back. He turned toward the hot hillside and looked intently between the boulders, into the black shadows. In memory he heard again the shots up among the rocks, and he knew what they had meant. Catching his breath in a sob, he ran to mount his *mehari*, forced it up, and already had gone several hundred paces before he was aware of what he was doing. He stopped the animal to sit quietly a moment, glancing back at the campsite with fear and indecision. If his uncles were dead, then there was nothing to do but get out into the open desert as quickly as possible, away from the rocks that could hide the Moungari while he took aim.

And so, not knowing the way to Tessalit, and without sufficient food or water, he started ahead, lifting one hand from time to time to wipe away the tears.

For two or three hours he continued that way, scarcely noticing where the *mehari* walked. All at once he sat erect, uttered an oath against himself, and in a fury turned the beast around. At that very moment his uncles might be seated in the camp with the Moungari, preparing a *mechoui* and a fire, sadly asking themselves why their nephew had deserted them. Or perhaps one would already have set out in search of him. There would be no possible excuse for his conduct, which had been the result of an absurd terror. As he thought about it, his anger against himself mounted: he had behaved in an unforgivable manner. Noon had passed; the sun was in the west. It would be late when he got back. At the prospect of the inevitable reproaches and the mocking laughter that would greet him, he felt his face grow hot with shame, and he kicked the *mehari's* flanks viciously.

A good while before he arrived at the camp he heard singing. This surprised him. He halted and listened: the voice was too far away to be identified, but Driss felt certain it was the Moungari's. He continued around the side of the hill to a spot in full view of the camels. The singing stopped, leaving silence. Some of the packs had been loaded back on to the beasts, preparatory to setting out. The sun had sunk low, and the shadows of the rocks were stretched out along the earth. There was no sign that they had caught any game. He called out, ready to dismount. Almost at the same instant there was a shot from very nearby, and he heard the small rushing sound of a bullet go past his head. He seized his gun. There was another shot, a sharp pain in his arm, and his gun slipped to the ground.

For a moment he sat there holding his arm, dazed. Then

swiftly he leapt down and remained crouching among the stones, reaching out with his good arm for the gun. As he touched it, there was a third shot, and the rifle moved along the ground a few inches toward him in a small cloud of dust. He drew back his hand and looked at it: it was dark and blood dripped from it. At that moment the Moungari bounded across the open space between them. Before Driss could rise the man was upon him, had pushed him back down to the ground with the barrel of his rifle. The untroubled sky lay above; the Moungari glanced up at it defiantly. He straddled the supine youth, thrusting the gun into his neck just below the chin, and under his breath he said: "Filali dog!"

Driss stared up at him with a certain curiosity. The Moungari had the upper hand; Driss could only wait. He looked at the face in the sun's light, and discovered a peculiar intensity there. He knew the expression: it comes from hashish. Carried along on its hot fumes, a man can escape very far from the world of meaning. To avoid the malevolent face he rolled his eyes from side to side. There was only the fading sky. The gun was choking him a little. He whispered: "Where are my uncles?"

The Moungari pushed harder against his throat with the gun, leaned partially over and with one hand ripped away his *serouelles*, so that he lay naked from the waist down, squirming a little as he felt the cold stones beneath him.

Then the Moungari drew forth rope and bound his feet. Taking two steps to his head, he abruptly faced in the other direction, and thrust the gun into his navel. Still with one hand he slipped the remaining garments off over the youth's head and

285

lashed his wrists together. With an old barber's razor he cut off the superfluous rope. During this time Driss called his uncles by name, loudly, first one and then the other.

The man moved and surveyed the young body lying on the stones. He ran his finger along the razor's blade; a pleasant excitement took possession of him. He stepped over, looked down, and saw the sex that sprouted from the base of the belly. Not entirely conscious of what he was doing, he took it in one hand and brought his other arm down with the motion of a reaper wielding a sickle. It was swiftly severed. A round, dark hole was left, flush with the skin; he stared a moment, blankly. Driss was screaming. The muscles all over his body stood out, moved.

Slowly the Moungari smiled, showing his teeth. He put his hand on the hard belly and smoothed the skin. Then he made a small vertical incision there, and using both hands, studiously stuffed the loose organ in until it disappeared.

As he was cleaning his hands in the sand, one of the camels uttered a sudden growling gurgle. The Moungari leapt up and wheeled about savagely, holding his razor high in the air. Then, ashamed of his nervousness, feeling that Driss was watching and mocking him, (although the youth's eyes were unseeing with pain) he kicked him over on to his stomach where he lay making small spasmodic movements. And as the Moungari followed these with his eyes, a new idea came to him. It would be pleasant to inflict an ultimate indignity upon the young Filali. He threw himself down; this time he was vociferous and leisurely in his enjoyment. Eventually he slept.

At dawn he awoke and reached for his razor, lying on the

ground nearby. Driss moaned faintly. The Moungari turned him over and pushed the blade back and forth with a sawing motion into his neck until he was certain he had severed the windpipe. Then he rose, walked away, and finished the loading of the camels he had started the day before. When this was done he spent a good while dragging the body over to the base of the hill and concealing it there among the rocks.

In order to transport the Filala's merchandise to Tessalit (for in Taoudeni there would be no buyers) it was necessary to take their *mehara* with him. It was nearly fifty days later when he arrived. Tessalit is a small town. When the Moungari began to show the leather around, an old Filali living there, whom the people called Ech Chibani, got wind of his presence. As a prospective buyer he came to examine the hides, and the Moungari was unwise enough to let him see them. Filali leather is unmistakable, and only the Filala buy and sell it in quantity. Ech Chibani knew the Moungari had come by it illicitly, but he said nothing. When a few days later another caravan arrived from Tabelbala with friends of the three Filala who asked after them and showed great distress on hearing that they never had arrived, the old man went to the Tribunal. After some difficulty he found a Frenchman who was willing to listen to him. The next day the Commandant and two subordinates paid the Moungari a visit. They asked him how he happened to have the three extra *mehara*, which still carried some of their Filali trappings; his replies took a devious turn. The Frenchmen listened seriously, thanked him, and left. He did not see the Commandant wink at the others as they went out into the street. And so he remained sitting in his courtyard, not knowing that he had been judged and found guilty.

The three Frenchmen went back to the Tribunal where the newly arrived Filali merchants were sitting with Ech Chibani. The story had an old pattern; there was no doubt at all about the Moungari's guilt. "He is yours," said the Commandant. "Do what you like with him."

The Filala thanked him profusely, held a short conference with the aged Chibani, and strode out in a group. When they arrived at the Moungari's dwelling he was making tea. He looked up, and a chill moved along his spine. He began to scream his innocence at them; they said nothing, but at the point of a rifle bound him and tossed him into a corner, where he continued to babble and sob. Quietly they drank the tea he had been brewing, made some more, and went out at twilight. They tied him to one of the *mehara*, and mounting their own, moved in a silent procession (silent save for the Moungari) out through the town gate into the infinite waste land beyond.

Half the night they continued, until they were in a completely unfrequented region of the desert. While he lay raving, bound to the camel, they dug a well-like pit, and when they had finished they lifted him off, still trussed tightly, and stood him in it. Then they filled all the space around his body with sand and stones, until only his head remained above the earth's surface. In the faint light of the new moon his shaved pate without its turban looked rather like a rock. And still he pleaded with them, calling upon Allah and Sidi Ahmed Ben Moussa to witness his innocence. But he might have been singing a song for all the attention they paid to his words. Presently they set off for Tessalit; in no time they were out of hearing.

When they had gone the Moungari fell silent, to wait through the cold hours for the sun that would bring first warmth, then heat, thirst, fire, visions. The next night he did not know where he was, did not feel the cold. The wind blew dust along the ground into his mouth as he sang.

a distant episode

The September sunsets were at their reddest the week the Professor decided to visit Aïn Tadouirt, which is in the warm country. He came down out of the high, flat region in the evening by bus, with two small overnight bags full of maps, sun lotions and medicines. Ten years ago he had been in the village for three days; long enough, however, to establish a fairly firm friendship with a café-keeper, who had written him several times during the first year after his visit, if never since. "Hassan Ramani," the Professor said over and over, as the bus bumped downward through ever warmer layers of air. Now facing the flaming sky in the west, and now facing the sharp mountains, the car followed the dusty trail down the canyons into air which began to smell of other things besides the endless ozone of the heights: orange blossoms, pepper, sun-baked excrement, burning olive oil, rotten fruit. He closed his eyes happily and lived for an instant in a purely olfactory world. The distant past returned—what part of it, he could not decide.

The chauffeur, whose seat the Professor shared, spoke to him without taking his eyes from the road. "*Vous êtes géologue?*"

"A geologist? Ah, no! I'm a linguist."

"There are no languages here. Only dialects."

"Exactly. I'm making a survey of variations on Moghrebi."

The chauffeur was scornful. "Keep on going south," he said. "You'll find some languages you never heard of before."

As they drove through the town gate, the usual swarm of urchins rose up out of the dust and ran screaming beside the bus. The Professor folded his dark glasses, put them in his pocket; and as soon as the vehicle had come to a standstill he jumped out, pushing his way through the indignant boys who clutched at his luggage in vain, and walked quickly into the Grand Hotel Saharien. Out of its eight rooms there were two available—one facing the market and the other, a smaller and cheaper one, giving onto a tiny yard full of refuse and barrels, where two gazelles wandered about. He took the smaller room, and pouring the entire pitcher of water into the tin basin, began to wash the grit from his face and ears. The afterglow was nearly gone from the sky, and the pinkness in objects was disappearing, almost as he watched. He lit the carbide lamp and winced at its odor.

After dinner the Professor walked slowly through the streets to Hassan Ramani's café, whose back room hung hazardously out above the river. The entrance was very low, and he had to bend down slightly to get in. A man was tending the fire. There was one guest sipping tea. The *qaouaji* tried to make him take a seat at the other table in the front room, but the Professor walked airily ahead into the back room and sat down. The moon was shining through the reed latticework and there was not a sound outside but the occasional distant bark of a dog. He changed tables so he could see the river. It was dry, but there was a pool here and there that reflected the bright night sky. The *qaouaji* came in and wiped off the table.

"Does this café still belong to Hassan Ramani?" he asked him in the Moghrebi he had taken four years to learn.

The man replied in bad French: "He is deceased."

"Deceased?" repeated the Professor, without noticing the absurdity of the word. "Really? When?"

"I don't know," said the *qaouaji*. "One tea?"

"Yes. But I don't understand . . ."

The man was already out of the room, fanning the fire. The Professor sat still, feeling lonely, and arguing with himself that to do so was ridiculous. Soon the *qaouaji* returned with the tea, He paid him and gave him an enormous tip, for which he received a grave bow.

"Tell me," he said, as the other started away. "Can one still get those little boxes made from camel udders?"

The man looked angry. "Sometimes the Reguibat bring in those things. We do not buy them here." Then insolently, in Arabic: "And why a camel-udder box?"

"Because I like them," retorted the Professor. And then because he was feeling a little exalted, he added, "I like them so

292

much I want to make a collection of them, and I will pay you ten francs for every one you can get me."

"Khamstache," said the *qaouaji,* opening his left hand rapidly three times in succession.

"Never. Ten."

"Not possible. But wait until later and come with me. You can give me what you like. And you will get camel-udder boxes if there are any."

He went out into the front room, leaving the Professor to drink his tea and listen to the growing chorus of dogs that barked and howled as the moon rose higher into the sky. A group of customers came into the front room and sat talking for an hour or so. When they had left, the *qaouaji* put out the fire and stood in the doorway putting on his burnous. "Come," he said.

Outside in the street there was very little movement. The booths were all closed and the only light came from the moon. An occasional pedestrian passed, and grunted a brief greeting to the *qaouaji.*

"Everyone knows you," said the Professor, to cut the silence between them.

"Yes."

"I wish everyone knew me," said the Professor, before he realized how infantile such a remark must sound.

"No one knows you," said his companion gruffly.

They had come to the other side of the town, on the promontory above the desert, and through a great rift in the wall the Professor saw the white endlessness, broken in the foreground by dark spots of oasis. They walked through the opening and followed a winding road between rocks, downward toward the nearest small forest of palms. The Professor thought: "He may cut my throat. But his café—he would surely be found out."

"Is it far?" he asked, casually.

"Are you tired?" countered the *qaouaji*.

"They are expecting me back at the Hotel Saharien," he lied.

"You can't be there and here," said the *qaouaji*.

The Professor laughed. He wondered if it sounded uneasy to the other.

"Have you owned Ramani's café long?"

"I work there for a friend." The reply made the Professor more unhappy than he had imagined it would.

"Oh. Will you work tomorrow?"

"That is impossible to say."

The Professor stumbled on a stone, and fell, scraping his hand. The *qaouaji* said: "Be careful."

The sweet black odor of rotten meat hung in the air suddenly.

"Agh!" said the Professor, choking. "What is it?"

The *qaouaji* had covered his face with his burnous and did not answer. Soon the stench had been left behind. They were on flat ground. Ahead the path was bordered on each side by a high mud wall. There was no breeze and the palms were quite still, but behind the walls was the sound of running water. Also, the odor of human excrement was almost constant as they walked between the walls.

The Professor waited until he thought it seemed logical for

him to ask with a certain degree of annoyance: "But where are we going?"

"Soon," said the guide, pausing to gather some stones in the ditch.

"Pick up some stones," he advised. "Here are bad dogs."

"Where?" asked the Professor, but he stooped and got three large ones with pointed edges.

They continued very quietly. The walls came to an end and the bright desert lay ahead. Nearby was a ruined marabout, with its tiny dome only half standing, and the front wall entirely destroyed. Behind it were clumps of stunted, useless palms. A dog came running crazily toward them on three legs. Not until it got quite close did the Professor hear its steady low growl. The *qaouaji* let fly a large stone at it, striking it square in the muzzle. There was a strange snapping of jaws and the dog ran sideways in another direction, falling blindly against rocks and scrambling haphazardly about like an injured insect.

Turning off the road, they walked across the earth strewn with sharp stones, past the little ruin, through the trees, until they came to a place where the ground dropped abruptly away in front of them.

"It looks like a quarry," said the Professor, resorting to French for the word "quarry," whose Arabic equivalent he could not call to mind at the moment. The *qaouaji* did not answer. Instead he stood still and turned his head, as if listening. And indeed, from somewhere down below, but very far below, came the faint sound of a low flute. The *qaouaji* nodded his head slowly several times. Then he said: "The path begins here. You can see it well all the way. The rock is white and the moon is strong. So you can see well. I am going back now and sleep. It is late. You can give me what you like."

Standing there at the edge of the abyss which at each moment looked deeper, with the dark face of the *qaouaji* framed in its moonlit burnous close to his own face, the Professor asked himself exactly what he felt. Indignation, curiosity, fear, perhaps, but most of all relief and the hope that this was not a trick, the hope that the *qaouaji* would really leave him alone and turn back without him.

He stepped back a little from the edge, and fumbled in his pocket for a loose note, because he did not want to show his wallet. Fortunately there was a fifty-franc bill there, which he took out and handed to the man. He knew the *qaouaji* was pleased, and so he paid no attention when he heard him saying: "It is not enough. I have to walk a long way home and there are dogs. . . . "

"Thank you and good night," said the Professor, sitting down with his legs drawn up under him, and lighting a cigarette. He felt almost happy.

"Give me only one cigarette," pleaded the man.

"Of course," he said, a bit curtly, and he held up the pack.

The *qaouaji* squatted close beside him. His face was not pleasant to see. "What is it?" thought the Professor, terrified again, as he held out his lighted cigarette toward him.

The man's eyes were almost closed. It was the most obvious registering of concentrated scheming the Professor had ever seen. When the second cigarette was burning, he ventured to say to the still-squatting Arab: "What are you thinking about?"

The other drew on his cigarette deliberately, and seemed about to speak. Then his expression changed to one of satisfaction, but he did not speak. A cool wind had risen in the air, and the Professor shivered. The sound of the flute came up from the depths below at intervals, sometimes mingled with the scraping of nearby palm fronds one against the other. "These people are not primitives," the Professor found himself saying in his mind.

"Good," said the *qaouaji*, rising slowly. "Keep your money. Fifty francs is enough. It is an honor." Then he went back into French: "*Ti n'as qu'à discendre, to' droit.*" He spat, chuckled (or was the Professor hysterical?), and strode away quickly.

The Professor was in a state of nerves. He lit another cigarette, and found his lips moving automatically. They were saying: "Is this a situation or a predicament? This is ridiculous." He sat very still for several minutes, waiting for a sense of reality to come to him. He stretched out on the hard, cold ground and looked up at the moon. It was almost like looking straight at the sun. If he shifted his gaze a little at a time, he could make a string of weaker moons across the sky. "Incredible," he whispered. Then he sat up quickly and looked about. There was no guarantee that the *qaouaji* really had gone back to town. He got to his feet and looked over the edge of the precipice. In the moonlight the bottom seemed miles away. And there was nothing to give it scale; not a tree, not a house, not a person. . . . He listened for the flute, and heard only the wind going by his ears. A sudden violent desire to run back to the road seized him, and he turned and looked in the direction the *qaouaji* had taken. At the same time he felt softly of his wallet in his breast pocket. Then he spat over the edge of the cliff. Then he made water over it, and listened intently, like a child. This gave him the impetus to start down the path into the abyss. Curiously enough, he was not dizzy. But prudently he kept from peering to his right, over the edge. It was a steady and steep downward climb. The monotony of it put him into a frame of mind not unlike that which had been induced by the bus ride. He was murmuring "Hassan Ramani" again, repeatedly and in rhythm. He stopped, furious with himself for the sinister overtones the name now suggested to him. He decided he was exhausted from the trip. "And the walk," he added.

He was now well down the gigantic cliff, but the moon, being directly overhead, gave as much light as ever. Only the wind was left behind, above, to wander among the trees, to blow through the dusty streets of Aïn Tadouirt, into the hall of the Grand Hotel Saharien, and under the door of his little room.

It occurred to him that he ought to ask himself why he was doing this irrational thing, but he was intelligent enough to know that since he was doing it, it was not so important to probe for explanations at that moment.

Suddenly the earth was flat beneath his feet. He had reached the bottom sooner than he had expected. He stepped ahead distrustfully still, as if he expected another treacherous drop. It was so hard to know in this uniform, dim brightness. Before he knew what had happened the dog was upon him, a heavy mass of fur trying to push him backwards, a sharp nail rubbing down his chest, a straining of muscles against him to get the teeth into his neck. The Professor thought: "I refuse to die this way." The dog fell back; it looked like an Eskimo dog. As it sprang again, he called out, very loud: "Ay!" It fell against him, there was a confusion of sensations and a pain somewhere. There was also the sound of voices very near to him, and he could not understand what they were saying. Something cold and metallic was pushed brutally against his spine as the dog still hung for a second by his teeth from a mass of clothing and perhaps flesh. The Professor knew it was a gun, and he raised his hands, shouting in Moghrebi: "Take away the dog!" But the gun merely pushed him forward, and since the dog, once it was back on the ground, did not leap again, he took a step ahead. The gun kept pushing; he kept taking steps. Again he heard voices, but the person directly behind him said nothing. People seemed to be running about; it sounded that way, at least. For his eyes, he discovered, were still shut tight against the dog's attack. He opened them. A group of men was advancing toward him. They were dressed in the black clothes of the Reguibat. "The Reguiba is a cloud across the face of the sun." "When the Reguiba appears the righteous man turns away." In how many shops and market-places he had heard these maxims uttered banteringly among friends. Never to a Reguiba, to be sure, for these men do not frequent towns. They send a representative in disguise, to arrange with shady elements there for the disposal of captured goods. "An opportunity," he thought quickly, "of testing the accuracy of such statements." He did not doubt for a moment that the adventure would prove to be a kind of warning against such foolishness on his part—a warning which in retrospect would be half sinister, half farcical.

Two snarling dogs came running from behind the oncoming men and threw themselves at his legs. He was scandalized to note that no one paid any attention to this breach of etiquette. The gun pushed him harder as he tried to sidestep the animals' noisy assault. Again he cried: "The dogs! Take them away!" The gun shoved him forward with great force and he fell, almost at the feet of the crowd of men facing him. The dogs were wrenching at his hands and arms. A boot kicked them aside, yelping, and then with increased vigor it kicked the Professor in the hip. Then came a chorus of kicks from different sides, and he was rolled violently about on the earth for a while. During this time he was conscious of hands reaching into his pockets and removing everything from them. He tried to say: "You have all my money; stop kicking me!" But his bruised facial muscles would not work; he felt himself pouting, and that was all. Someone dealt him a terrific blow on the head, and he thought: "Now at least I shall lose consciousness, thank Heaven." Still he went on being aware of the guttural voices he could not understand, and of being bound tightly about the ankles and chest. Then there was black silence that opened like a wound from time to time, to let in the soft, deep notes of the flute playing the same succession of notes again and again. Suddenly he felt excruciating pain everywhere—pain and cold. "So I have been unconscious, after all," he thought. In spite of that, the present seemed only like a direct continuation of what had gone before.

It was growing faintly light. There were camels near where he was lying; he could hear their gurgling and their heavy breathing. He could not bring himself to attempt opening his eyes, just in case it should turn out to be impossible. However, when he heard someone approaching, he found that he had no difficulty in seeing.

The man looked at him dispassionately in the gray morning light. With one hand he pinched together the Professor's nostrils. When the Professor opened his mouth to breathe, the man swiftly seized his tongue and pulled on it with all his might. The Professor was gagging and catching his breath; he did not see what was happening. He could not distinguish the pain of the brutal yanking from that of the sharp knife. Then there was an endless choking and spitting that went on automatically, as though he were scarcely a part of it. The word "operation" kept going through his mind; it calmed his terror somewhat as he sank back into darkness.

The caravan left sometime toward midmorning. The Professor, not unconscious, but in a state of utter stupor, still gagging and drooling blood, was dumped doubled-up into a sack and tied at one side of a camel. The lower end of the enormous amphitheater contained a natural gate in the rocks. The camels, swift *mehara*, were lightly laden on this trip. They passed through single file, and slowly mounted the gentle slope that led up into the beginning of the desert. That night, at a stop behind some low hills, the men took him out, still in a state which permitted no thought, and over the dusty rags that remained of his clothing they fastened a series of curious belts made of the bottoms of tin cans strung together. One after another of these bright girdles was wired about his torso, his arms and legs, even across his face, until he was entirely within a suit of armor that covered him with its circular metal scales. There was a good deal of merriment during this decking-out of the Professor. One man brought out a flute and a younger one did a not ungraceful caricature of an Ouled Naïl executing a cane dance. The Professor was no longer conscious; to be exact, he existed in the middle of the movements made by these other men. When they had finished dressing him the way they wished him to look, they stuffed some food under the tin bangles hanging over his face. Even though he chewed mechanically, most of it eventually fell out onto the ground. They put him back into the sack and left him there.

Two days later they arrived at one of their own encampments. There were women and children here in the tents, and the men had to drive away the snarling dogs they had left there to guard them. When they emptied the Professor out of his sack, there were screams of fright, and it took several hours to convince the last woman that he was harmless, although there had been no doubt from the start that he was a valuable possession. After a few days they began to move on again, taking everything with them, and traveling only at night as the terrain grew warmer.

Even when all his wounds had healed and he felt no more pain, the Professor did not begin to think again; he ate and defecated, and he danced when he was bidden, a senseless hopping up and down that delighted the children, principally because of the wonderful jangling racket it made. And he generally slept through the heat of the day, in among the camels.

Wending its way southeast, the caravan avoided all stationary civilization. In a few weeks they reached a new plateau, wholly wild and with a sparse vegetation. Here they pitched camp and remained, while the *mehara* were turned loose to graze. Everyone was happy here; the weather was cooler and there was a well only a few hours away on a seldom-frequented trail. It was here they conceived the idea of taking the Professor to Fogara and selling him to the Touareg.

It was a full year before they carried out this project. By this time the Professor was much better trained. He could do a handspring, make a series of fearful growling noises which had, nevertheless, a certain element of humor; and when the Reguibat removed the tin from his face they discovered he could grimace admirably while he danced. They also taught him a few basic obscene gestures which never failed to elicit delighted shrieks from the women. He was now brought forth only after especially abundant meals, when there was music and festivity. He easily fell in with their sense of ritual, and evolved an elementary sort of "program" to present when he was called for: dancing, rolling on the ground, imitating certain animals, and finally rushing toward the group in feigned anger, to see the resultant confusion and hilarity.

When three of the men set out for Fogara with him, they took four *mehara* with them, and he rode astride his quite naturally. No precautions were taken to guard him, save that he was kept among them, one man always staying at the rear of the party. They came within sight of the walls at dawn, and they waited among the rocks all day. At dusk the youngest started out, and in three hours he returned with a friend who carried a stout cane. They tried to put the Professor through his routine then and there, but the man from Fogara was in a hurry to get back to town, so they all set out on the *mehara*.

In the town they went directly to the villager's home, where they had coffee in the courtyard sitting among the camels. Here the Professor went into his act again, and this time there was prolonged merriment and much rubbing together of hands. An agreement was reached, a sum of money paid, and the Reguibat withdrew, leaving the Professor in the house of the man with the cane, who did not delay in locking him into a tiny enclosure off the courtyard.

The next day was an important one in the Professor's life, for it was then that pain began to stir again in his being. A group of men came to the house, among whom was a venerable gentleman, better clothed than those others who spent their time flattering him, setting fervent kisses upon his hands and the edges of his garments. This person made a point of going into classical Arabic from time to time, to impress the others, who had not learned a word of the Koran. Thus his conversation would run more or less as follows: "Perhaps at In Salah. The French there are stupid. Celestial vengeance is approaching. Let us not hasten it. Praise the highest and cast thine anathema against idols. With paint on his face. In case the police wish to look close." The others listened and agreed, nodding their heads slowly and solemnly. And the Professor in his stall beside them listened, too. That is, he was *conscious* of the sound of the old man's Arabic. The words penetrated for the first time in many months. Noises, then: "Celestial vengeance is approaching." Then: "It is an honor. Fifty francs is enough. Keep your money. Good." And the *qaouaji* squatting near him at the edge of the precipice. Then "anathema against idols" and more gibberish. He turned over panting on the sand and forgot about it. But the pain had begun. It operated in a kind of delirium, because he had begun to enter into consciousness again. When the man opened the door and prodded him with his cane, he cried out in a rage, and everyone laughed.

They got him onto his feet, but he would not dance. He stood before them, staring at the ground, stubbornly refusing to move. The owner was furious, and so annoyed by the laughter of the others that he felt obliged to send them away, saying that he would await a more propitious time for exhibiting his property, because he dared not show his anger before the elder. However, when they had left he dealt the Professor a violent blow on the shoulder with his cane, called him various obscene things, and went out into the street, slamming the gate behind him. He walked straight to the street of the Ouled Naïl, because he was sure of finding the Reguïbat there among the girls, spending the money. And there in a tent he found one of them still abed, while an Ouled Naïl washed the tea glasses. He walked in and almost decapitated the man before the latter had even attempted to sit up. Then he threw his razor on the bed and ran out.

The Ouled Naïl saw the blood, screamed, ran out of her tent into the next, and soon emerged from that with four girls who rushed together into the coffee house and told the *qaouaji* who had killed the Reguiba. It was only a matter of an hour before the French military police had caught him at a friend's house, and dragged him off to the barracks. That night the Professor had nothing to eat, and the next afternoon, in the slow sharpening of his consciousness caused by increasing hunger, he walked aimlessly about the courtyard and the rooms that gave onto it. There was no one. In one room a calendar hung on the wall. The Professor watched nervously, like a dog watching a fly in front of its nose. On the white paper were black objects that made sounds in his head. He heard them: "*Grande Epicerie du Sahel. Juin. Lundi, Mardi, Mercredi. . . .*"

The tiny inkmarks of which a symphony consists may have been made long ago, but when they are fulfilled in sound they become imminent and mighty. So a kind of music of feeling began to play in the Professor's head, increasing in volume as he looked at the mud wall, and he had the feeling that he was performing what had been written for him long ago. He felt like weeping; he felt like roaring through the little house, upsetting and smashing the few breakable objects. His emotion got no further than this one overwhelming desire. So, bellowing as loud as he could, he attacked the house and its belongings. Then he attacked the door into the street, which resisted for a while and finally broke. He climbed through the opening made by the boards he had ripped apart, and still bellowing and shaking his arms in the air to make as loud a jangling as possible, he began to gallop along the quiet street toward the gateway of the town. A few people looked at him with great curiosity. As he passed the garage, the last building before the high mud archway that framed the desert beyond, a French soldier saw him. "*Tiens*," he said to himself, "a holy maniac."

Again it was sunset time. The Professor ran beneath the arched gate, turned his face toward the red sky, and began to trot along the Piste d'In Salah, straight into the setting sun. Behind him, from the garage, the soldier took a pot shot at him for good luck. The bullet whistled dangerously near the Professor's head, and his yelling rose into an indignant lament as he waved his arms more wildly, and hopped high into the air at every few steps, in an access of terror.

The soldier watched a while, smiling, as the cavorting figure grew smaller in the oncoming evening darkness, and the rattling of the tin became a part of the great silence out there beyond the gate. The wall of the garage as he leaned against it still gave forth heat, left there by the sun, but even then the lunar chill was growing in the air.

BOOKS BY
PAUL BOWLES

DAYS
A Tangier Diary
ISBN 0-06-113736-7
(paperback)

THE DELICATE PREY
And Other Stories
ISBN 0-06-113734-0
(paperback)

A DISTANT EPISODE
The Selected Stories
ISBN 0-06-113738-3
(paperback)

LET IT COME DOWN
A Novel
ISBN 0-06-113739-1
(paperback)

POINTS IN TIME
Tales From Morocco
ISBN 0-06-113963-7
(paperback)

THE SHELTERING SKY
A Novel
ISBN 0-06-083482-X
(paperback)

Printed in the USA
CPSIA information can be obtained
at www.ICGtesting.com
LVHW031131310824
789807LV00005B/150